BLOOD AND FAITH

A NOVEL

BILL KANE

DEDICATION

This book is dedicated in loving memory of my mother
Theresa B. Kane, the kindest, most selfless and giving person
I've ever known.

ACKNOWLEDGMENTS

It's long been said that a writer draws from a well of experience and personal knowledge. Despite the ups and downs of life, luckily, mine has been filled by an interesting cast of characters over the years.

First off, I would like to thank my wife Tracey and my two daughters, Rachel and Natalie for putting up with me. Without them in my life, I have no idea where I would be. Secondly, I would like to acknowledge my father Bill Sr. who at the ripe old age of 93 still works 2 days a week and is a constant inspiration to anyone on two legs. A big thank you to my siblings and their significant others; Sue and Brian Crosby, Kathy Kane & Phil Tordella, Karen and Jim Hovey, Maureen and Joe Labricciosa, my sister-in-law Sue Kane and, especially, my brother Mike who, through thick and thin, has always had my back. Also, I imagine I wouldn't be a very good uncle, without mentioning my nieces and nephews; Scott, Kevin, Erin, Meghan, Danny, Mikey, Allison, Nicole and my fishing buddy Jack. Other individuals who have had an impact on my development as a human being are Sifu Pedro Cepero and my two Si Hings; Mike Burnett and Roberto Alicea.

With regards to my writing itself, I would like to recognize Cindy Burns who has always been a solid source of support over the years as well as Barry Sheinkopf at The Writing Center who, I believe, did a great job editing my work. A tremendous thank you to Nicole Sausville for her professionalism and helping me make this 25 year project a reality.

Although I am probably missing a few, I would like to mention the many childhood friends who, at one time or another, have made me laugh to no end: Jim Sausville, Tony Ludwig, Kurt Cieszko, Jody Hnat, Rachel Whiteman, Nancy Miles, Dave Caiazzo, Scott Cooper, Mark Malcolm, Steve Cochran, Bob Gold, Barry McNamara and Jackie Sumanis

Blood and Faith

CHAPTER 1

It was a wet summer night in New York City, a long depressing day marked by sweltering heat and staggering humidity. A pale crescent moon, tilted on its back, fought to pierce the thin curtain of slow-moving clouds. The monsoon-like rain that had been soaking the city for days showed few signs of letting up.

The streets of Times Square were nearly empty, save a few tourists and needy peddlers hawking stale car fresheners and tired roses out of old five-gallon buckets.

Gone from the surface were the pimps, whores, and pickpockets; the days of pissing bums and lunchtime blow-jobs were over, sent underground by the opaque promise of bright lights and bigger money.

A dented yellow cab darted recklessly across three lanes of Broadway traffic, eager to unload a restless fare; a cloud of mist from a nearby manhole engulfed the rear of the ride.

With difficulty, the passenger climbed out and closed the door, offering a farewell in a rapid exchange of Arabic. As the cab pulled away, he lit another cigarette and walked off into the darkness. He hadn't paid.

Emerging like a moth to a flame, he was drawn by the people and the lights that lined the busy street. Once he had been a man of wealth and privilege, bathed in luxury, in a place where nepotism and oil were one. But the rigid rules that bound his position in society reached across the lines of blood, beyond wealth and power, to the very doorstep of a God whose judgment was swift and penalties severe. But those dangerous days were long gone. Soon it would be their turn.

Strolling the wet sidewalk, oblivious to the rain, he stopped by a light post to catch his breath; chin up, he inhaled deeply through wide nostrils, the cool moisture on his face. He clenched his eyes tight, and his senses flowed with an energy that pushed him ahead. There was no repression here. It had become his new Mecca, the Kaaba of his redemption. But he didn't feel like himself, nor had he for days. Nausea had become his constant companion, and his nose ran red.

Reaching the door of a nearby bar, he again stopped to catch his breath; the multicolored lights above the awning flickered rhythmically, casting a thick halo of red on his cloth covered head.

He pulled an ornate metal container from his pants pocket, put it to his nose, and sniffed quickly. Feeling recharged, he flicked the butt of his cigarette at the feet of a man with a darker complexion who had been taking up space next to the entrance. Sensing a confrontation, he whipped opened the door and hurried inside.

It was as dark as a moonless night inside the smoky bar, and the blend of poppers, cigarettes, and stale leather assaulted his senses.

In the rear, bar stools were occupied by men of varying ages whose postures suggested intimate conversation. A red, white, and blue Budweiser clock that hung behind the bar read 11:35 p.m. Noting the time, the Arab hurried across the floor for a pack of smokes.

He tried to make eye contact with each man he passed, needing to get close to see. His night vision had been failing. The abundance of pierced body parts and bare stomachs gyrating on the dance floor tickled his fancy. But there were no overt invitations. For the moment, he would be sitting alone.

But Allah heeds those who wait, he thought as he reached the bar where the lighting was a little better. Finding a vacant stool, he sat and turned to face the door. He lit a Camel, drew on it, pulled the smoke up from his mouth to his nose, and waited.

Three cigarettes later, he began to grow bored with the unexpected delay. Silence and the inactivity were, in such a target-rich environment, beginning to take their toll. He tried striking up a conversation with a thin, pale, bartender whose short green hair, shaved neatly to a point, suggested an Irish vampire on a calorie-free diet.

The lone man spoke softly, reaching for another ashtray. He motioned towards the door. "Have you seen a woman….a blonde?" He coughed.

The bartender, faintly repulsed, shook his head. "Not a chance."

Disappointed, the bearded man, drawing heavily on his cigarette, eyed the other. With nothing but the side of his face to look at, he began to think the bartender might not be pouring drinks much longer: his meager frame and ashen pallor explained the anger. The other, on whom these insights were not lost, set down a pint of beer and walked away.

Turning his back to face the door, the Arab lifted the mug to his lips, unaware of the blood that was running from his thick roman nose to the upper leg of his stone-washed bellbottoms.

His anxiety mounted further with each sip; again he checked his watch. The satisfied looks of the male patrons leaving the men's bathroom caught his attention. If his date didn't show, he'd have to see what all the excitement was about.

A few minutes before midnight the door opened and a tall, buxom woman in a dark raincoat entered, eliciting little response from those around her.

Waiting for her eyes to adjust, she lit a cigarillo, removed her wide brimmed hat and then moved forward, floating across the dance floor towards the bar. Without a word, she unbuttoned her coat, draped it on the stool beside him, placed the hat on the bar, and put her arms around his neck. She immediately noticed the blood. Pulling a cloth from her glove, she lightly dabbed at it, cooing in a voice roughened by tobacco. "My poor baby. Let Mamma have a look at you."

"Where have you been?!" he barked, the bass of his accent underscoring his anger, as he tossed his right arm at the galloping row of Clydesdales above the bar.

"Baby had trouble finding a spot," she whined. "Miss me?" she asked, leaning in close, wanting to apologize further. "Where is it?" Again, she raised the handkerchief to his nose.

Ignoring her, he yanked the blood-stained cloth from her hand and dropped it onto the bar. His look of desire, and the lump in his drawers, was overpowering. At first, she resisted, avoiding a scene. This brought a smile to the man's face.

"You've been a bad boy, Salaam. Our delivery boy's gonna want his dough," she whispered as her grip on his ego eased, her attention returning to the blood running from his nose. She reached out for the handkerchief.

"Daddy's going to be in town soon," she purred, dabbing at the blood. "You said everything was taken care of. D-day is just around the corner. Now is not the time to lose focus. There are to be *no* loose ends."

"It will be done," he replied, pulling away abruptly. Touching was the kind of contact he could do without--and she was right. The clarity of his thoughts, his reasoning, had deserted him; but there were more important reasons for his delay, and they unnerved him.

"This has *never* been done before. There are many risks. Some I'm sure I've missed," he said, drawing heavily on his cigarette, hoping to calm his nerves. Exhaling, he again wrested the handkerchief from her hand and stuffed it into the pocket of his dampened shirt.

"The risks *are* the reward. Now let's get out of here," she begged, licking her thick lips suggestively. "I want to see it."

Stepping back, her coat over her arm, she allowed him to slip off the stool. He finished his beer, and they left as quickly as she had come.

A light foggy rain had replaced the torrent, casting a thin gray haze on the night. Arm-in-arm the two walked, avoiding the angry pimp outside the bar and a few stumbling couples who had had too much to drink.

The bearded stranger thought she looked stunning, as she always did when they were together. They walked until they came to a late-night drug store. His head was beginning to throb.

It was 12:10 a.m. He grabbed her gloved hands playfully, and whispered in her ear, the shiny gold earring he'd given her on a whim tickling the hairs of his nose. He laughed half-heartedly, offered an apology, and said he needed something for the pain.

Before he could take a step, she grabbed his arm firmly, her lips pursed, brow rising provocatively above a wagging finger that

4

motioned him towards the alley. He couldn't resist the opera-length white satin gloves and her unusual aggressiveness. If she wanted to be the charmer, he would gladly provide the snake. They hurried into the darkness like newlyweds.

Halfway down the alley he turned, smiled and started to undo his pants. His eyes, wide with anticipation, never left hers until she fell eagerly to her knees.

The pressure of his bladder prevented him from truly enjoying the pleasures of her lips. With reluctance, he stopped and pulled her face up to rise. She seemed content to oblige.

"Can I see it?" she asked warmly, before he turned to urinate.

"No!" he replied sternly over his shoulder, widening his stance. "It's safer at the apartment."

"Then you should have stayed there."

The struggle that ensued was violent, yet brief; the soft tissues of his neck no match for the thin wire that soon robbed him of his breath.

The Arab managed to land a blow to his attacker's right ear, causing her to stumble and kick her purse, spilling some of its contents on the alley floor. The unexpected blow so infuriated her, she smashed his face into the nearest wall, the garrote nearly ripping through his spinal column before letting his body slump to the ground with a lifeless thud.

She dropped quickly, methodically gathering up her things. Stunned by the unexpected reaction, she rose slowly and glanced around her feet. The alley was short on light. What little there was gleaned on the instrument she had removed from her purse. Finished, she rolled him over and robbed him of his billfold and the contents of his pockets. The ornate container would make a great keepsake. Giving the area one last look, she moved to the street and waited.

CHAPTER 2

His day long over, Detective Bill Masters was on his way home when the call came. Handing him an armful of mail, the exhausted desk sergeant provided an approximate address and a few details, one of which was that units were already on the scene. He'd look for the flashing lights.

Speeding up the wipers, he eyed the acreage of colored bulbs that blinked and raced, hoping to hide the stark realities that lurked just below the fancy veneer of lights. Absent were the custom Cadillacs and pink fedoras, mutated by greed and the insatiable desire for flesh, replaced with dresses by Gucci, watches by Cartier, and convertibles by Mercedes. Vice, like politics, was an eternal masquerade whose masks changed with the necessities of time.

As with any homicide, Master's arrival was always preceded by short bouts of nervousness--like a quarterback in a bowl-game with no rules, clock, or mercy; one of the few professions where death and loss were the prerequisites for a paycheck. With the latest economic downturn, he was getting a lot of practice with the poor and unskilled paying the biggest price.

A new game was well underway in an alley a few blocks from the protection of the Times Square precinct. The chatter he was hearing over the radio set his heart pounding. The perp seemed to have been unusually angry. Coming off the bench, he would need to be on top of his game.

At that late hour, there was not much fanfare. For a crime scene, it was ordinary--dead person in the heart of Gotham, four o'clock in the morning. There were a few interested freaks milling around on the sidewalk, beyond the blue wooden police dividers, hoping for a chance to look death straight in the eye. A yellow spool of crime scene tape was being unwound to cordon off the entrance to the alley, hoping to contain the evil waiting within.

For those who lived in the neighborhood, it was the status quo, once the sun went down. A few blue-and-whites lingered at different angles with their lights flashing. The men from the ME's office had yet to arrive. As usual, Master's partner was late.

Anxious about the integrity of the scene, yet unwilling to proceed without his partner present, Bill flicked on the overhead light and reached down for the bundle of mail tucked against his hip. Leafing through it quickly, he tossed everything on the seat except for a weathered, dog-eared postcard. Instantly, a smile spread across his face.

The author was unknown to those who had never held his hand or seen his smile but Bill knew in his bones the occasional correspondences were from his estranged father; a tall, painfully devout family man with strong ties to his community, who, since the untimely death of Master's mother, had left abruptly, like a wounded animal crawling off to die.

But, like a good son, Bill had always dreamed that with the money from her indemnity, he was traveling the world like a nomad, never settling down for much longer than a month, because there had been no note, no goodbyes—he was just gone.

The first card was a view of the Sistine Chapel ceiling. After that, it was one or two a year, usually around Bill's birthday, sent from major cities around Europe, plugging pictures of famous people or landmarks.

Although the postmarks were different, the content was always the same—*Nothing*. No lengthy body, no sentiments. This one was a bit different--a yellow cab with the legend *Welcome to New York*. Bill flipped it quickly, in anticipation of something new. His pupils narrowed. . . .

"Hey, Lieutenant Masters!" yelled a young patrolman named

Anthony Piazza, banging on the window with the heel of his flashlight, causing Bill to jump. "Sorry to bodda you so late," he said apologetically, realizing his mistake, "but the captain got a call from the chief sayin' to bring yous two in on this ASAP."

Masters liked the patrolman and his dense Brooklyn accent. He was as young and green as he himself had been when he first started on the job. He had guts and knew how to take charge of a situation when he had to. He had won the Golden Gloves as a teenager and could use a nightstick like a pro--in a pinch, the man to have backing you up.

"No problem Piazza, I was just reading some mail," Bill replied with a mocking smile. "Just don't let it happen again," he added, swatting at a fly in a holding pattern around his face. "The mayor's office for *this*? Something definitely stinks in Denmark," he said, under his breath, emerging from the car. "So what do we have on the menu tonight? Another high priced hooker?" Masters asked, as he bent under the tape and entered the alley, his heavy flashlight probing the darkness, careful not to step in or on anything.

"No, sir. Male, dark-skinned, about five feet ten, one hundred and seventy pounds, black hair, mustache. With that turban look-ing thing, I'm guessin' Middle-Eastern descent."

"You mean he's a hack?" replied Bill. "Any I.D.?"

"Nah. . .he was, ya know, layin' face down when I found him. Just a little blood running out of his nose and a shitload out of his mouth and chest. His right ear's gone, there's a deep laceration on his left forearm and I'm not sure, but I think he's missing his tongue. Also, there is some indication he was throttled. Deep ligature marks on his neck. Someone was making sure this guy stopped breathin'."

At the body, the detective squatted down, pulling at the base of his tan trousers, crushing something under his foot. The mixture of urine and garbage was unmistakable. Quelling the urge to vomit, he directed his Mag light revealing the broken remains of a pink pistachio nut resting neatly atop a quarter.

The victim, his fly still open, was lying on his side, eyes wide with terror. His tone rising, Masters looked up to Piazza and bark-ed, "Someone touch the body, or did it get the urge to roll over?"

He rose slowly and smoothed out his pants. His knee was bothering him.

Cringing, Piazza replied, "Um, sorta."

"Sorta? What kind of fucking answer is that? How long you been on the job?"

"Uh. . .six years," stammered the patrolman, staring at the tips of his shoes.

"Six years, and you turn over a fucking corpse before anybody's had a chance to take pictures, or get samples, or do the slightest cursory inspection of any kind?"

Before he could finish, the patrolman lamented, "Sorry sir, I just thought I recognized 'im."

"*Well*, do you?"

Shrugging, Piazza replied, "Maybe. I think he was busted for meter tamperin' a while back. He had a full beard then. I was in on the collar. But to me dese guys all look the same."

"Really? Nice memory. Anyway, it's a start," sighed the lieutenant, checking his watch, now conscious of the water hitting his shoulder. He looked at the leaky gutter above his head; the rain was not cooperating.

"Let's get back to the street. Secure the area and have someone get on the roof and throw something across the alley--the rain's killin' us. But next time, *wait* until a detective arrives before you start molesting the victim. Be patient. This is how scumbags walk. That guy's going nowhere, and he doesn't look like he'll be giving any speeches any time soon. When you're done, I want you to question everyone on that corner over there. See if they saw anything."

"Sorry, sir. It'll neva happen again."

As Masters walked off, the patrolman wondered why the lieutenant always busted his balls when he saw him, even when he *wasn't* moving the evidence. Maybe they were trying to make him a better cop, because he was slowly becoming a student of details, an area where, in his mind and many others, Lieutenant Masters was second to none.

Masters was leaning against the Pontiac, arms folded, checking his worn Timex. It was close to 4:30 a.m. The weather, as predicted, turned foul. Personally, Bill didn't mind the rainy days. A ray of sunshine never brightened the horror of a slit throat or reduced the lasting impact of a shotgun blast to the face. But as a professional, the thought of evidence, and a possible conviction, running down the gutter angered him. In the presence of DNA evidence, contaminants had become the cornerstone on which to build a solid defense.

"Patrolman, did *anybody* get in touch with Lackey?" he inquired, somewhat perturbed, adding, "Maybe you should go to that crime scene he calls his bed and drag his fat ass down here. God, does he love to sleep!" For no apparent reason, Bill broke into a sweat.

"They called him five minutes before you," the patrolman replied with a defensive smirk. "He shoulda' been here by now."

At that moment, the dim headlights of a late model, two-tone Chevy Caprice Classic rounded the corner and pulled up to the scene. Judging from the wealth of dirt and bird droppings, Bill figured it hadn't been washed in months.

Detective Jim Lackey, a gritty, fair-haired behemoth of a man, labored out of the front seat, his right hand vigorously mining the crack of his ass. His penchant for alcohol, and adversity towards dry-cleaning, gave him the perpetual look of an unmade bed. Irascible and innately rude, he'd been Bill's partner for fifteen years, and nothing ever changed but his excuses. Since his aging divorce, he had been going through life with the direction of a balloonist.

"Listen, Bill, sorry I'm late, but my fuckin' 'roids are killin' me. I've got an ass like a baboon," he said wincing apologetically, smoothing out his pants. He paused, glancing at his sweating partner, and asked, "Christ, did you run here? Personally, I could barely lift myself off the crapper."

"Gee, I'm shocked," replied Masters with an added dose of sarcasm, wiping his forehead with a napkin pulled from the pocket of his raincoat.

Raising his nose to the sky, he added, "Smells like you mighta' tagged one on." He leveled an accusing stare at his partner.

"*Please*, cut the shit? It's late!" Jim remarked, reaching into his pocket. "So what do we got?" he added, through teeth clenched around the butt of a cheap cigar, its clear wrapper tumbling to the curb.

"Besides Patrolman Fuck-up over there? We got one dead Arab-looking male, possible cab driver, with a massive chest wound, no I.D., and no right ear. There's also a possibility he lost his tongue in the scuffle. There are some *deep* ligature marks visible around the neck and a ton of blood coming out of his nose and mouth. Bear with me, I just got here myself. Besides waitin' for *your* fat-ass, I've spent the last few minutes lecturing the boy blunder over there."

10

"What he do?" Jim asked gingerly, knowing there was more to Bill's ire than routine tardiness and a dead foreigner.

"Moved the body before you, me, or the lab boys could get here. Said he thought he recognized the guy, just wanted to make sure. We'll find out later."

Bill held out his palms. "We'd best get a move on. This rain's gonna pick up. It's already ruined most of what little we got, so watch your feet."

A moist, warm wind began to blow; creating eddies between the rain-soaked buildings. Papers and loose flyers danced small minuets cut short by a length of chain link fence. The sky got darker, and the rain picked up.

The spot where the body lay was surrounded by graffiti covered brick and cinder block walls spalled by years of leaking gutters and rusting conduit that snaked along the roofline and off into the darkness above. The rotting down-spouts were scarred by holes filled with dirt and decaying leaves that nourished a broken row of weeds that inched skyward. The rear of the alley was cut off by another chain link fence topped by broken strands of barbed wire, beyond it the back alley of another street.

On the ground, fronting the chain link fence, sat the makings of a small time capsule: old papers, garbage, and used condoms that hung from the fence and walls like ornaments from Christmas trees past.

Returning to the body, Masters inadvertently stepped into a puddle and almost slipped. Probably water, he thought, but the smell and experience told him otherwise.

"This place is god-awful," he barked to his partner, checking the sole of his shoe. "Seriously, how can people have sex like this?"

Lackey, numbed with indifference and three bed-time martinis, replied suspiciously as he came upon the body, "You, kiddin' me? Welcome to Club Head, my friend." The beam of his flashlight fell on the victim's face. "Jesus! Guy looks a friggin' Pez dispenser."

"All right already....enough! You write, I'll talk," ordered Bill, closing his dampened notepad. "Let's start with the fact the guy's junk's still hanging out of his pants."

"Check out the shoes," added Lackey, noticing the stained arches of the tan cowboy boots.

Bill inspected the blood around the victim's mouth. Forcing open the lips with the end of his pencil, he instinctively opened his own mouth, dropping his chin to his chest as if he were at the dentist. "This guy is, without question, missing his tongue." He stood slowly, tilting his face to the rain, adding, "Gonna' be a long fuckin' night."

CHAPTER 3

The slow pace of the night yielded to the dawn as the two detectives, aided by a team of colleagues, completed the job of collecting and documenting evidence and, along with the ME's men, carried the stiffening body toward the street.

Leaving the alley and removing his rubber gloves, Bill turned to his partner, paused, and pointed across the street. "Go see what those shop owners have to say. I'm goin' back inside one more time, just to make sure we didn't miss anything."

"Why, I'd love to," offered Jim, shaking his head in disgust. "So much in common." He turned, buried his hands in the pockets of his wrinkled raincoat, and headed across the street.

Bill, trying to dismiss the odor of his partner's breath, moved slowly down the alley, his eyes scanning for anything he might have overlooked.

The morning sun remained shielded by the low, slow-moving clouds that offered nothing but hints of shadowless light. The gutter above had stopped dripping. The weather had held, but a new storm was coming. The lingering smell of garbage and dispensed bladders was all but gone.

Pulling on the knees of his trousers, Bill dropped to a catcher's stance and reinspected where the body had been found. The bloody stain on the soil, still moist, was as large as the man who had left it. From the wall above his head, where soft cartilage had met brick, flowed a thin stream of blood crossing over a few loose papers that had defied the forces of the wind.

Most murders, given a witness or a clue, were easy to solve. The motives were endless -- the jealous lover, the drug-crazed lunatic, and the occasional psycho that drifted into town. This one had been planned to include every ingredient of a violent death but the precision and location of the wounds suggested a profession-alism reserved for operating rooms, not seedy alleys. Looking about the scene, the anger was palpable, but as he digested the view further, he couldn't help but feel there was an overwhelming sense of pleasure involved. It was certainly a message -- sent with the accuracy of a sniper.

As he rose to leave, another burst of wind rustled the strewn papers around his feet. Some rolled, others took flight and bobbed and weaved for a moment, before settling back to earth.

Something in the rubbish to his left caught his attention. Bill squatted, brushing away loose debris with the back of his fingers.

Experience stopped him from picking it up. Removing a small plastic bag from his front pocket, he scooped up the object with the tip of his pen and dropped it in. It looked like an earring. It was not only fancy, but unusually heavy.

"Solid gold," Bill muttered, as if the find was more treasure than clue. Closer inspection revealed an intricate picture of a Bengal tiger on one side and an inscription he didn't understand on the other. Definitely not New York, he thought as he headed out of the alley.

Returning from across the street, Jim met his partner at the hood of the Pontiac, chomping on a wad of gum.

"Any luck?" asked Bill, still elated by his find, thoroughly convinced spearmint wasn't the answer.

"I don't know if you would call it luck. But do you see that troll sitting in the bus stop over there?"

Bill shrugged. "He have an extra martini?"

Jim ignored him with a deep breath and lidded eyes. "When he wasn't assaulting the nostrils of the people walking by, he says he saw a Martian jump out of a black van and go into the alley."

"Did he say what time or how long it stayed?"

"Christ, Bill, you're not serious! Look at the guy. He had the attention span of an infant and probably hasn't left that spot he calls a toilet for days."

"I'm sure," replied Bill, writing in his pad. "What else did he have to say?"

Jim grinned and mumbled reluctantly.

"What?" pressed Bill.

"He said he has the same suit," Jim replied, insulted. "Imagine that guy? Friggin' loser."

From the second they met, Bill had known his partner was domestically challenged the kind of guy who needed a tailor to match a pair of socks. Bill looked at his wrinkled partner and said with a smile, "Loser? You *paid* for yours." He pulled the plastic bag from his pocket and dangled it in front of his partner's face. "Check it out."

Chewing feverishly, Jim pulled his head back to focus. Inspecting the contents for a moment, he snapped, "So what? An earring. Anybody could have dropped it."

"Look at the design. This thing isn't cheap. It's a work of art. You lose it, you look for it. Unless, you're in a hurry. We match this to the other one, we have our woman."

Jim wasn't buying it. "So you've narrowed the field of suspects to people with earrings. That means you can include every hip '90s guy, girl, and drag queen from here to Fire Island. Christ, this day and age, that thing coulda been hangin' from the head of some guy's dick. We have to do better than that."

After another hour in the alley, they were ready to wrap it up. All the evidence had been collected, tagged, and bagged. Other than the earring and the body itself, there was not much to discuss.

At the detectives' request, Patrolman Piazza and his partner took down the police barriers, prepared statements from possible witnesses, and had the alley temporarily sealed. An unmarked patrol car would remain for a few hours, to see if anyone was foolish enough to return.

As the two detectives headed for their cars, something occurred to Masters. "Yo, Jimbo--by the way, I forgot to mention it, but we were called in special by the mayor's office."

"Great! What is it now? No dead johns in *my* backyard!....

15

Christ, I hate election years," whined Lackey. "These suits are worse than the pimps. At least with them you know what you're getting for your hard-earned dollar, and they don't bitch-slap the constituency. Never know what City Hall's got to ram up your ass."

"It does seem like that on the surface.... Whoever said this guy was even a john?" asked Bill with a shrug. "Hookers usually kill in self-defense. Why make it something it's not by cutting off the body parts? Christ, his fly's open, and whoever it was left behind his dick.... This guy's no john, my friend. He was probably taking a leak when someone nailed him from behind."

"Why don't you look in his shorts?" interjected Jim with a smile. "I'm willin' to bet he has ring around the root." He reached into his pocket for change.

"No, that's okay. I'm trying to quit," answered Masters, stepping back, both palms up.

"Gotta be done."

"Call it!"

Flipping the coin, Jim yelled, "Heads….you lose my friend. Dig deep."

Bill, pulling on a pair of fresh surgical gloves, unzipped the body bag and leaned over the victim. A powerful flashlight, supplementing the morning light, provided ample coverage.

Masters found what they were looking for. "You're the expert. What do you think? Skoal or lipstick?" asked Bill, displaying the base of the organ to his cringing colleague.

"With boots and pants like those, chewing tobacco can't be ruled out. But, *I'd* say lipstick."

"Me, too. . . . But I don't know, man. A dead john, and the *mayor* drags *us* in?"

Unless, of course, there was something the mayor knew that they didn't. And if the mayor's office knew, the feds were involved. Masters and Lackey hated working with the feds: It was always a one-way street headed in Uncle Sam's direction.

Masters reached a conclusion. "If the feds are around, we'll know soon enough. Look, I'll call you in a few hours. There are some errands I need to run. Have Piazza call His Honor's people and let them know we'll be downtown around eleven."

"Errands my ass. You're going home to that beautiful gal of yours. It's amazing what a few minutes down here will do to a guy."

Leaning out the Pontiac's window, Masters said, "*Adios*. See you in about three or four hours--and *please* don't be late. You can sleep it off later."

Lackey held up a finger. "C'mon, it was only a couple."

"Just be there."

Tires squealing in protest, Detective Masters was gone in a flash.

CHAPTER 4

If there was one thing Bill loathed about city life, other than dangerous levels of overcrowding and the tendency for ethnic makeups to change like the weather, it was the lack of ample parking. He could *never*, for the life of him, find a spot anywhere near his apartment. Opting for the space in front of the hydrant across the street, Bill picked up the postcard, checked his mailbox, and headed inside.

At the fourth floor, he exited the elevator and trudged down to the end of a short hall. The dirty, oxidized plaque above a brass knocker, surrounded by a half-dead Christmas wreath, read 401.

His two-bedroom apartment was modest at best--marked by a taste for old furniture developed over the years as a result of refusing to buy anything new. Aside from the weak attempt at faux painting and the faint mix of scented candles and Marlboro Reds, it was nothing extravagant: a Sony wide-screen Bill had scored at a PBA raffle, above which sat an accompanying sound system that, except for the 100-disc CD player, was a hybrid of outdated components. Music, sports, and sex were his passions. Sports for the man in him, sex for the women on him, and music for when the other two were in short supply.

He'd lived there for ten years, having had the economic collapse of a previous administration to thank for the perfect asking price. Otherwise, he'd have been like the rest of his colleagues living along the fringes of New Jersey.

He dropped his unwanted mail in the Yankee trash can near the door, save for an additional postcard that, upon further inspection, was postmarked the same day as the one he had in his other hand. It was a photo of the Statue of Liberty. Another *welcome to New York*. It was the first communiqué he'd received at his apartment, and like a low-voltage shock, it gave him a jolt. Setting aside a pile of newspapers, he moved to the couch, cringing at the sight of one of his CD's substituting as a wine coaster. Moving the empty glass to the end table, he turned on the table lamp, leaned elbows on knees, and inspected the two postcards a bit closer. From the mantle above the fireplace, he retrieved a small wooden box, removed the lid and the rest of his collection.

Bill had never made any *real* sense of the lifetime of cards. Pictures of ancient battlefields, religious icons. Copernicus, Alexander, Einstein, Mozart--people whose remarkable achievements had come at a tremendous price to themselves.

Everyone had a theory about his father's disappearance — depression, guilt, despair, even shame. Some said it was *he* who had been responsible for his wife's death.

But the remaining family knew it ran deeper than anything they could fathom. No one--especially a man hardened by a childhood of polio and softened by the love of family--abandons his children to the care and geriatric dalliances of his seventy-five-year-old mother. He'd given it all up: family, a fledgling real-estate business, gains as a local politician and, ultimately, the respect and admiration of his fellow parishioners. But Bill's father hadn't just left his family; he'd abandoned his country—the love of which he had worn like a crown.

The latest cards had been signed, "*Love, Janus*", an eerily misspelled version of his mother's name, and *both* had been sent from the same post office in Milan three weeks earlier.

Staring blindly at the pile of cards, Bill knew there was meaning in the pictures and the paucity of words. His father loved mind games--and the one he was playing, he was playing to win.

Exhausted, Bill sat back and closed his eyes. One of the things he most remembered about his father was his uncanny ability to make right out of wrong, by diverting the futilities of blame, focusing on the root of its existence.

Bill let out a sigh, unconscious to the fact that he would be willing to settle for a mere sound of his past. But his father, a man who left nothing to chance, had taken those with him as well.

Through the remaining images of childhood that blazed through his head, he wondered how a man with a photographic memory could forget the spelling of his wife's name. Regardless, given the latest card, there was a chance the missing-link was in New York. Like an old astronomer, Bill bowed his head and did what he had done every day since childhood — he prayed for contact.

In the warmth of the back bedroom, Bill's girlfriend, Kathleen Wheeler, Esq. was fast asleep under a pile of soft pillows and thick blankets. Greeted with a muffled snore, Bill believed the term sleep applied to everyone *but* the woman hibernating under the covers. Standing at the bottom of the bed, he couldn't tell where the head started and the feet ended. He flicked on the air conditioner; lifting the covers at the head of the bed, he saw a beautiful pair of women's feet. He decided to tickle them, to see if the owner was awake, for which he received the normal response: her foot snapping to attention, her screaming angrily through a sweaty mass of tangled hair, half of which was stuck in her mouth. She was beautiful, though, and after a few more syllables spat through strands of moistened hair, the voice began to take on a more human tone. "How many times do I have to tell you not to *do* that shit, Bill? Jesus, am I hot!"

He knew she was talking temperature.

"Nice mouth, babe! You talk to your colleagues like that?" he asked with an air of disapproval, his head shaking playfully in disgust. Although she sounded like a longshoreman, she had been for the last five years an assistant D.A. for the City of New York.

"How about *I* tickle *your* feet every time I come into the room while you're sleeping?. . . .Did you get my cigarettes?" she added, rubbing her eyes, again changing the subject.

"No, and no," he teased, amazed at the thick red crease the pillow had put in her cheek. "And how was *your* day, scarface?" He eyed his wrist for the date, sensing the onslaught of another painful period for them both.

"What?" she said, rubbing life back into her face.

"Never mind counselor. How was your day?"

"Terrible. Some scumbag rapist got off on another bogus technicality. Judge Wilson—the old fart—rather let a rapist go than have the case overturned on appeal," she said, trying to roll to the edge of the bed, the pile of blankets restricting her movement. Bill gave her a playful nudge.

"I'd rather see that piece of shit spend six months to a year on Rikers awaiting an appeal. With any luck they'd have to surgically remove his hands from his ankles. It's a sin to let that monster walk."

He watched intently, as she squirmed for a seat on the edge of the bed. He loved the way she looked in her leopard thong.

He sat next to her, wrapping his arm around her shoulders as he did, pulling her close. "How about a quick roll in the hay, counselor, ya know, to forget your problems?"

"C'mon, Bill, it's my day off. I don't need *sex* to forget my problems. I need a fuckin' *cigarette!*" she said with a painful sigh as she flopped back, spread-eagle, onto the bed. She started to whine. "You promised you'd pick me up a carton! Besides," she said, crinkling her nose, "you smell like a back alley."

"Forget it," he said, rising with a sigh. "Yeah, I did say that, didn't I? But as fate would have it, I was at the precinct late when some towel-head got fleeced of his sensory organs. So, shoot me, if I forgot."

"Where, Forty-second and Eighth?"

"Everyone's a detective these days. What makes you say that?" he asked, making his way down the hall to the bathroom.

"Heard it on the radio, when I got up to pee," she called out. "Quick report. Figured you'd be there."

"You're very funny, counselor. Somebody cut that poor slob's tongue out and sliced off his ear." He added offhandedly, "How's that for a bad night?"

In the bathroom, he lathered his face in the small mirror above the sink. Drawing the razor across his chin, he suddenly realized, although it was the middle of the night, he *had* recognized his favorite ambulance chaser from the *Post* behind one of the barricades, snapping pictures, digging like a mole. The word was out.

Kathleen, still mulling the details, said, "Thanks for the gory tidbit."

"I assure you, the pleasure is all mine," he said, talking to the mirror with a devious smile. "Hey, smokey, did you happen to catch the final score of last night's Yankees game?" he asked, admiring himself further, his vanity deflating as he ran his fingers through thinning brown hair.

She shook her head and flopped back onto the bed; he heard nothing but a grunt.

"Well, *did* you?" he snapped, pondering the freshly opened box of tampons and the lengthy strands of Kathleen's hair dusting the toothpaste mottled sink and brown tiled floor.

"No! Try reading the fuckin' paper!" she screamed, rising to rummage around the night-stand for her brush.

"No, I think I'll just unwind with a cool shower, thank you," he mumbled under his breath, as he pulled back the shower curtain and kicked the door shut with his heel.

With the shower out of the way, he brushed his teeth, pulled on a pair of dark slacks and a thin red cotton pull-over that hid his growing waistline, and headed for the kitchen, where Kathy, clad in nothing but slippers and an oversized oxford, was preparing frozen waffles.

"You want to read the paper?" she asked, approaching him for a kiss, a cup of fresh coffee in hand.

"Let me guess. '*Israeli rocket hits car full of children*' or '*Palestinian gunmen attack Tel Aviv bus*'?" asked Bill, slipping on his shoulder holster as he took the mug from her hand.

"Sorry. I didn't know you were so sensitive to world affairs," she replied. He eased in behind her and gently placed his arms around her shoulders as she leaned over the counter to retrieve the waffles from the toaster. "I'm sorry, it's just senseless aggression. Killing for the sake of killing."

"It's religious apartheid, nothin' else," she pushed, adding, "What would happen if outsiders came and told *you*, Bill Masters, that it was time to leave *your* home, give up *your* job. All because you had placed your faith in the hands of another, less desirable, God."

Turning her around, drawing her near, he said lovingly, "Listen, woman, *ground* ain't worth killing over."

She stared up into his eyes. "*Everyone* deserves a safe place to hang their hat."

Bill really wanted to fuck, not fight. Bending, he dismissed the dialogue and pecked her on the lips as both their hips rocked in unison. "Listen, one more thing. How about, ya know, later?" he asked, grinning as he raised and lowered his eyebrows.

Seeming disinterested, she turned her attention back to the counter and purred as she licked syrup from her fingers. Pulling up the back of her shirt, she exposed her number one asset and said, "Not this week."

Fighting off an urge to scream, he returned to the living room, found the old phone on the end table next to the couch and made a call.

Across town, Detective Lackey lay peacefully on his California king-sized bed, snoring like a pig. The phone rang. It was Bill. He didn't sound at all satisfied.

"Hey, chief, what's a matter?" Jim asked, up on an elbow, his free hand kneading his balls. "Go it alone again, did ya?"

"Forget it. Just meet me downtown in an hour."

"Sure. Why not?"

"Just be there, smart ass." Bill hung up.

CHAPTER 5

The traffic heading downtown was light for a late Saturday morning. Probably people sleeping off a little TGIF Bill thought as he tried to recall the last time he'd taken Kathy out on the town just to watch her dance. He got aroused just thinking about it. She was either working crazy hours, schmoozing some ass-grabbing politico, or sweating through the bed. It was sad, but he had pretty much the same schedule. Routine was the biggest killer of love, his life the biggest routine of all.

They needed a change, something: it was no fun being alone together any more. He wanted to share his past, how it had affected and shaped him, but the lack of memories, or the warmth of a parent's touch, left him empty inside--a void she or a lifetime of blank postcards could never fill.

At the mayor's office, he was surprised to find his partner waiting for him on the front steps, fumbling with what looked to be the remains of a hot dog loaded with sauerkraut.

Pulling the Camaro up to the curb, he turned off the radio, placed his placard on the dash, checked for any valuables, and headed for the steps.

Lackey approached, arm extended, his voice muffled by the

previous bite. "Want some?"

"Nah, only Bratwurst before ten."

"Sorry. Just being polite," Jim said, before stuffing the rest into his mouth. "What crawled up your ass?"

Bill took a step back. "Nothing." Hands in his pockets, he paused momentarily, kicking some debris that had stuck to his foot. He had to get it out. "Ah, shit. I didn't get any because of a carton of cigarettes. How fucked up is that? She's the one smoking, and I'm the one dying." He bent over and cleaned off his shoe.

"Sounds like she's on the rag."

Bill exhaled quickly. "Just drop it. Let's see if we can't get some solid answers out of these guys."

After the short climb to the entrance of the building, the two detectives flashed their shields to the guards at the door and headed through the main lobby and down the corridor to the elevator.

"What's up with the guard?" Bill muttered, stepping inside. "I've seen 'im a hundred times, and he always gives you the same old shit, 'What's doin'?' What kind of crap is that?"

Following, Jim replied, "If you sat in a chair and did the same thing day in and day out, you'd need a personality adjustment yourself."

"Adjustment? Guy needs a fuckin' transplant."

"Maybe it's the heat. This place feels like a friggin' sauna."

"Feels like *Hell*."

They stepped from the elevator, suspecting that most of the building would be empty. They were wrong.

The mayor's outer office was abuzz. Odd for a Saturday, thought Bill as they approached the secretary.

The wood paneling, as well as the lights hanging from the ceiling, looked in need of cleaning. The only decorations were pictures of the city's past mayors, the impact of civic duty showing profoundly on their stolid faces: none wore a smile.

The mayor's middle-aged secretary, a full-figured woman flushed from the heat, sat panting like a dog as she applied a final coat of enamel to her stubby nails. The color, like the roots of her hair, matched the uppers of her shoes.

Bill offered a fake smile and his shield. "Hello, I'm Detective Masters, and this is Detective Jim Lackey. We're here to see the assistant to the mayor or deputy mayor, if they're around."

Fanning her nails wildly, she replied in a robotic tone, "Deputy maya's on vacation, but the maya will see yous now."

So it was no ordinary homicide, Bill thought; entering the mayor's office, he noticed that the decor had been drastically changed since his last visit. New curtains; a short, gray muslin, provided a better view of the East River and greatly reduced the need for artificial light. A pretty ritzy renovation for an administration with a budget deficit especially since the man they were visiting had griped so much about it during his campaign.

The usually unshakable Abraham Kravitz was seated behind his large mahogany desk, barking orders into the phone. To his right, seated at the conference table, slumped the chief of police Willie Jones, dressed in what looked like golfing attire. His right leg, flung over his left, shook impatiently as he sipped a glass of water. Bill recognized his uneasiness as a harbinger of reproach.

To Jones's right sat Commissioner Al Agnew, another snappy dresser willing to pay a premium for a soft pair of shoes and a tidy divorce. To his right, admiring the new artwork and paying little attention to their arrival, stood their federal nemesis, Agent Willard of the F.B.I., fronted by his latest sidekick Agent Patterson, a deceivingly tall, middle-aged man of few words and fewer emotions.

Presently, Willard's subordinate, dressed in a blue off-the-rack suit, was stooped picking up loose change from the floor around his feet.

Dark suits, dark glasses, impeccable to look at: The quiet one appeared to be older, a bit more distinguished. He politely covered his mouth with a handkerchief, as he coughed heavily behind his hand.

To their left, nearest the door, stood the assistant to the mayor, Mr. Nates Johnson; a man in constant battle with a feminine side that sprinted to the forefront every time he opened his mouth. Or maybe he was content; they couldn't tell. He had suffered a nasty break, turning an ankle on a hike around the pyramids. Despite two months of rehab, he still required a metal cane for support.

The detectives had taken a liking to him from their first introduction. He wore his black hair back in a short pony tail, dressed impeccably, was as thin as a string bean and spoke with a voice like a mouse on steroids. He could also take it as well as dish it out.

"Hey, Nates," Jim teased, offering his hand. "Leg must be getting better. You seem much lighter in your loafers."

"God, you're incorrigible!" Johnson shook the hand and went back to pouring water into the deep purple vase on the mayor's desk.

Bill pulled out a chair and sat. Jim followed suit.

"Can I get you gentlemen something to drink?" Nates asked, returning to the table.

"Two coffees, cream and sugar," requested Bill, settling into his chair.

Nates poured the coffee, handed it over, and went about his business.

"Nice office, sir," observed Bill, stirring his joe. "New interior decorator, or has Nates made that career change he's always wanted?"

"Enough!" the mayor snorted, as he moved from behind his desk and took a seat next to the commissioner. "What do we have on the dead guy?"

"Well, not much," Bill admitted. "We're still waiting on the ME's report. There are a few tentative witnesses. One is a high-priced hooker, the other a bum."

The mayor rubbed his forehead as if it hurt. "Of course, who else?"

Checking his notes, Bill continued. "The guy was strangled, and the perp took the time to cut out his tongue and remove his right ear. All three are still at large." Puzzled, Bill paused. "Excuse me, if I'm outta' line, but what is the interest in this particular stiff, in this particular alley, on this particular night? Who is he, some dignitary's cab-driving son?"

The commissioner leaned forward in his chair. "Pardon me, Detective. Allow me to introduce Special Agents Willard and Patterson. They'll be assisting in the investigation."

"*What* investigation?" Bill protested, raising his hands. He turned to Willard and added, "When we arrived on the scene, the guy couldn't have been dead for more than three hours, tops! We haven't had a chance to write up any in-depth reports or interview any credible witnesses. Obviously you know who he is. *Please*, enlighten us Willard--the suspense is killing me!"

The agent, a tall, fit, middle-aged man with a weak chin and lips as thin as dimes, got to his feet and made his way to the slide projector set at the head of the table. Bill thought the man's new-wave hair style belonged on Nate's head. He had been a federal fixture for years—a byproduct of a Hampton socialite and an Ivy League wonder boy whose ass had chaired many of Wall Street's most prestigious institutions.

Willard popped the clasps on his briefcase and removed a few documents and a carousel of colored slides. He dropped the tray onto the projector and, motioning for the lights, picked up a remote, pressed a button, and headed for the side of the portable screen.

Immediately, a mug shot of the deceased appeared, the photo taken in a New York City station house six years before.

The only thing visible, other than the photo, was the light on Willard's face. His eyes, somewhat dim, gave him a jaundiced appearance. He cleared his throat and began to speak in deadly earnest.

"Gentlemen, what you're about to hear is for our ears only. Should you feel pressured in any way to share this information with anyone outside of this room, don't!"

He seemed very convincing, as the slouches in the leather chairs began to disappear. Unless there was a political advantage to be gained, security was always the first priority of Uncle Sam.

Bill, out of habit, preferred to slouch, tilting his head back as he hummed softly the theme to *Mission Impossible*. Jim playfully slapped his head back to the upright position.

"This is Malik Abdul Salaam. He is, or shall I say *was*, a government informant working in conjunction with myself, Agent Patterson here, and others in the F.B.I., aiding us in our efforts to combat terrorism."

His eyes narrowed on Bill and his humming.

"*Some* of you may not have been aware of this, but Mr. Salaam was instrumental in foiling certain plots by Middle Eastern terrorists to bomb various sites around the City of New York, including the Statue of Liberty. You remember that, don't you, gentleman?" He offered a half smile.

"Anyway," he continued, "I, personally, had a meeting with Mr. Salaam set for twelve o'clock last night down in the Forty-Second Street area. He was a no-show. One thing that I and the Bureau liked about Mr. Salaam--he was prompt in his dealings with us. We waited patiently for some time. Naturally, we suspected foul play and got in touch with the commissioner." He offered a smile that could have passed as a leer and motioned to the commissioner, who, like any politician, nodded selflessly in agreement.

"We asked the commissioner to keep the department's ears open for any information regarding a suspicious death or other act of foul play in the area. When the call came in with the description, we thought we might have our man."

Bill thought about this for a second. "How did *we* learn of your boy's demise?"

Leaning forward, smoothing out his silk power-tie, the commissioner replied, "Anonymous tip. Call came in around two. After being contacted by Agent Willard, I immediately woke the mayor and arranged for you two to get down there ASAP."

"I don't recall hearing his name mentioned in the papers or any of the court proceedings concerning the Statue of Liberty investigation," said Bill, elbowing Jim for additional support. It was a detail they would've never overlooked.

"That's because he *wasn't*," replied Agent Willard. "He was our ace in the hole, when dealing with these guys. They don't live by our rules. He was our low-profile line to the inside. He didn't participate in any of the planning, or the attempt. He was on the fringe. He lived with half of those guys for two years just listening, going to school, driving his cab, attending to his studies."

"They just let him hang out, like one of the guys, huh? A student?" asked Bill, unconvinced.

"The Islamic people are very trusting of one another, Detective," explained the agent, forcefully. "He wasn't an active participant, but they feel they are *all* in the struggle together to bring about the demise of the Great Satan. So, yes, he was left to himself, left to his studies."

"How did you get your hooks into him, then?" Jim asked, slurping his coffee, as he reached for the glazed bear claw that beckoned him from the center of the table.

"We had New York's finest help us out on that one. We'd been keeping loose tabs on the entire group when your people busted him on that meter-tampering charge. Given his background, we took the opportunity to step in and turn him. We told him we'd pull his green card and have him deported. The I.R.S. folks are amateurs compared to the I.N.S., when it comes to ruining people's lives."

"Holy shit!" Bill murmured. "Not sent back home to his Jihad brothers? Say it ain't so."

Agent Willard ignored him. "Unfortunately, Mr. Salaam's father had a falling-out with the ayatollah, resulting in the whole family being butchered in their sleep. Somehow, Salaam got out. He wouldn't have lasted a day back in his own country. We felt obligated to give him an offer he couldn't refuse."

The rest of the men in the room seemed to be analyzing the information in a calm silence. The commissioner asked, "What did his father do for a living?"

Willard was not eager to be specific. "Let's just say, he set policy for the Shah, and others, when it came to American oil interests in the Middle East."

Most of the older men digested this with visual disdain; the two detectives thought it had merit. He might have looked like a bum, but Salaam came from money.

The commissioner's usual aplomb was marred by a bead of sweat; the chief, handkerchief in hand, dabbed lightly at his brow as the room grew warmer.

The mayor signaled to Nates, who, looking shaken, moved towards the thermostat on the far wall near the door. Agent Patterson rose and removed his jacket. The commissioner did the same. Patterson's short-sleeved shirt looked silly, com-pared to the neatly pressed and starched oxford of the wilting commissioner.

The pallor of the older man's skin, and the band-aid in the crook of his arm, suggested to Bill he had a health problem.

"So," Jim went on, "what protection strategies did you use for his overall safety? Look and leave?"

"Sounds more like you-scratch-our-back-and-we-get-you-dead," added Bill derisively. "I surmise, from the outcome, his choice of destination made little difference? Here, there, he's still a corpse."

"Listen, you two jokers!" said the agent, agitated, "he didn't *need* constant Bureau protection, because no one ever knew about him but us. You *got* that?" He had motioned to himself and his assistant Patterson, whose phlegmatic demeanor drew little attention.

"We had the whole thing set up. No other control agents. Just our little secret, up until now."

The commissioner, sounding like the political beggar that he was, asked, "Are, or were, you running any active operation with the deceased, Agent Willard?"

"That's strictly a need-to-know basis for now, sir," Willard said. "I assure you, we have our reasons. What we *can* tell you is that he was still living, until recently, with those who escaped prosecution in the original investigation. They have been, understandably, lying low. He kept a watchful eye and let us know what was going on."

The police chief rose slowly, wincing as he did. Rheumatism, from years on the street, had taken its toll. He had seen a lot during his tenure, but there were still a few things he didn't digest easily. Bullshit was one of them. His graying hair could vouch for it.

He nodded respectfully to the mayor and the commissioner as he picked up his hat. He stared at the agent with an austere look in his eyes, beads of sweat still dotting his brow--a look Bill had seen before.

His jaw and disposition firm, the chief spoke softly. "From what I've heard and seen so far, it's highly probable that the security of your witness has been compromised, Agent Willard."

"Maybe it was just a random killing, Will?" interrupted the mayor, trying to avert a showdown. "It happens all the time down there, God help us!" Bill thought he heard him mutter something else in Yiddish, but the mayor was always muttering.

The chief continued unswayed, "Unfortunately, the victim, regardless of his identity, or past transgressions, was a citizen of our fair city. Therefore, he is entitled to an unfettered investigation into his untimely and, may I add, brutal death. . .*wherever* that may lead." He looked directly at Willard. "The New York City Police Department will not be able to conduct an effective investigation without the full cooperation of the F.B.I. He was your boy, Agent Willard, someone who happened to be acquainted with some pretty bad people. This concerns me, as I'm sure it does the rest of the gentlemen in this room. The killer's method reeks of a hit. The question remains, whose mob? That should be our main concern.

"If the F.B.I. wants access to our information and resources, we must have complete access to theirs. Until you're willing to play ball and put your cards on the table, you're just wasting my time. Therefore, I must excuse myself from further discussion. I have other pressing matters."

He turned, tucked his hat under his arm and strode across the brand-new carpet towards the door. Grabbing the knob, the mayor offered him a friendly recommendation, "Remember, Willie, keep your head down and open your stance."

Without turning, the chief raised his hand over his head, waved, and left.

Jim felt a surge of respect for his boss. He also knew the display was standard horse-and-pony--fiery rhetoric that carried little or no weight.

The commissioner, his own response muzzled, thought it therapeutic for the chief to let off a little steam now and again. Bill contemplated blowing off a little of his own. Usually, an FBI ass-kissing was required before they'd come around. This time he wasn't so sure--the agents had their own asses on the line.

Nates instinctively closed the door behind him as the commissioner leaned over to the mayor and whispered quietly into his ear. Then he too rose from his chair, shook the mayor's hand and took the same path out the door, leaving Kravitz looking disturbed.

The agents, through with their speech, were collecting their belongings, readying to leave.

Leaning in, Bill whispered to Jim, "It's obvious they had something going with this guy. Saying it's classified is the same as saying we were actively using him. But what could have happened? More bomb activity going on? A war between factions? The guy was a *cab* driver, for Christ's sakes. What could *he* possibly know?"

Bill looked up at the two agents and asked, "Where was this meeting to take place? If it's not too much to ask? A deserted wharf, the dark recesses of a parking garage?" Patterson had a puzzled look on his face, of which Bill took notice.

Willard said firmly, "Sorry, Detective. Again, you don't need to know."

"With all due respect, sir, but how can we put together an investigation if you won't share any of the pertinent information with us? I believe we have a right to know!" Bill added, getting pissed off.

"Detective," the agent replied, his own voice beginning to rise, "this individual was a federal witness under my aegis. And I stress federal, because that is the jurisdiction under which that information falls. I brought you in because he was killed, as far as we see it, outside our sphere of influence. Therefore, until I hear otherwise, he's your problem. You do your job, and I'll do mine. Do I make myself clear? I want to catch whoever did this more than you. Knowingly or not, they have cut my line to the inside. Besides, the mayor and the commissioner concur on this matter. Why can't you?" Taking a deep breath, he returned to his business.

Masters looked as if he'd just seen a ghost. The government *never* handed the reins to local law enforcement and they both knew it.

Jim, shaking his head in disbelief, picked up the coffee mug resting on his knee and finished it. "Let's get the fuck out of here."

"I'm with you, partner," replied Bill, looking to rise.

The mayor had other plans. "Wait one minute, detectives!" He waved them back to their chairs, the mood brightening as the feds gathered their belongings and headed for the exit.

Agent Willard turned and addressed the mayor one last time. "He's all yours. We'll fax the specifics on Mr. Salaam by the end of the day. No promises, but we'll share what we can. Give our regards to the commissioner and Chief Jones." The two put on their dark sunglasses and passed Nates on their way out the door.

Jim and Bill were standing. The mayor sat back in his chair, eyed them up and down, and said, "The old dynamic duo." His tone, attempting respect, leaned heavily towards the fatuous.

"I want you two to know the three of us agree only on one thing, that the F.B.I. is hiding a lot more than this 'classified' shit. No federal witness gets brutally murdered, and they just walk away. Something's not kosher.

"I spoke briefly with the commissioner. He has a few friends at the Bureau who might be willing to lend a hand." He lowered his voice. "Listen, Agent Willard gives me the creeps. I want to be briefed on the progress of your investigation *daily*. . .hourly, if need be, cause I got a bad feeling about this one. People are still on edge as it is. The UN will renew hosting ceremonies next week. The president and every dignitary known to man is scheduled to visit. If there's going to be any more activity by these whackos, we need to know *now*, not after it's too late. The feds may have taken themselves out, but this is my city, and as long as I sit behind *this* desk, things will be done *my* way. We're going to have to beat them at their own game. I'm sure after this display, you two *will* see to that."

"You've got to get up pretty early to pull one over on old Mayor Kravitz," joked Bill. "And that was one hell of a slide show."

The mayor was squirming in his seat; Bill held up his hands in mock assurance.

"No problem, sir--you seem to be one step ahead of us anyway. Listen, we'd love to stay and chat, but there is an investigation to conduct."

With that they turned to leave. As they approached the door, they were met by Nates, who excitedly said to Bill as he brought the pinky of his hand to the corner of his mouth, "Wasn't Agent Willard just *striking*? I wonder how much he weighs?" He gave Bill a strange look, as they slipped out the door.

With a worried look on his face, the assistant leaned back on the closed door, crossed his arms, and sighed, "Savages!"

The mayor shook his head and dragged his hands through his remaining hair. He paused momentarily, and in a polite tone, added, "Nates, would you please reschedule my haircut for after lunch. If that's at all possible?"

"Don't be silly, sir. I'll have my man here in a jiff."

Without hesitation or a need to look up the number, he picked up the phone and began to dial.

CHAPTER 6

"Where do you want to go from here, partner?" Bill asked, his eyes circling the large, pillared rotunda, finally settling on a beautifully tanned, civil-servant as she headed for the street.

"I'm starving. What ya say we grab some chow, head to the station house, and start piecing together what we've got?" Jim replied, doing the same. "Obviously, we're not gettin' any help from anybody else."

"You got that right. Willard's a prick--name reminds me of that rat in the movies." Bill paused briefly, dismissing his next thought.

"What's up?"

"Ahh, never mind. Wong's again?" Bill asked, disappointed.

The two headed for their cars and drove to the station house. Wong's Chinese kitchen was within walking distance. Jim and half the others in the station house ate there religiously. He ordered ahead on his car phone.

"Isn't Saturday's special pork fried rice and an egg roll?" asked Bill, plucking a rose from one of the racks outside a bodega on the way to the restaurant. Bringing the flower to his nose, he offered a genial smile and the correct change to a smooth-skinned woman in a blue sari standing watch just outside the door.

"Does that really work for you?" Jim turned to admire the woman's ass. "Never does for me."

"It helps to have a friend to give it to," Bill teased, amazed at his partner's lack of class.

"Very funny. I'm in a transitional stage. I can't seem to get back in the game. I've forgotten how, ya know, to pick up women." Jim looked down, almost ashamed, but his thoughts returned immediately to food. "Forget the special. I ordered from the car."

Bill should have known. "*Why* do you insist on ordering my lunch? And secondly, forgive my insensitivity but, transitional stages don't last five fuckin' years. Did the court award her your balls 'r what?"

"It was the betrayal, ya know?" said Jim, his eyes distant. "She ripped my fuckin' heart out, man. . .pure and simple. Before the legal apologies arrived by certified mail, I just wanted to bury it, forget it ever happened. If not for me, for the kids. But something deep inside always told me to make it right or never live it down. Why would a man who worked hard and provided for his family be blessed with a woman like that? I gave her everything the job allowed, and she rammed it down my effin' throat. You know, the booze is the only thing that's kept me sane."

"*Please* don't be a schmuck!" replied Bill. "If that's the worst of your past, you can only hope for a brighter future. Sometimes you just have to cut your losses. Trust me, the hand's been dealt. Put down the bottle. . .you'll get to lay your cards on the table."

Bill paused momentarily, sidestepping a runaway garment rack. "A long time ago, my father told me--and *please* don't get offended--'Battle the past, forfeit the future.'"

The few remaining blocks left the two deep in thought, both detectives teetering between the task at hand and the irrepressible desire to get laid. The next twenty-four hours would be sure to fly by; they would have little time for socializing.

Just before they entered the restaurant, Jim broke the silence. "Sometimes, the losses are just too much." A bell rang wildly, as they went inside.

Wong's Chinese Kitchen was like a lot of others: Previously cooked duck with crunchy brown skin hung on metal hooks inside windows decorated with broad Chinese characters singed and sooted by the heat of flaring woks. The heavy mixture of hot oil and ginger lingered in the air like an aromatic fog as the rapid staccato sounds of another tongue melded with their own.

Inside, Bill's eyes fell on a long wall decorated with a silk mural of mismatched peacocks battling among the limbs of a willow tree, their faded plumage reddened by the fiery warmth of the setting sun.

Not knowing the battle's outcome was the beauty of the piece–but its impact was being slowly eroded by the growth of celebrity photos receding from its borders, back to the wall behind the register.

As Bill inspected them for any he might have missed, Jim haggled over the bill with an old, round-faced woman in a blood-stained apron who glared at him as she yelled, "You *pake*! Now you go!" Her additional barrage, only the grimacing cook could understand.

"Yeah, yeah. Whatever," Jim muttered, as he pocketed his change. "You have a pleasant day, mamasan."

He headed for the door while Bill, looking to make nice, offered her the single rose as she wiggled angrily behind the counter like an undercooked eel.

"What'n-the-fuck does '*pake*' mean?" asked Jim out on the sidewalk.

"I may be going out on a limb, but I think in Mandarin it translates into 'cheap bastard.' Don't you ever quit?"

"Cheap? Why do we have to drop twenty bucks every time we want to eat rice?"

"It's called New York," replied Bill, starting to walk.

"There you go--someone gives me shit, and you say nothing, you just stare at pictures."

"Pictures are worth a thousand words."

Outside the station house, cops between shifts came both ways through the tall swinging doors. Some loitered on the steps, making small talk and smoking cigarettes as others returned wearily, their self-proclaimed innocents in tow.

Ascending the crowded steps, Bill turned, cupped his hands around his mouth, and cried, "Any of you villains catch last night's Yankee game?"

"Yanks crushed, mon!" answered a dark-skinned perp with perfect Caribbean English. "I tell ya, mon, they be on fire. Twelve runs on fifteen hits. Dis be da year, mon! Jah has predicted it."

"Excellent, and thank you, Mr. Marley!" said Bill, admiring the length of his dreadlocks. "I'm. . .they're on a roll," he added with a pumped fist.

"Betting again?" nagged Jim, wrestling with the belt of his pants.

"Of course not," insisted Bill, grabbing the handle of the thick double doors of the station house. Inside, their ears were bombarded by unpleasant sounds: people yelling, patrolmen screaming; organized chaos.

Making a bee line through the crowd, they marched up to the uniformed man at the desk--Sergeant Harry Sprague.

"What the fuck is going *on*?" Bill shouted over the din.

"Nothing much. Protest at an abortion clinic went sour. Protesters don't like that late-term shit. Can't say as I blame them, but just the same. . . ."

Peering through his heavy bifocals, he leaned forward and, in a tone of secrecy, added, "A little teargas, a few bumps and bruises, and presto, end of story."

Sprague had been a fixture behind that desk for almost twenty years, one of the few guys from the old school who wasn't afraid to make tough decisions and didn't take shit from anybody. He had no other aspiration than to run his section of the precinct with an efficiency and professionalism beyond the lure of office politics. Which was why he was still a desk sergeant--he didn't care, and everybody knew it.

Looking up a moment later as he shuffled aimlessly through his growing paperwork, he realized the two detectives were still standing in front of the desk.

"Hey, what are you two dickheads waiting for? Don't just *stand* there--captain's been waiting for you over an hour! You know how he loves to wait."

"Jeez, take a Valium. No one told *us*," Jim protested. He turned and followed Bill up the stairs.

Up the four flights that led to Homicide, glass cases lined the stairway filled with the pictures, trophies, and awards of those men and women who were the promise of the future. Near the top, a section had been expanded to commemorate those heroes fallen in the recent past.

When they reached the fourth-floor landing, Jim muttered something about a quick jog to the can as he disappeared around the corner.

Standing outside the main doors of the division, Bill was greeted by the unenvious stares of a few departing colleagues. Masters wasn't quite ready to meet with the malignantly miffed man that he called his boss. Sneaking into the room, he sought the solitude of the worn metal desk in the opposite corner.

Masters had sat there, across from Jim, for over fifteen years; it had become a second home furnished with a few framed photos and a ragged throw pillow stuffed in the bottom drawer.

The rest of the room had its ceilings and half its walls decorated in white, or at least that'd been the original color. The remaining wall space consisted of a four-foot stained oak wainscot with a dull varnished finish that ran the perimeter of the room. Deep grooves and rounded corners suggested a Victorian substantiality. The only other wood in the place was the line of creaky, old floor boards and the green chalkboard that occupied the far corner. From where he was sitting, it looked as if it had been hastily wiped clean.

The opaque windows that lined the far wall on the street side were covered with dirt and soot concealed by partially raised Venetian blinds that contained a few seasons' worth of cobwebs and dust. Unlike the posh reserves of the mayor's office, the city's maintenance budgets had come under the axe in recent years. Occasionally, people volunteered their time to do a little house cleaning. Lately, charity had fallen to an all-time low.

Bill's distant eyes refocused, returning to the chalkboard. A smiled appeared, as he finally grasped the source of Captain Jackson's woes.

A rare product of Benson Hurst, Leon Jackson was a man who had risen above the ethnic and social adversities of the street only to drag them behind him wherever he went. Office door open, he sat rigidly behind his desk, his nose buried in a large book.

When Jim returned, Bill rose and the two headed in his direction. Lackey placed the take-out on the counter next to the coffee machine outside the captain's door. Grease had seeped through the bag, soiling the stack of napkins as well as the upper leg of Jim's faded gray pants. They entered the captain's office and closed the door behind them.

"Well, I'm glad that you two could make it," Jackson drawled, closing his book. "Where have you two been hanging out? Over the belt?"

"Sorry sir," replied Bill respectfully, "we didn't know you were waiting. We just left the mayor's office and picked up a quick bite to eat."

"Yeah," said Jim, easing himself and his 'roids gingerly into the chair.

"Well, fill me in. I want to know why the FBI finds this stiff in *my* alley so important." The captain had a cagey look as he leaned back in his chair, hands folded neatly behind his head. "As you may already know," offered Bill, "Agent Willard and his boy Patterson were in attendance. The deceased is--was a federal snitch, who, according to Willard, was acquainted with those responsible for the Statue of Liberty bombing. Late last night, the feds had a meeting set in the Times Square area, and he was a no-show. Turned up dead in an alley on Eighth, strangled, stabbed, cut up, *and* he no longer had any use for his right ear and tongue. We'll know more, after we get the Medical Examiner's reports."

"Well, how in the hell did the F.B.I. get involved so fast?" asked the captain.

"Willard gloated over the fact that the guy was unusually prompt when summoned," interjected Jim. "Feds got spooked, called the commissioner, the rest you already know."

"And Willard? What's that prick up to?"

"'Classified', I believe was the term he used, Captain," replied Bill, with an expression of fake surprise.

"The usual stone-wall," chimed Jim, wiping his hands on a tissue he had pulled from his sauce-encrusted pocket. "I thought the chief was going to blow a gasket."

"Well, what do you guys think?" asked the captain. "Any ideas?"

Bill shrugged. "Mob hit maybe, gambling debts. . .from what Willard described, it was more than likely one of his own."

"And Willard doesn't care?" asked the captain, rocking nervously in his chair.

"To be honest, we haven't had any time to do anything. Personally? I think Willard's diffusing some other cluster fuck, and he wants us to do the dirty work for him. We came in to start our preliminary reports, review the evidence, and see what we can come up with. We need that ME's report, and I imagine it won't be ready until sometime tomorrow. You'll be the first to know about anything we come up with, Captain."

"I'd better. Come Monday morning, the hotline's gonna' be ringin' and I don't want to be looking like a dick." His accusing eyes were locked on Bill, as he rocked slowly in his chair. Breaking eye contact, he picked his book back up off his desk, and added firmly, "Dismissed!"

The two detectives rose from their chairs and headed towards the door. Lackey, eager to get to his lunch, left first. As Bill reached the door, he turned back and asked, "Catch the score of last night's game?"

"Yeah, yeah," replied the Captain with disgust.

"Losers paid a hundred," said Bill with a toothy smile.

"Get out, Detective! And one more thing," he added, pointing a finger. "Only a retard'd leave odds on the board. IAD would just love to pin that on somebody. Thank you, and be gone!"

CHAPTER 7

"There are a few possibilities," Bill observed, pocketing the crisp c-note stashed in the top drawer of his desk. "First, instincts tell me Willard's snitch had his cover blown and was butchered as a warning. The guy lived here a long time. Driving a cab exposed him to every miserable low-life imaginable. I don't think he was in the alley by accident. He knew his killer."

"Probably right," said Jim, tossing the remains of his lunch into the garbage can at his feet. "There didn't seem to be much of a struggle. Nothing at the entrance or on the way to where he fell. So he wasn't dragged in or dumped. He entered under his own steam."

"Drug deal gone sour?" Bill pondered, looking for another angle. "Or maybe he was there to pay a debt and got whacked anyway."

"Robbery?"

Bill curled his lip and took a second to look about. "Sure, but why was his fly down and his pants unbuckled?" he asked. "He did have traces of 'whatever' around his knob."

"Maybe a hooker popped him," Jim suggested, eyeing the

plump blonde secretary approaching with a few files under her arm.

"Captain asked me to pull the victim's jacket," she offered robotically. The paperwork landed with a thud, as she cast a narrow gaze in Bill's direction. Spinning on her heels, she returned to her desk.

"What do you think my chances are with Nancy?" Jim asked with raised eyebrows. "I dig blondes."

"Nurse Ratchet?" asked Bill, amazed, sifting quickly through the paperwork. "Slim to none. I think, from the ring on her finger and the frown on her face, she's married. Besides, if you like blondes, I can *guarantee* the rug ain't matchin' the curtains." With a wink and a grin, he continued organizing the papers on his desk. Peering under a few files, he asked, "Where the hell are those Polaroids of the scene?"

Jim picked a file from the stack in front of him and produced the photos. He took a few and handed the rest to his partner.

"Shit," Bill said, leaning over. "Look here. The piss stains are down towards the base of his legs, and they're pretty large. It's like he fell into it."

"Maybe someone killed him and took a piss on him. Or maybe the uniformed fuck-up rolled him in it.

"I bet the doc forgets to do the pants," added Bill, still eyeing the photo.

"Look, I'm sure he will—at his size, his brain is like his body. But I think we're looking at this all wrong," Jim concluded. "Pissing in an alley is a common occurrence. So are open flies. He was probably getting his knob gobbled, and the chick whacked him."

"Had to be a pretty strong hooker to do that."

"Hey, stranger than fiction, but I've worked vice and there are some toughies out there. Besides, a sharp knife is a great equalizer."

"Well it's a good place to start," Bill admitted, "but what kind of hooker cuts up a john like that? I could understand loppin' off his dick. Maybe it was payback from another trick, an angry pimp? A disease? Maybe it was his wife or girlfriend. I'd expect traces of semen, not urine."

Bill came around his desk, picked up a pencil, and put the eraser end in his mouth, dropping deep into thought. He started turning slowly. "By the looks of him, and all the preliminary guesswork from the ME's guys, we place time of death at approximately--what? Between twelve and twelve-thirty?"

"Yeah, probably. But if you ask me, he looked like he'd been dead for days." Jim was looking at another photo, turning it slowly on its side for a better perspective.

"You're right--did look a little pasty, didn't he? Probably a junkie, too." Bill paused to check his watch. "Anyway, it's a busy street, nearby corner's a hangout for the ladies. . .get in touch with Vice and see who works that corner. Somebody had to see something. Piazza come up with anything?"

The phone on Bill's desk rang. He picked it up as Jim listened in. Suddenly, Bill's interest piqued and he sat up, pulling his chair closer to the desk.

"What? *Really*?. . .okay. We'll be down shortly." Replacing the phone, he offered Jim a set of pursed lips. "That was the ME's office. Apparently, after hearing from the FBI, Kravitz got him out of bed to work on our body. Everything's preliminary, but he has some information he'd like to share."

"Such as?"

"The fresh traces of lipstick and perfume on his clothes suggest the perp's a woman. White satin fibers were found on the handkerchief, with the initials R. W. It seems we may have a woman scorned."

"Couldn't he have just faxed us the report and saved us a trip?"

"There's more, but he didn't want to talk about it over the phone." Bill's eyes narrowed, his attention was elsewhere. "We better get going."

"Park here. I want a knish," ordered Jim, pointing to the spot across the street from a bus-stop where a tall jittery man, clad in a purple tank-top, was hawking imitation watches from a three-legged card table.

Knish in hand, Jim and his partner hurried through the ME's side door at 31st and First. An attending guard checked their identifications and waved them on. Through the aluminum doors at the end of the corridor, they entered the silent world of the dead.

The large, shoebox-shaped room, awash in bright lights and the repelling scent of formaldehyde, was quiet and devoid of life save a hunched lab-coat staring into a large microscope in the corner. Centered on the floor, lined up like sleeping dominoes fashioned from polished aluminum, were ten separate autopsy stations. Each table had low walls, a shallow draft, and a wide drain at both ends. Above each table hung two adjustable sets of halogen lights, its octopus-like frame supporting a small bank of microphones. Along the left wall, stacked four high and five across, humming softly, stood the refrigerated coolers that preserved the departed until they were summoned to tell their tales.

Taking up the right side of the room, along most of the wall into which it was built, ran a large table that accommodated four microscopes of varying sizes. Adjacent to those sat an array of machines capable of analyzing any fluid the human body was capable of producing.

Filing cabinets along the far wall, closer to the Medical Examiner's office, contained the records. Drawers and cabinets, filled with the necessary tools with which to carry out the procedures, took up the rest of the available wall space. Presently, there were two shrouded works-in-progress occupying the tables, their identities indicated by white tags strangling their big toes.

Resisting the urge to look, the two detectives moved on. Bill noticed one of the refrigerated boxes was sealed with a padlock and a red sign that read "*Do Not Touch*". Under that, a name: *John Doe*. Jim, finishing the last of his knish, took little notice as he passed.

Dr. Robert Wallace, M.E. was sitting quietly behind his enormous metal desk, enjoying a late afternoon snack. He was, as they say on the street, gravitationally challenged--a man built from fat.

The detectives entered and took seats opposite him. They knew better than to disturb the man while he was still eating. Until he was done, they glanced aimlessly around the room, examining his various diplomas and awards.

The big doctor had a thin beard that covered the purled, teetless udder that comprised his many chins. A slight gasping sound escaped, as he breathed heavily through a broad, porcine nose.

Bill found it odd that a man of that size and occupation couldn't grasp the frailties of the human heart—but here he was in the flesh. As the M.E. dabbed at his thick lips with a napkin, Bill asked, "*Well*, what's the big secret?"

The doctor, doing his best imitation of leaning forward, replied through a swallow, "First, I'd like to discuss the certainties of the case. Then I'll get to the one that presents a serious problem for all of us."

Scratching his graying beard with uncertainty, he breathed heavily as he spoke. "As you may have already perceived, the primary cause of death was strangulation, as revealed by the deep ligature marks encircling the neck. The blow to the chest, although secondary, split his heart in two." Pausing briefly, he handed them each a close-up Polaroid.

"The victim was strangled from behind with a braided wire, the kind one might use to hang a picture. It's very strong and pliable, easily coiled if you wanted to conceal it. It incised the larynx and crushed the hyoid bone. Victim's nose was broken. We found minute traces of masonry, old paint, and mildew spores in a few of the lacerations along his nose that confirm your prelim report that he was slammed against the wall. We also found cocaine residue inside the nasal mucosa. So the perp—well, I would have to suspect this woman was very strong."

"Are you sure, doc?" asked Bill, skeptically.

"There were lipstick marks on his face and neck, and perfume on his clothes. We have a partial lip print, and a good one."

Jim added, "Guy's neck looks like it could use some cleaning. What's that white ring above the wound?"

"That's white marine paint that covered the cord. It's oil based, with concentrations of lead not seen legally since the sixties."

"Anything else?" added Bill, his crossed leg bouncing impatiently.

"Individual was most likely a bisexual, if you discount the presence of the lipstick. There's conflicting pubic hair evidence to suggest the victim had been intimate with someone other than a woman in the hours prior to his death."

"There's more?" asked Bill, sensing the man was holding something back.

"As I mentioned earlier, he had high levels of cocaine in his system. . .as well as other contaminants of profound consequence. That's why you're here."

The detectives adjusted themselves in their chairs.

"First, we checked his clothes," he went on, "and found urine covering his pants and plenty in his bladder, suggesting the deceased was urinated on. We'll screen the pants again, just as a precaution. The results should be back later on today."

Jim shot Bill a glance, reminding him of his earlier hypothesis.

"What about the bloody handkerchief and his missing body parts?" Bill asked, hoping to get to the meat of the matter. His ass was about to fall asleep.

With a deep breath, the doctor replied, "The blood on the handkerchief was the victim's. It, too, contained minute traces of cocaine and beer. You said you found it away from the body. It had urine on it as well. The missing organs were removed with an extremely sharp instrument--a filet knife, razor knife, or some kind of military blade. The wound on his arm was probably made with the same instrument. The precision of that testifies to the blade's quality. A scalpel couldn't have done much better. I would say from experience that whoever did this was taking these pieces as a memento of his or her act. We see it all the time."

"Why the forearm?" asked Bill, his wheels beginning to turn.

"Deceased may have had a tattoo, or some other distinguishing mark, on which the killer had placed some value."

On more than one occasion, on the whims of drunken friends, Bill had considered getting a tattoo, finding them fascinating by design but ultimately repelled by their sense of permanence.

"Anything else?"

"He was also a heavy smoker, probably the no-filter type."

"Doc," protested Jim, throwing up a hand, "you didn't drag us all the way down here to tell us the victim should have smoked a milder cigarette. What's the skinny?"

"The initial examination of the victim, as I just explained, showed obvious signs of death by strangulation--the ligature marks, broken blood vessels in the eyes, et cetera. But as with any autopsy, we opened the victim up, and what we found was, to say the least, alarming. He might have died from strangulation, but he would have expired in two to four days anyway." Jim shrugged. "Guy have cancer?"

"Listen to me carefully," said the big man, pausing to inhale most of the oxygen left in the room. "The guy was strangled and stabbed, but had end-stage pulmonary edema. . .excess fluid in his lungs. You could argue he had pneumonia or had suffered a heart attack, but he didn't. You might say lung cancer, but there are no cancer cells present. This man's body tissue was breaking down, and at a rapid rate. There's a possibility he wouldn't have lasted until lunch."

Bill asked, "Did you find anything wrong with his intestines."

The big man's eyes narrowed. "Very good, my talented detective. We did happen to find something interesting in his lower cavity--cell damage to the walls of his gastrointestinal tract. But the victim was in his forty's. There are only a few instances under which he would have developed such a condition."

"Radiation!" exclaimed Bill, rising, his thoughts reeling in his head. "I don't believe it," he added in a surreal calm.

"Yes," said the doctor, the load finally off his chest. "Radiation. The only question is what kind. Lab's working on that. But he *was* exposed, and to a very high dose. Otherwise, death would have come much slower."

"Do you mean like cancer or leukemia?" asked Bill, probing carefully.

"Exactly. But I've ruled out a few on my own. It's not the sun. It's not electromagnetic. And he didn't have a job working around x-ray equipment or a nuclear facility. Safe to assume he wasn't at Chernobyl, either.

"Cab driver, I believe, was the word used to describe his profession. So we're left with exposure to certain radioactive elements or, dare I add, isotopes not typically available to the general public.

"Happens like this. A perfectly healthy human is exposed to high doses of subatomic radiation--alpha, beta or gamma particles. These rays pass through the living tissue, ionizing it--put simply; it gives the molecules a positive or negative charge. Depending on the dosage, this breaks down chemical bonds that are important to the survival of any biological organism. For example, DNA is in our chromosomes. It makes us who we are. When it's exposed to radiation, cell division is affected.

"The cells that multiply the fastest—like tissue in bone marrow--are affected the most. That's why leukemia and other blood cancers tend to arise when radiation is a factor."

Sweat ran off the tip of his nose onto his aqua colored doctor's gown, adding to the stain growing around his neck. He had been doing some serious thinking of his own, and he didn't like it.

Bill began thinking about an earlier time, an earlier case. He wasn't smiling.

The two had been called in to lead the local leg of the investigation into the bombing of the Statue of Liberty. A group of terrorists had placed a bomb halfway up the spiral staircase, anchored to the statue's metal rivets with a powerful magnet. Since the assailants hadn't done all their metallurgical homework, the bomb had torn a hole through the Statue's weak copper plating, most of the force pushing out, sparing all but the lives of three children.

The killers had stuck another knife deep into the side of the great Satan, on American soil and with additional targets in mind, but they hadn't been very smart.

They'd rented a large boat to go crabbing, not an unusual activity during the summer season, except their rented van had been loaded with diving gear. The owner of the boat had a problem with the idea of three hairy foreigners crabbing with scuba tanks in two feet of water. As was customary with all his rentals, he had a license plate and the driver's license number on file.

Later in the day, a few tug captains spotted the boat joy riding in the shipping lanes where it didn't belong, and passed the bow numbers onto the harbor master.

The group had quickly determined which days and times would provide them with a window of opportunity to plant the explosives, installing the bomb within a week of renting the boat. None of the witnesses had, of course, reported any of this information until it was too late.

Jim and Bill had done the necessary leg work, again working with the feds, and apprehended the suspects rather easily—in Bill's mind, rather too easily.

But their follow-up investigation had ground to an abrupt halt when the lead investigator for the F.B.I., Agent Bob Willard, arrived and shut them out, taking credit for the arrests. Bill and Jim hadn't cared that much about the collar, but they were numbed by their increased sense of vulnerability--a condition Washington insisted had been legislated into a decline.

Jim, who had been silent, asked, "By isotopes, do you mean nuclear material. . .bombs? If you do, we need to get the F.B.I. in on this A.S.A.P.—preferably ones from Washington. What the fuck do we, or Willard, know about dealing with radioactive materials?"

Bill thought about it. "We *can't* let them in on this," he finally said, "until we talk to the mayor. We have to do a better background check on this victim and his acquaintances. There are other possibilities that need to be examined first. We don't want to hit the panic button."

"I would have to concur," said the ME. "Besides, the results won't be back for a day or so."

"What are the other possibilities?" asked Jim.

The doctor leaned forward. "One, maybe he was exposed outside the United States. Two, he might have been exposed in some medical foul-up that no one caught. I have his prison medical file here, and two and a half years ago he was healthy upon release. He had to have been exposed to high doses of radiation, and recently. You have to find out where he's been. I can only keep this quiet until the results come back."

"Understood," Bill replied, eyeing his partner. "Three days should be enough."

"We should hope."

The two detectives thanked him and left. Heading for the Pontiac in stunned silence, each man recalled the scene at Liberty Island. Things could get much worse.

CHAPTER 8

Outside the hospital, the sun was trying to pull through the clouds, and a slight breeze was teasing the humid air as people passed, oblivious to what was happening around them.

The shock and seriousness of what they had just heard was beginning to settle in like an addiction. It was entirely possible that the deceased, a federal snitch, had been in contact with weapons-grade material, probably plutonium. The two had to assume they were dealing with the same network that had been involved in the Statue bombing, a group that had progressed a long way from tossing stones.

Bill burned rubber pulling onto Broadway.

"Hey," objected Jim. "Is there a fire?"

"Yeah--we need a pay phone."

He found one, jumped out, dropped in two quarters, and dialed. Putting a finger to his ear, he said, "Hello. This is Detective Masters. I need to speak to the mayor." There was a short pause. Bill's patience had eroded. "Listen, sweets, I don't care if he's in a meeting with the pope--get him on the phone!" After another delay, Nates picked up.

"Mayor's office. Can I help you?"

Bill recognized the voice. "Nates, this is Bill Masters. I need to speak with Kravitz."

". . .Certainly, Detective. One moment," he replied, sensing the urgency in Bill's voice."

With a picture in his head of bombs leveling the city, the mayor got on. "There's been some unexpected developments in the John Doe case," Bill told him.

"I'm in a meeting. Can it wait 'til this afternoon?"

"Sir, my partner and I just received a disturbing report from the M.E.'s office. . . ." He hesitated.

"Well, spit it out."

"We're on our way to your office. Call the commissioner and pull the chief off the course. We have a *major* crisis brewing. And leave Willard at home. If—uh—you please."

For a stable cop, the mayor was thinking Masters sounded mildly hysterical.

"All right, I'll clear my schedule. This'd better be good."

"Far from it."

They headed towards the mayor's office, eyeing the wary crowd of New Yorkers with modest sorrow.

"Well partner," Jim said, "it's had time to sink in. What do you think?"

"Panic mostly. If *you* had possession of weapons-grade material, and a way to detonate it, wouldn't that make you a world power? It's either blackmail or superpower diplomacy. Regardless, we have to keep a lid on it. If this gets out, there'll be an exodus Moses would be proud of."

Jim nodded in agreement, as they reached the office.

They took the front steps three at a time, flipped a badge and, for the second time that day, rode the elevator to the fourth floor.

They burst into the office and almost knocked over the secretary, who was standing on a chair, rolled newspaper in hand, attempting to kill a fly.

"He's still *busy!*" she protested, as they pushed past her.

"Save it sister!" Jim called back.

The mayor, contemplating his shrinking budget, was practicing his putting on the tan carpet; his thinning hair was neatly cut. Nates, perched on the edge of the desk, was talking quietly on the phone. When he saw the two detectives, his face grew firm. The commissioner was seated, hoping to be somewhere else, and the chief, still in his golf attire, looked seriously disturbed.

The two took the seats they'd had at the earlier meeting. Willard and his partner were not in attendance.

Bill looked around the room and said to no one in particular, "Pardon the interruption, but we've been told by the medical examiner that the victim of last night's homicide, although savagely butchered, would have died shortly as a result of *severe* radiation exposure."

An eerie calm immediately descended on the room, as the astonished men eyed one another, wrestling with what that revelation meant. The mayor, leapt to his feet. "I *knew* Willard couldn't be trusted! The FBI knew about this all along. We'd every right to know." He sank back into his chair, tossing up a hand. "Let's hear the rest of it."

Jim rose and addressed the uncertain faces. "We've had a few minutes to think about this on the way over. Medically speaking, there are numerous ways ordinary people could come in contact with radioactive material. But they probably wouldn't be exposed to this high a level of contamination. Our immediate problem stems from the fact that, below the surface, the deceased was no ordinary guy."

The commissioner, looking ever so neat in his tailored suit, cleared his throat. "Gentleman, this is very dangerous ground we're on here. Reports from the Justice Department indicate that weapons-grade seizures are not as prevalent as one might think."

The chief, scratching the back of his neck, added skeptically, "I don't know. . .the thought of a cabdriver constructing a nuclear device seems unlikely. I could see them introducing the material into the water supply, or maybe burn it so it would enter the atmosphere. But a full-scale nuclear explosion?"

Suddenly, everybody was talking at once, throwing ideas into the ring.

Bill had been sitting quietly, conscious only of the fact that what they could be facing wasn't in any field manual or departmental circular. Something dawned on him, and he barked, "*Whoa*, gentlemen! Let's take turns! Each one of you has a point, but this is the way I see it playing out. Let's say you're a person or organization who's come across some weapons-grade material and you intend to harm a large population. Certainly, a bomb would be your first choice, assuming you have the financial backing and the network required to take it out of the country and bring it into another, not to mention the skill to contain it during transit. I'd like to agree with the chief, but radioactive isotopes are higher on the periodic table, so they're much denser than say, iron. If you put them in the water supply, you'd get *some* contamination, but most of the material would sink to the bottom and join the sediment. On the other hand, if you burned or detonated the substance, it would enter the atmosphere and return as fallout. Each scenario is scary. People would die, and cancer pockets will certainly arise, but let's face it--nothing would capture the attention of the world like the threat of a full-scale nuclear explosion. If you dump poisons in the water or release them in the air, you are just a terrorist. If you have the weapon and you *don't* use it, you become a second-rate world power. People *will* have to listen to you.

"A nuclear device has only been used twice on human beings, and that was during wartime. Common sense tells us you'd have to be a madman to arbitrarily detonate a nuclear device among innocent civilians. Once it's done, you're back to being a terrorist. This whole thing reeks of blackmail. The question is—what will they want in return?"

The mayor turned to the window. "We don't need to be reminded about the whims of madmen." Staring through the gap in the skyline, he rolled his arm and displayed the concentration camp numbers that had seemed much larger once. "Child's gift from a madman . . . Al, any luck with your pal in the FBI?"

The commissioner, looking uncomfortable, straightened his tie and uncrossed his legs. "No, Abe, I was, ah. . .getting a massage. I'll call him immediately after our discussion. You can bet on it."

Excellent, thought Jim, eyeing the soft Italian leather on the commissioner's feet, wondering what a pair would cost. He couldn't even afford to massage himself. "This guy supposedly wasn't involved with these others," he said uneasily. "Willard would have known. Maybe he was exposed to something else, or he has a disease. A few hours ago, we thought he'd gotten whacked by wise guys. Can't you develop pulmonary edema any other way? The guy smoked unfiltered cigarettes, for Christ's sake!"

All heads seem to nod in unison. It made some degree of sense, and it was certainly safer than what his partner had proposed.

The mayor reclaimed the floor. "I'm sure by now *everyone* realizes this cannot become public knowledge. . . .I'm giving you guys twenty-four hours to come up with something concrete. I know it's not much, but that's *it*. Then we call in the cavalry." Turning his attention to the chief, he continued, "This guy is to remain a John Doe until I say otherwise. No squad cars, no forensic teams, no reporters, nothing. We need answers. Al, get on this FBI thing. Use some tact—it's gotta be bigger than Willard." Eyeing the two detectives, he pointed toward the door and added, "Time's a wastin'."

As they left, he said, "Good luck and keep us posted. And *remember*--just you two." The assistant had been trailing the detectives, trying to get Bill's attention, but the mayor cut him off and closed the door behind them. "Nates, I need those disaster response figures, pronto!" Turning back to his colleagues, "Gentlemen, about the security for Monday morning's briefing with the President. . . ." The meeting continued, as the assistant looked on impatiently.

CHAPTER 9

Back on the street, their tension had eased a bit. It was the politicians' problem now—but deep inside they knew, with no outside help, they were going to be the only hope of stemming the growing crisis.

"Jimmy, it's time we get a cup of coffee," said Bill through a yawn. "You might want to call both your bed and toilet and let them know they won't be needed for a while."

"Shit, this whole thing sucks! I'm going to need more than a cup. I'm behind on my sleep, as it is."

"Where to?" asked Bill, looking for the nearest coffee shop.

"Let's go find John Doe's cab and impound the thing. Maybe squeeze the owner, or whoever's there, and see if we can't come up with something, *anything* on this guy Salaam. If he's covered with radiation, he can't be clean."

"*Really*?" asked Bill, wide-eyed.

"*Really.*"

The Pontiac swerved lazily down Broadway, running lights with the rest of the traffic. They pulled to the front of a mom-and-pop shop, allowing Jim an opportunity to resupply for a twenty-four hour, full-court press.

Returning with two cups of coffee, a box of chocolate-covered donuts, and a minor look of disdain, Bill knew he would have to relive the experience.

"What is it with those places?" Jim complained, falling into the car with the grace of a Brahma bull. "You can buy ice cream, you can buy coffee. Feeling a little horny? Rent some porn. Copped a bag of grass? We have the bong for you. Nitrous oxide, Amyl nitrate. . .I mean, what the fuck?"

"Guess you gotta love New York," Bill said with a smile.

On a busy side street lined with double-parked cars, the detectives pulled to the curb in front of a leaking hydrant, hurried out, and entered the New York City Cab Company.

The motor pool, dimly lit and heavy with the stench of exhaust and gasoline vapor, was similar to the one at the station house—same make of vehicle, the same steady stream of traffic.

Single-file, the two detectives marched down the entrance ramp, steering clear of the racing taxis that arrived and departed like bees from a hive.

Rounding the bottom corner, they were two lanes away from the dispatcher's cage. Aside from the fungal smell, the cigarette butts, and the used chewing gum that littered the ground, they had the impression that the reinforced cage wasn't meant to keep criminals out but rather the dispatcher in.

At the moment, he was standing under the dim light of a single bulb ranting like a maniac into the phone. His enormous, middle-aged frame, covered by an undersized cotton shirt, sagged under the weight of a swollen paunch riddled with a vertical pattern of stretch marks.

The dispatcher failed to notice the two men approaching, as he crammed the crumbling remains of a sausage and pepper sandwich into his chomping jowls. With each bite, the retreating end of the sandwich offered a glob of tomato sauce and double Provolone to his heaving chest, leaving the rest to collect on the dog-eared sheet of tin foil crumpled on his desk. Without a care, he wiped the remains off with the palm of his left hand, smearing a stain across the front of his shirt. He took a seat.

As the two lawmen stared in amazement, he was writing with his right hand and cradling the receiver between the thick folds of his neck. As a string of expletives exited his mouth, his thick

Brooklyn accent was barely intelligible through the mouthful of food.

"Listen to me, you cocksucka! Yous three weeks overdue. I betta see some green from yous soon, like today, eh, or my ortho-pedist's comin' ova for a little visit. *Capisce*? You're lucky I don't rip out your tongue!"

Slamming the receiver in disgust, he rose to his feet, laboring a final swallow. Tiny pieces of food that had clung to his shirt jumped ship, sprinkling the desktop colored black by years of falling cigarette ash.

Soaking up the conversation, the two detectives moved forward, eager to see if anyone else needed to have their tongues ripped out.

The dispatcher raised his head slowly, noticed them and asked in a tone lacking respect. "Yeah, what can I do for yous two?"

Looking to adjust his attitude, the two men showed him their shields. The dispatcher, exiting the cage to the garage floor, responded immediately by putting up one of his own.

Standing directly in front of Jim, his bravado still unchecked, he asked irritably. "Weren't yous guys just in here? I told em' everything I know."

The two detectives shared a confused look.

"Who was just here? New York City detectives?" asked Jim, eyeing the disturbing sight.

With some hesitation, he replied, "Yeah, I think so. Der was a red haid guy and one who didn't talk so much. They was askin' about an employee. Wanted to know if he had any gamblin' debts. . .did he do any drugs? The usual bullshit."

"Well, what did you tell em'?" pressed Bill, feeling like he was wrestling with a giant clam.

"The same thing I'm gunna tell yous two. I don't know shit! I'm a dispatcher, not a fuckin' priest. So if yous don't mind, I got woik ta do." He looked Jim up and down, adding, "Whoa, tumble-dry silk, go figia."

Jim moved quickly to the business end of the fat man's nose. "Listen, you walkin' napkin! I've had about all I can smell of you, so I'm gonna make this short and sweet. One, we want his fuckin' cab! That baby's coming with us. If it's out, get it back! Secondly, you're gonna tell us what we want to know, or I'm going to have the city inspectors come down here with a fuckin' microscope. Are we making contact?"

"Yo, Vinnie," snapped the large man. "I got problems. Take over da desk." The moist, yellow rings beneath his arms began to grow.

Vinnie, a slight, black-haired Italian with a nose like a beak, was sitting calmly at a small table to the right of the cage, sipping a diet soda, reading the *Daily News*. Flipping to another page, he replied without looking up, "Hey, *stunad*, I'm on my fuckin' break! So why don't you give me one?"

The big man took two labored steps in the direction of his unsuspecting colleague and started to yell. The barrage came so fast that neither detective understood a word.

Vinnie turned white and replied, palms up. "Okay, okay, go easy, don't have a fuckin' heart attack! I got ya covered, but you owe me anudda' break." He entered the cage, banging his head on the light as he locked the door behind him.

Fats turned to the detectives. "Listen, Malik was a good driva. What can I say? He got busted for tamperin' wit his meeta. He also...."

Sighing, Bill held up a hand. "Listen, we're detectives, not fuckin' retards. Give us something we can use. Was he a gambler? Did he talk about his friends or women? Did he have enemies, do drugs...*anything?*"

"Well, I don't think there's anybody in this city who don't place a friendly wager now and again," said the dispatcher, his temperament beginning to soften. "Yous two hearda Lotto?"

Jim, unamused, gave him a steely smile. Fats continued. "Malik talked a lot about this chick of his. I've neva seen her. I don't know of anybody who has. Supposedly, she's a real looker. But aren't they all?"

"What about his friends? His likes and dislikes? We also need a current address, if you have one." Bill was upset with himself for not having written it down already. "One more thing--was he driving last night?"

"Now that you mention it, he was working last night, and he hasn't brought the cab back. What he do now?" asked Fats, pretending not to care.

"You mean the two other guys didn't tell you?" asked Jim, surprised.

"Those two pricks? No. They told me to mind my own fuckin' business. What he do?" asked Fats, his thick fingers kneading the tip of his chin. Arrests were bad publicity.

"Stopped breathing."

"Aw, no fucking way!?" Fats screamed, surprised. Bill sensed the sudden concern had little to do with the welfare of his ex-employee. "Is there a problem?"

The big man's eyes narrowed with indecision. "Ah. . . Fuck him. That scumbag was into me for two large!" He paused, as if it mattered. "Listen, Malik always talked about women, but I suspected he was half a fag. Some of da guys told me he roamed the Village bars a lot."

"Hey, that's *real* good for a guy who could make an onion cry," teased Jim. The plot was beginning to thicken. "Since you're the expert on the gay scene, what were the names of some of these bars? You know. . .if you can remember?" His insinuation irked the fat man.

"Hey, I don't have to take this crap from you! I got rights, ya know. Are you two *finished*? I've gotta get back to woik."

Bill took a long step closer. "Listen, my friend. Yes, we're through. . .for *now*. But we'll be back. *That* you can bet on. The offer still stands. If we suspect you're hiding anything, the inspectors will give you such a reaming, you'll beg for the familiar sound of a fart." The two turned to leave.

"All right, already," lamented Fats, moving forward, his hands in the air. "He used to go to the Backdoor a lot. That's all I know. I swear on my mutha." He looked to see what was occupying Vinnie, before returning with an address card and plate number of the cab.

"Listen," he said quietly, again looking back at the cage. "Malik owed people money, but not enough to get himself whacked." Bill's eyes locked with Jim's.

Jim replied sourly, "Sure, sure. Coming from a man of your stature, we're both more than satisfied. But who mentioned he got whacked?"

"Well, I. . .I . . .I figured if yous two and those *other* guys were askin' all these questions, something bad musta happened to him, *right?*"

"Very observant," said Bill, heading for the ramp.

"Let's get out of here," said his partner. "My eyes are beginning to water."

With the detectives out of sight, Fats re-entered the cage, ushered Vinnie aside, and was immediately on the phone.

Masters and Lackey retraced their steps up the ramp, making mental notes of the various violations that they could use to feed Fats if he was lying, which both knew he was. A missing wheelchair ramp was a good place to start. The above-ground fuel tanks looked terribly unsafe. One spark and it would be wall-to-wall Fats.

Reaching the street, they milled around the hood of the Pontiac contemplating their next move. "Twenty pounds of shit in a five-pound sack," offered Bill with a grin.

"That idiot couldn't kill time. I'll bet you fifty bucks he's on the phone right now talkin' to a silk suit."

"Probably," said Bill, scanning his surroundings, "and he *definitely* knows more than he's giving up. Can't say I blame him, though—he's fucked either way."

Out of the mass of people passing on the sidewalk appeared a young Caucasian male who stopped at the entrance to the garage. Talking to himself under his breath, a determined look on his face, a pink piece of paper in hand, he inhaled deeply and headed for the darkness of the ramp.

Bill immediately caught up with him.

"Excuse me! Sir?" he shouted, slowing as he approached, barely dodging the front end of an exiting cab.

The young man turned slowly, waving him off. "No, I don't want any of your drugs, or watches, or whatever. So fuck off!"

Bill flashed his badge. The man stopped, dropping his hands to his sides, twisting about like a sheet in the wind. Jim approached slowly with his hands in his pockets.

"Where ya' headed?" asked Bill, returning the identification to his breast pocket.

The young man had been staring at the ground, his back against the stone apron of the building. He caught Bill's gaze. He didn't flinch.

"I'm gunna' collect my last paycheck from these scumbags. They gave me no notice and no reason. You have a problem with that? Is that some sorta crime?" He was not a happy man.

"How long have you worked here?" Bill asked, readying his pen. He was beginning to like the guy already.

"About six years come September. Driving a cab's become a very popular profession with the immigrant population. There's no room for whitey anymore. Nah, the land of opportunity now lies beyond this melting-pot of shit." He paused to reflect on his future.

When his focus returned, he asked impatiently, "What's it you want?"

"We're here to inquire about a co-worker, one Malik Salaam." Bill said, adding, "We're investigating his death."

The young man's face turned to stone. He took a step closer and whispered, "Then if I'm seen talking to you, I could be next. Listen, I'll answer your questions. Just not here. I'm gonna get my check and give that fat, waste of sperm a piece of my mind. Then I'll meet you at the coffee shop on the corner." He turned on his heels, disappearing into the abyss.

"I hope he doesn't do anything stupid," said Bill, looking over his shoulder, moving down the sidewalk. "This place is controlled by one of the five families. You heard the conversation that fat fuck was having. He's not running his own book. Piazza grew up with one of the sons of Don Sciaffa. Maybe he can get us in to see him."

Don Sciaffa, known for his dull wit and fiery temper, possessed a certain charm and twisted wisdom that he called upon when doling out colorful tidbits to the daily newspapers, was addicted to money and dressed like an ambassador. Rare, tailored suits and fancy cars were his trademark.

CHAPTER 10

The two detectives entered the corner coffee shop and headed towards a booth across from the kitchen. A tall elderly waitress, her black hair pulled back in a bun, approached the table lifelessly, as Bill studied the legible part of the coffee-soiled menu. Thinking better of it, he ordered two coffees. Adjusting himself under the table, Jim gazed through the window at a girl waiting on the corner.

After the waitress left, Bill murmured, "Seems to be right up your alley. Sleazy and cheesy. You have some time—go outside and get her number."

An overweight customer in the next booth, his view blocked by the tines of his fork, lifted his massive head only to burp.

"I'm not going out there, so cool it! Kid's going to be here any minute. What about the waitress?"

Bill rubbed his chin. "Don't know. Too tall, plus I'm not yet ready for senior citizens."

"She's not *that* old," replied Jim in her defense.

"Body's okay, but another face lift and she'll have a bush for a chin."

The two shared a laugh as the waitress returned, coffeepot in hand, offering a robotic frown that matched Jim's own smile in emotional intensity. Without a word, she shuffled away, the coffeepot dangling listlessly at her side.

"That'll reflect in her tip," said Jim irritated.

The ex-cab driver entered, looking disheveled as he moved quickly through the eatery, planting himself firmly into the seat next to Jim. He was thin, but fit, around one-fifty, with short red hair and sturdy shoulders. His lively brown eyes matched his freckled complexion. His right eye, shut from a punch, was red and swollen, his brow sported a mouse.

"Looks like your last paycheck was a painful one," said Jim, welcoming the thought of his own fists bouncing off the fat Italian's face.

"Yeah. Well, he's not long for this earth anyway."

"What makes you say that?" asked Bill, more than curious.

"Just look at the size of the guy. Compared to the rest of his ass, his heart has gotta be the size of a pea.

The comment reminded Jim of the medical examiner, and he had to agree. "You're right, but, just the same, what's your name?"

Full of apprehension, the kid replied, "Ryan, Mike Ryan."

"Oh, a nice Irish boy?" asked Jim, still eyeing the waitress.

"Aye, but what do you want with me?"

Bill reentered the conversation, sipping his coffee. "This guy Salaam, what can you tell us about him? You've worked there a long time. You heard about the tampering case, right?"

"Who hasn't? Salaam was less than functional when it came to his sense of direction. Fares want the Seaport--Salaam's in Queens, his head spinning, lost as fuck. Customers were constantly complaining, accusing him of increasing the fares. So what does the guy do to cover his ass and save his job? Moron sets the meter back."

"What else?" Bill asked, taking notes.

"Salaam had a strangeness about him, he was always borrowing other people's things. . .nice things, personal things. Some thought he was a thief. I just think he was just used to getting what he wanted."

"For instance?" growled Jim, adjusting the tension on his belt.

"Like. . .if you left a shirt, jewelry, or a pair of shoes laying around, or a comb even, Salaam would be wearing it, or using it, a week later. He'd even give them to others in the garage as presents. If you mentioned it to him, he'd apologize like a madman and then return it. After a while, no one cared and left him alone, like he'd planned it all along." He waited for either man to respond.

Bill changed the line of questioning. "What kind of action goes on in the garage? Big time, or small stuff?"

Ryan replied, "Are you kidding? Those sick fucks would bet on anything."

"What kind of action did Salaam take?" asked Jim, stirring his coffee. "Was it baseball, basketball, hockey, ponies, what?"

"I think he bet baseball. He liked the Yankees."

The kid was looking around uneasily, his head low, as if waiting to come upon a familiar face. He knew his limitations. "Guys, can we make this quick? I'd love to help you more. But the fact of the matter is, I don't care if somebody whacked that fucker. Go talk to his buddies at the clubs. They know him inside and out. Get my drift?" He looked at Lackey, grinning like a snake.

Jim leaned forward, lowering his voice. "What a...kind of clubs...eh, should we be looking at?"

"He talked about a club called the Backdoor. I'm a little unsure about the name. Could be a clue."

"Okay, Mr. Ryan, the fun's over," said Bill, ending the interview. "If we need another statement from you, we will give you a call. Give Detective Lackey here your address and telephone number.... Don't worry, this investigation will remain confidential." He thought, he was beginning to sound a lot like Agent Willard.

Complying, Ryan slid from the booth. He'd barely taken a few steps when he turned around.

"One more thing. He might've been gay, a gambler, and couldn't find his way out of a paper bag, whatever, but I do know one thing--he always had money, and he was as smart as they come."

"Obviously, not street smart," said Bill with renewed interest. Recalling the carnage of the crime scene photos--that wasn't the vibe he'd been getting.

"Book smart. How many people do *you* know who could tamper with an electronic meter? He said he took night classes. Studied chemistry, or something. Carried a journal everywhere he went. He was always thinking, always writing."

"Journal? What kind of journal?" asked Jim, raising his arm, check in hand. The waitress ignored him.

"Nothing fancy. Binder type, the kind you'd take to class. I used to see him write formulas and shit when we'd eat lunch next to the cage...."

The young man had become alarmed and preoccupied by the group of well-dressed men now coming through the door. "Listen, I gotta go--my wife is expecting our first child any day now. If I can remember anything else, I'll give you a call. Do you have a card?" Jim handed him one. Covering his face with his hand, he turned, waited for the men to pass and hurried for the door.

Jim, eyeing the group of well-dressed suits settling into a booth, paid the bill, minus a tip which produced a leer a bit worse than the first.

Making their way back to the Pontiac, Bill asked, "What's with the tip?"

"She can get it from those greaseballs," replied Jim, closing the car door.

The light rain had resumed, as they pulled to the front of the precinct. The usual act was playing out on the front steps among the dampened newspapers, umbrellas, and colored rain suits moving about in a cloud of cigarette smoke.

The abortion fiasco had died down. The desk sergeants were between shifts. Masters and Lackey headed up the stairs.

Bill turned towards the bathroom. "Listen, Jim, call Piazza. He's always wanted to play detective. Get his ass down here quickly and see who called. I'll be with you shortly."

Jim checked their messages first. One, from Nates, was brief and to the point. "Detective Masters, call me at once, very important."

Jim thought the call strange, as he thumbed quickly through the Rolodex and removed Piazza's card.

"Hello," answered a young woman, presumably his wife.

"Yes, good afternoon, sorry to bother you. This is Detective Lackey. Is the patrolman in?" inquired Jim, putting his feet up on his desk. He could hear Piazza in the background, pleading with his wife to say that he was not home.

"Yes, Detective Lackey, he's right here," she replied, handing him the phone.

"Yeah, detective...what can I do for you?" asked the young patrolman, his deep voice sounding both nervous and displeased.

"Tony, Bill and I need you to get down here ASAP. I know

you're off, but we need your help investigating that stiff you were rolling around with."

"Yeah, sure," he muttered. "Whatever. Gimme thirty." He hung up.

Bill caught up with his partner.

"Nates called for you," said Jim through a snicker. "You two have a date?"

"No. I told him you were considering a lifestyle change. Thought maybe he could offer you a hand. . .or two." Grinning, Masters dialed the mayor's office.

"Nates Johnson please. Oh. . .he isn't?" he asked. "Is there a number where he can be reached?"

Another pause. Bill was getting restless scribbling on his notepad, as Jim got up to refill the coffee pot.

"Thank you very little," replied Bill, hanging up. He turned his back in his chair to face Jim. "The mayor's secretary should be shot. No wonder nothing gets done at City Hall. She wasn't sure if it was okay to give me Nates' number." He pulled his phone closer, pushed an extension and began to dial. He got Nates' answering machine. Bill left a pager number. It couldn't have been that important, he told himself.

Jim poured two cups of coffee and sat down across from his partner.

"Nothing seems to fit here," said Bill in frustration. "This guy is covered with radiation. He gets killed, and the perpetrator cuts off his ear and tongue, filets his arm, and stabs him. Why?"

"I'm telling you, Bill," offered Jim, sipping his coffee. "This mutilation thing reeks of the mob. Relatively sane people just don't hack up their fellow man. It takes too long and it's sloppy. There's a definite message here. Anyway, maybe this guy was never clean and had access to these materials. Do you think Sciaffa would or could move that shit without drawing any attention?"

Masters drew a frustrated breath. "Jim, I'm not trying to insult you, but this is not your luggage we're talking about. Ya just don't throw it in a trash bag and mosey around town. They're kept in regulated and monitored containers made of lead, transported under strict conditions."

Bill had other ideas. "I was thinking about what the kid said at the diner about New York being such a melting pot. We keep talking about an Italian syndicate. Every ethnicity, including the

Arabs, has some sort of secret society. Maybe dicing up a man is the sign of some Middle-Eastern mob? Personally, if nuclear materials are involved, maybe it's a government thing. I bet you, at this very moment, the CIA is all over this stuff. Which would lead me to believe that they are nearby, waiting. Call it a gut feeling. Maybe they popped this guy and made it look like a hit. But again, if they knew anything about this material, they would have never let it in the country. They'd have to bed down with the Feds. And we know how uncomfortable that can be."

Sipping from his cup, Bill's face betrayed the taste. "What did you put in this shit?"

"Sugar," Jim replied with a grin. "And lots of it. How do you know about this stuff?" he asked, dismissing the complaint.

"Basic reading, and a few dinners with my godfather, who's a professor at the university."

"In New York? You never mentioned him."

"Yes I did, you just didn't listen. Besides, he prefers his privacy. Regardless, this stuff is based on years of study and testing. It took some of the best minds in math and physics to bring us into the atomic age. Didn't you pay *any* attention in school? There's a big difference between harnessing nuclear power as an energy source, and using it as a means of mass destruction."

Math, physics, and attending class had never been one of Jim's strong points. "Well, now we have that blurb out of the way, do you think Salaam had the knowledge to make this thing happen?

"Possibly. But statistically, not likely. The guy drove a cab, for Christ's sake."

"He was a foreigner. It would make a great cover."

"*Touche'* my large friend. . .that it would. I guess we need to find out a bit more about him because. . . ."

"Why was Willard and his boy at the garage?" Jim interrupted, "It was our case, remember?"

"They're into this shit up to their necks, and like fats, Salaam wasn't running the show," replied Bill. "Whenever Kravitz pulls the plug on this, we got problems. There's something about Willard I just don't understand. How can anyone be an asshole twenty-four seven?"

"Practice."

The outer doors opened and in strolled Piazza, clad in jeans, a white T-shirt, and a foul disposition. He talked briefly with the plump secretary, as he passed and approached the two detectives, stopping at Bill's desk.

"Good evening, gentlemen," he began. "How can I help you?"

"Tony, my man," said Bill with mock excitement. "Is it true you grew up with Carmine Sciaffa?"

"Yeah. So what?" he replied defensively.

"Tony, lighten up. We didn't ask if you were a made guy. We just need to get in touch with his old man," said Jim reassuringly. "That's all. You'll be outta here in no time."

"Oh. Okay. No problem. I'll give Carmine a call right now. But if yous don't mind me asking, why not jus' roust his ass at his club?"

Bill, who had been leaning back in his chair, said, "You get more bees with honey. We could barge in, but what is that gonna get us? But if you call on him and show him the little respect that he thinks he deserves, maybe he'll cough something up. Play to his vanity."

Jim nodded with an evil grin.

"Besides, we're not sure about this at all. If we do it any other way, I can see a harassment suit on the horizon. He beat that federal racketeering rap just last week. I don't think he wants to see any cops for a while, ya know what I mean?"

"Sure. What criminal does?"

Sitting on the corner of Jim's desk, Piazza picked up the phone and dialed.

Carmine Sciaffa was nothing like his father; the infamous don. He wanted to be a wise guy, but his father wouldn't have it. He had been sent to an Ivy League school, graduating into the legitimate side of the family business -- cabs, a string of pizza parlors, and a few funeral homes throughout the five boroughs. The feds believed he knew a little about the art of money laundering. But as was true of his father, so far, they could prove nothing.

Tony was soon shaking his head in agreement. "Sure, Carmine, that'd be great. Call me back as soon as you can?"

He gave Carmine the number and hung up.

Jim, who'd been heading for the coffee maker, turned to Tony and asked, "You have something going with the secretary? I noticed you two laughing."

"Nah, she was just joking about your suit," replied the patrolman with a devious smile.

Ten minutes later the phone rang. It was Sciaffa calling with a message. His father, the unflappable don, would be delighted to meet with the two detectives. He intimated further that his father was elated that, like gentlemen, they had requested an appointment. He would entertain them any time after 8:00 p.m.

"Where is this place?" Bill asked, patting himself on the back.

"It's a men's club on Mulberry Street. There's no sign or address. I'll go with yous guys and point it out," Tony said, eagerly.

"Sorry. I don't mean to bum you out, but you're going to grab that high priced hooker you have in your report. What's her name? Candice? Sounds like a real cream puff. What do ya say?"

"It's gunna cost me a hundred bucks!" he whined. "Besides, I'm done with my shift."

Jim was heading back to his chair. "Then make her earn it, son."

Bill reached into his pocket and handed Tony five twenty-dollar bills. "She'll probably be just hittin' the streets. Tell her whatever you have to, but get her ass in here by 9:00 at the latest!"

"No problem, lieutenant," said Tony, hands raised in resignation. He turned for the stairs.

Setting up a workable strategy on a case of such magnitude usually took a few days. They had less than twenty-four hours before turning what little they had over to the feds. Not a lot of time to get the big break they needed.

The next few hours were spent talking methods and motives, plotting their course through the myriad of old files, pictures, and other information in the hope that they would find a concrete place to start. Most theories bordered on the ridiculous: spies, women, hit men, and ruthless assassins. Yet, the only connection they had between Salaam and his untimely demise was the don. Over the years he'd made a friend of death. He was the place to start.

CHAPTER 11

The ride to Little Italy took less than fifteen minutes; they pulled to the front of a single-story, plain red brick brownstone that lay sandwiched between two apartment buildings fronted by a row of double-parked Cadillacs. Oddly enough, there was a parking spot waiting for them in front.

The building, clean and devoid of pomp was unremarkable. With his exploits often on the front page, the don didn't attract any undue attention.

The only sign of life was the soft glow of a spot light in the window that fell on a lone statue of the Madonna perched on the sill, her hands out to greet those who were welcome, and offer a final blessing to those who were not.

The heavy front door was made of metal, painted brown to match the color of the building. The vertical row of locks underscored the occupant's concern for security. Bill sensed eyes upon them--Jim, the sweet smell of sausage. As they were getting out of the car, Bill's pager went off.

Bill issued directives over the roof of the car. "I know you don't dig the mob scene, so let *me* do the talking. If we run into a brick wall, then manners'll no longer matter."

"Sure, sure, whatever. What about the page?"

Bill checked his watch and pager. He didn't know the number; it would have to wait. Eager to get inside, he grabbed his belt and pulled up his trousers. It was almost dark. "We'll worry about it later."

Bill adjusted his attire and knocked on the door. It opened immediately. The welcoming committee was a large, muscular Italian gent with sandy gray eyebrows that merged above his eyes like charging moles.

"Good evening," said Bill, holding out his badge. "We've an appointment with Mr. Sciaffa." The man said nothing that could be confused with speech, simply motioning the two through the door with a wave of his arm.

Entering, they were met by an atmosphere both cool and dark; cigar smoke filled the air. Playing cards shuffled and poker chips jingled over the soft hum of merriment and the smooth, olive-oil voice of Tony Bennett.

The tables, covered with red-and-white checkered cloth, were neatly arranged amid the shiny black and white squares of the linoleum floor. Each table had its own light, shaded by imitation stained glass flaunting a Royal Flush.

A real collection of vowels thought Bill as he noticed the absence of female participation. It seemed a place one could get used to.

Moving towards the back, across from the kitchen, the sound of a knife could be heard falling heavily upon a chopping block. Oil seared, tomato paste bubbled, and short bursts of laughter rose from various points behind them. Bill sensed they were the brunt of the joke.

The only individual in the room, *not* finding humor in their presence, was the crooked-nosed bartender, leering at them through dark caustic eyes as he slowly cleaned a tray of mugs. Bill had him marked as a traditional cop hater as he welcomed them with a solid wink and a shot from the barrel of his thumb and forefinger.

In a side room, Bill recognized the don in a corner booth, his back to the wall. He seemed bigger on T.V. One of his men leaned over and whispered into his ear. His face was expressionless, as he replied. The escort cautiously approached; the two detectives waited awkwardly at the edge of the room.

Sciaffa was a small man teetering on the cusp of old age. With his graying hair and perpetually tanned skin, one could have mistaken him for a Florida retiree. He was dressed more casually than the public was accustomed to seeing—in a silk shirt with a dark paisley design and a pair of unassuming black dress pants. His feet, elfish in size, were covered with soft leather lounge slippers. He looked relaxed, as if celebrating. Like most of the men in the room, he was puffing on a cigar. A cloud of smoke hung listlessly in the air. The don had been talking with one arm slung along the back of the booth, the other, bearing an array of gold and diamonds, lazily gripping a nearly empty glass of Chianti.

At the sight of the detectives, he dropped the commanding pose, sat upright and lay smallish hands on top of the table, readying himself for business. The men who had been seated with him vacated their chairs and took flanking positions against the wall.

"Welcome, gentleman," he said, rising courteously, pointing to their chairs. "Have a seat." They obliged.

"Thank you for calling in advance. Men with badges have a tendency to be, shall we say, impatient, and appointments without subpoenas are a rarity. You read the papers?"

Stifling a reaction--the cigar smoke was killing him--Bill asked, "Could I get a glass of water?"

The don looked at one of his men standing in the entrance way; he left without a word and returned with a pitcher of ice water. Bill and Jim's pagers went off again. It was the office.

"Forgive me, Detective Masters. These latest unpleasantries have hardened my manners. My son's friend speaks highly of you and your partner. Says you are both fair and honorable men... men of your word."

The don's sermon was just starting when Jim rudely interrupted. "We'd love to sit here and jerk each other off, but frankly, we're in the midst of a murder investigation. The victim--one Malik Abdul Salaam, was an employee of yours. Name ring a bell?"

Sciaffa, a devout Catholic, and an old pro at not recalling incriminating details, turned his head towards his minions and winked playfully, producing a restive look from Bill and his cagey partner.

Over the years, Sciaffa had complemented this vital attribute by logging more hours in a New York City court room than the average attorney. Jim's tactical blunder summoned this disposition to the forefront.

The don leaned over, looking right into the patchy hairs of Jim's stubbly chin. "Do I *look* like a fuckin' rag-head, detective?" Satisfied, he relaxed. "Never heard of 'im."

With the hopes of salvaging the occasion, Bill took a deep breath and, using his right heel, applied pressure to the toe of his partner's left foot. Putting his hands gently on the table, he cracked an apologetic smile and addressed everyone in the group around him. "Please excuse my over-worked partner. He meant no disrespect. He just hasn't had much sleep lately. Maybe *I* can refresh your memory?"

The don welcomed the invitation with a nod.

"Mr. Salaam was an employee of yours--a driver for one of your cab companies. We were hoping you might have some information that might assist us with our investigation...maybe shed a little light on things. Someone garroted him and cut out his tongue."

"First of all, detective, I'm sorry I didn't recall the name when you first mentioned it. Perhaps the name does ring a bell." The little man looked around at the heads already shaking in acknowledgment. "Matter of fact, that's the *same* guy that stole my fuckin' cab!"

Jim rubbed his thick palms over his face, shaking his head in disbelief, "Are you telling us you reported the car stolen? Your guy failed to mention it." That fat son-of-a-bitch, Jim thought--he would be seeing him again.

"That's exactly what I'm telling you. If I'd a dollar for every time a cabbie was joyriding around, attending to personal matters, I wouldn't have to hump pizzas. Company policy clearly states that a cab more than an hour late, and the driver hasn't radioed in any problems, will be reported stolen. Check with your department." A contentious smile appeared on his mousey face.

Bill felt that special rapport they had been working on begin to slip over the edge. He'd give it one more shot.

"You know anything that might help us? We don't have much time."

The tan Italian seemed confused by references to time. Justice was short on time when it came to the victim, but they were always willing to dish it out to the likes of the don. And he resented it. He knew they would take all the time they needed to solve the murder of a minority immigrant. They wanted something else. Whatever it was, it was going to cost them. Quid pro quo. In Sciaffa's world nothing of value was free.

"Detective," he said, his sympathy ringing hollow. "It sounds like you've a serious problem on your hands. But I, like yourself, have problems as well. I'm out an automobile." He put his hands back on the table and reached for his cigar. The dance had begun.

Relighting his stub, the short man blew a large smoke ring in his direction. "I have city inspectors constantly coming into my pizza parlors looking for roaches. I hear threats of tearing apart cabs. . .sodomizing my employees."

He turned to Jim, who seemed a bit embarrassed. "Maybe, if we had some cooperation, we could solve this murder together."

Not likely, Bill thought, but he would see what he could work out. "It's unfortunate that the city singles you out. Maybe all these federal investigations, well founded or not, have gotten the ball rolling."

"Maybe." The man's smile faded, as he got the picture. "If you can talk to certain people and have them cut back on these inspections, I'll see if I can't dig up some information that may be of help to you. I don't expect the inspections to stop. Safety is important." The don was looking directly at Jim, who turned to his partner and said, "Let's get the fuck out of here." He rose and gave the little man an aggressive stare. "I'm tired of all this *small* talk."

Bill's pager went off and again, a number he did not recognize.

The don was used to people not agreeing with him. They just never said so, openly. All the others in the room had, for just a moment, stopped breathing. But he just grinned.

"Before you two scurry off? You ought to know that the police and men such as myself have much in common. We depend on each other in certain respects. Your job is to protect and serve. I'm no different. The neighborhood feels safe and secure knowing that I and my men are close by. The crime rate in this area is lower than any other place in the city. My presence has something to do with that. All I ask in return is a little respect." He paused to refill his glass from the wicker covered bottle. "You and those federal prosecutors need people like me and my associates. Without us, you're out of a job. You put me in jail, there are slaps on the back, maybe a judgeship. But so far, promotions have been like witnesses. *Capisce?*"

The don's men laughed in unison, as he returned to his glass of Chianti, his wry smile beaming in their direction. "One final thing. I don't know a *thing* of what happened to that greasy camel jockey, but I will say this--whoever clipped him?--I do love their style." Grinning from ear to ear, he basked in the glow of homage that radiated around him--a necessity that ranked only second to breathing.

Bill was disappointed the meeting hadn't gone as planned. He had hoped the don was going to play ball. He'd called him in good faith, showed him some respect, yet received nothing in return. The detectives had misjudged the man—something they would never do again.

Pushing back his chair, Bill rose, placing his knuckles down on the table. He leaned forward, mere inches from the don's face. "I was hoping for a constructive meeting between two businessmen, but apparently that's out of the question. I'll say this--*I* do need you. . .as a constant reminder of why I take my job as seriously as I do. You're a fuckin' cancer, a nasty little parasite, feeding off the vices of men, intimidating the weak and undermining the strong. You sit here amongst your goombahs, sipping Chianti, sharing your *sfogliatelle*, thinking life will last forever. But a wise man once told me," he said, pointing to the cross around the don's neck, "In the presence of God, *nothin's* safe."

Tossing his head over his shoulder towards the door, his gaze transfixed on the smaller man like a laser, he added, "Those locks are useless against an enemy that's on the inside, waiting, transforming their fears into loathing and indifference. Lucky for me, I've had a head start."

Jim took the slack jaws and Bill's echoing silence as an invitation to exit.

The men in the room rocked uneasily on their heels as Sciaffa, the veins bulging in his neck, entered into a tirade that resulted in contents of the table hitting the floor. For New York's finest, it was time to go.

Moving quickly through the muted crowd, Bill found the gaze of the glass-drying cop hater. At the door, he aimed his own thumb and forefinger and fired. "Bull's-eye!"

Out on the sidewalk, they could still hear the don screaming frantically over the cackle of youngsters playing stickball under the light across the street. They jumped into the Pontiac and took off.

"Where the fuck did *you* learn to negotiate?" Bill muttered, a bit miffed. The whole adventure had been a waste of time. "I told you not to get started with the guy!"

He checked the rear view mirror. Though the don was angry, he was not stupid.

"Well, you could've explained that you were going in there like Mother Teresa, for crying out loud. Maybe I would've genuflected to the righteous little fuck. But you showed the man the error of his ways. The beauty is, there's no question of harassment; *he* invited us." Jim slapped his knee in excitement.

Bill offered his reflections. "That man's as cool as they come. I'm sure it comes from years of experience. Show weakness, and you're dead. It's sad. He leads a life based on beliefs he knows are false."

"All criminals do," Jim said. Their beepers went off again.

"It's 8:45," Bill observed, checking his watch. "Piazza will be back soon with our hooker."

CHAPTER 12

Back at the precinct, the duty sergeant handed Bill a few messages, as Jim made his way up the stairs to the office. "We got a page earlier," Bill murmured. "Know anything about it?"

The sergeant, a middle-aged Mississippian, replied through a yawn, "Murder victim matching your M.O. turned up outside some dump in the Village. Initial unit responded half hour back. When you two didn't call back, Diaz and Hicks went to check it out. They left about ten minutes ago for a place called the Backdoor."

"Shit! What were you *waiting* for?" Bill asked angrily.

The sergeant shrugged with indifference.

The other message he provided was from Kathleen, wanting to know if he was coming home.

He took the stairs two at a time, until he reached the landing. The door to the homicide office was open and Jim was at his desk talking to Patrolman Piazza. To his right, beside the desk, sat a tall, slender woman holding up the back of her hand to admire her nails. As Bill approached, their three-way conversation came to a halt. The young patrolman rose and introduced her to Bill.

"Detective Masters, this here's our witness, Miss Candice."

"Good boy, Tony. You get an 'A'." Turning to the woman, he

added, "Would you give me a few minutes while I make a call?"

She replied with a disinterested snap of her gum.

The second number on the pager rang many times, but no one answered. Out of curiosity, he dialed the first. It too rang for a while before someone finally picked up. The voice seemed a bit out of breath. "Hello. . .uh, Backdoor." There was a lot of commotion in the background.

"Yes--I'm returning a page?" said Bill loudly over a commanding voice screaming for the person to hang up.

"I'm sorry," said the one who'd answered the phone, "but we are closed for the night. I gotta go." The line went dead.

Bill stood and moved to the coffee maker, nudging Jim as he passed. Grabbing a cup, he leaned in close. "Page Diaz and give him a 911. I think we have a problem."

"What's goin' on?"

"A body was found in the Village, outside a gay bar called The Backdoor. Heard of it?"

"Oh yeah. . .Fats and that kid mentioned it. I'm on it."

Jim paged the other detectives as Bill turned to Miss Candy and her suitor, Tony the Patrolman, who had by now resumed his conversation.

Bill thought she was beautiful--tall, with a thin face, her skin café au lait, the contacts in her eyes turning her natural brown a shade of jade, her sensuous lips accented with a bright red lipstick, the color of which highlighted the rest of her ensemble. Her chic Versace dress, trimmed with thigh-high stockings and lace garter, was consummated by the gold points of her stiletto heels. An outfit for a *last* date, Bill thought to himself, but, she was, after all, a hooker.

"I'm going to make this interview short and sweet," he said, "the way you ladies prefer it."

"Oh, aren't you a funny man, detective," she replied, her voice rising slowly. She crossed her legs. "I didn't catch your act at the Apollo."

She rolled the watch on her wrist and sighed. "Listen, unlike you and hard-on over here, I have work to do and children to feed. I came down here on my own. Unwise to be talking to cops in the street, *especially* if I'm not gettin' busted. It might give folks the impression that I'm goin' soft."

Jim, who was waiting for the return call on his page, barked,

"Hey, toots, if the job's so dangerous, why don't you quit?"

"If you must know, detective," she replied in a soft purr, "I'm a compassionate and caring woman who believes that divorcees, like yourself, have a right to feel the touch of a woman now and again. Think of me as a sexual philanthropist."

She turned her attention back to Bill, dismissing Jim with a wave of her hand.

"How did you know I was divorced?" asked Jim.

"Honey," she replied, returning to her nails, "I've been around the block. If there's one thing I know, it's men and all their slippery traits and nuances. In another setting, I guarantee you'd take time out from stroking the face of your child, or hugging your wife, just to get a glimpse of me."

"Lady, please! You're a *whore*, a warm body," Jim protested angrily.

"And you're a '*Dick*!' So what? A label, a word to describe an occupation. *Not* the summation of some sorry-ass life floundering at the bottom of a bottle. You see, they already have a word for that—it's *di-vor-cee*." She paused, reacting to Bill's attempt to conceal his eyes. "You see what you *want* to see, detective," she said, sounding apologetic. "And for a man of *your* occupation—who's the warm body?"

Jim stood, bit his lip, and stomped out of the room.

"Can we get started?" Bill asked, eyes wide, grabbing a small note pad from his desk, as the woman's gum snapped in defiance. "Tell me what you remember about last night."

Candy thought for a moment. "Some of the girls and I were on the corner near the drug store, jus' waiting for the next john, when we saw this new girl with this Arab fellow."

"How do you know she was a hooker?"

"Honey, with the outfit she was wearing, she had to be sellin'."

"Any details you can recall?"

"Yeah. She had a European look and wore a big-brimmed black hat that bounced up and down, covering most of her face."

"What color was her dress?"

"Black and orange. . .a striped pattern, like a tiger. She was also wearing white arm-length gloves. Pretty tacky."

Piazza, eager to leave, impatiently interjected, "Did you have an exchange or talk with them as they walked by?"

Bill gave him a stare. The woman had started to answer but,

seeing Bill's response, replied, "We just sorta' jeered at her, cussed at her, you know, commented on her dress. Some do that sort of thing when new girls come around. There are only so many eligible johns."

"Is there anything about this woman that you found odd, other than her dress?"

Candy thought about the question for a few seconds. "Besides the fact that she was escorting a *total* scumbag? She walked funny, like her shoes were too small. The streets require a comfortable pair of shoes."

"Anything else?" he asked, staring down at her four-inch heels.

She paused momentarily. "Yes. They seemed to be enjoying themselves. There was some laughter. Tricks're not so apt to cause a commotion, unless they're high or had a few too many. The last thing a lady needs is to be noticed. I'd say they knew each other."

Bill, sensing her growing unease, decided to let her go. She was as smart as most witnesses were dumb. Anyone with half a brain knew it was safer to stay inside. But she was right. They weren't just two ships passing in the night. They needed to find the killer, and fast--before she ran into any more of her old friends.

"This has been an interesting evening. Thank you. I appreciate you coming in. If I have any other questions, I'd like to give you a call, if that's okay? You can give Tony here your number." He handed her his card and added, "*My* number--if anything else comes to mind."

She accepted the card, looked directly into his eyes, and asked hesitantly, ". . .Can I make a suggestion?"

"Why, certainly," he replied. She had the decisive look of a cobra--seductive, tense, and ready to strike.

"I *know* why you don't eye me the way the others do. Women are mere distractions to a man who has replaced the warmth of life with the cool solitude of death. Remember, tomorrow is *not* always another day." She glanced at her watch. "Well, gentlemen, time to bring home the bacon." She looked relieved.

Piazza, eager to get back to his wife, asked for permission to leave.

The hooker had it right: Kathy was beautiful, but lately they seemed to be migrating in opposite directions--and he just didn't care.

Jim returned from the rock he had crawled under and sank into his chair as the phone rang. It was Detective Diaz.

"Hey, yo-yo! What does 911 mean?" asked Bill lightly. He didn't like to be out of the loop.

Diaz was a block from the bar, on a pay phone, outside a deli closed for renovations. Bill had told him, when things needed a muzzle, to avoid the new cellulars and turn down the radio. Who knew who was listening, these days?

"Sorry for the delay, but this thing is ugly. I called back as quickly as I could. Hicks just finished puking. I've done all I can to keep a lid on this, but you need to get down here right away. I'm too old for this shit."

Some muffled cries could be heard beyond the echo of his voice. Bill thought he'd heard the whirling blades of a helicopter. That could only mean one thing--the media had already gotten wind of the story.

"Yeah, no problem, Rico. Just sit tight. You have a name of the victim?" asked Bill, crossing his fingers.

"Some middle-aged guy named Johnson. . .Nates Johnson."

Bill said nothing.

"Hello? Hello. . .Bill, you still there?"

With his feet up on his desk, Jim tried to gauge his partner, having seen that look before--every time he opened the bottom drawer of his desk.

Jim dropped his feet off the desk and mouthed silently. "What?"

"Sorry, Rico," said Bill, tossing his pen down in disgust. "We'll be there shortly." He slammed the phone down. "Fuck!"

"*C'mon*--what's up?"

"Nates Johnson's been murdered."

They grabbed their gear and quickly headed for the car.

CHAPTER 13

Bill pulled the Pontiac to the curb on Greenwich Street, two blocks shy of the scene. A big crowd of pedestrians and hawkers had gathered, like a stampede of lemmings looking for a cliff.

Greenwich Village, for as long as he could remember, had been wired into the more progressive pulses of the city--an endless wealth of actors, artists, musicians, and Wall Street types looking for a leg up.

One of the local news teams was already on the scene trying to pry the lid off the story. The ME's vehicle and men were visible on the other side of the crowd, readying to load a shrouded corpse into a black body bag.

As the detectives hurried, they were met by the horde of TV reporters whose bright lights and cameras were obstructing their advance.

A staccato of "No comments" rolled off Bill's tongue as he and Jim pushed by, making their way under the barrier of yellow tape, toward Diaz and Hicks.

Acknowledging the two, Bill muttered, "What happened?"

"It's an ugly scene." Rico pointed at the blood-covered phone and the ground around it, and pulled a tired hand through his thick brown hair. "First man on the scene heard the phone ringing, but he was too busy controlling the crowd to answer it."

He pointed at the ground. Before them lay a thick puddle of blood oozing from the base of the public telephone, out across the sidewalk, and into the darkness of the gutter. A streetlight above was reflected clearly in the dark pool, shimmering in the misty breeze.

Bill pulled the others out of earshot and asked, his hand covering his mouth, "You *do* realize this guy was the assistant to the mayor? He was at the mayor's meeting this morning and had tried to contact us just prior to us getting here."

Bill matched the number on the phone to the second call he had received on his pager. "We can assume he was calling us from here when it happened. Keep a lid on this thing. If the mayor hears it on the news, we've had it."

Something wasn't right. He waved a finger at the growing number of cops lingering in the wings. "Tell all these men to button their traps," he said, raising his voice. "Look busy, or get the fuck off my crime scene!" With his arm around Diaz, he added softly, "Tell the photographers to get close-ups of the crowd. Maybe our suspect's still around." He paused to think. "Let's see the body."

With Bill standing over him, the ME's driver unzipped the bag. The body of Nates Johnson was there. His head was missing.

"Close that thing," Bill ordered in disgust. "Rico, please tell me there was a witness to this. It's only 9:30, for God's sake!"

Rico shook his head. "The only witness to anything outside was that guy over there." Diaz pointed to a thin young Latino, neatly dressed, crying softly into a tissue.

"What'd he see?"

"Not much. Just a woman, carrying a shopping bag, getting into a cab down the corner. I can't understand this myself. Somebody had to see *that*. There was just too much blood, and he was lying in plain view."

"Was she wearing a floppy black hat?"

"Why, yes, she *was* wearing a hat. How'd you know that?"

"Don't fret, Rico. After tonight, there'll only be one case we'll be working on. I'll give you my report when I get the go ahead from the captain. I can tell you this, though: We got big fuckin' problems."

Jim had returned with Detective Hicks behind him, his hand busy on his notepad.

Noticing the confused look, Bill asked, "*What?*"

"I don't understand. . .all this, and nobody saw a thing. I talked to a few people in and around the bar. Johnson was a regular. Everybody knew him. The bartender told me that he'd mentioned he was waiting for someone."

"Who's that?"

Jim glanced at his notebook. "His roommate, Bruce Philips. They met here occasionally during the week. According to Johnson's ID, they live nearby."

Jim rolled his eyes.

"Come on, Hicks. What ya got?" spat Bill, eyeing the line of reporters hogging the sidewalk beyond the tape.

"He'd been seated alone at the end of the bar, watching the news, when in walks a tall woman wearing a large-brimmed hat and white opera-length gloves. She sat down with her back to the bartender."

"Bartender hear anything?"

"He said he pulled some nuts across the bar for a nearby patron and he saw Nates stop talking, rise, and hurry out the door. Next, the woman helped herself to the bar phone, then the ladies room. After that, he doesn't know. I told him to relay the message to his employees that they're to talk only to cops or I'd shut him down. So far, everyone has amnesia. From what I've seen, can't say I blame them."

"Anyone else see this woman leave? Was there anyone in the bathroom at the same time? *C'mon*--there's got to be *something!*"

Bill headed for the door. Inside, he went straight for the phone. It still needed to be dusted, but opera-length gloves wouldn't offer a clue unless strands of fiber had been left behind. The number on the bar phone was identical to the first one he had received earlier on his pager.

"If you think we had problems before, think again."

"I don't get you," said Jim, following him like a puppy, as he retraced his steps from the entranceway to the seats at the bar. "What is it?"

"I'll tell you later--not here."

Bill pressed his stomach against the waitress station of the copper-covered bar and took in the cramped expanse of the room.

It was a little dark for his liking, but cozy. Yet, *he* didn't fit the profile. "How is it a woman can walk into this bar and not be noticed?"

"Maybe she figured she would be noticed--by those who would want her to be seen," Jim answered without really knowing why.

"Exactly. Just like Miss Candy. . .in this place, she was no one."

"Do you think Nates knew who we were talking about today in the mayor's office?" asked Jim, jotting in his notebook.

"I doubt it. Nates was smart. He would have gone immediately to the mayor. I think he was more reserved than frightened."

"Well, regardless--her presence didn't make him run or panic. He just went outside to use the phone. Who'd he call? His roommate, who hadn't arrived yet? We could check the records."

"I told you outside--he was calling *us*."

They left the bar and found Rico, who had been briefing four other officers who had just arrived on the scene.

"Rico, you didn't call us from the bar phone, did you?"

"No, but one of the first patrolmen on the scene told some asshole who picked it up to put it down."

"I figured as much. Listen, you know the drill. Have the forensic guys check the phone, the bar, the bathroom for anything and everything. I don't care if it's a fuckin' short and curly. If they find one, tag it and bag it. I want it all. Have that phone removed and taken as evidence. Tell the phone company that they'll get it back when we're through."

Bill was considering what to do next when another thought dawned on him. "Rico, did the roommate ever show?" If Nates had been in danger, who had led him to the source?

"No, I don't think he did. At least, we haven't spoken to him. For all I know, he's still on his way--or he's the sick fuck that did this," Diaz added with a shrug. "Should I send a patrol car over to his place?"

"Hicks," Bill replied, "give me the address of the deceased. I think I'll go take a look myself." The detective handed him a piece of paper from his pad. "Rico, I have a hunch. Take over for now. With any luck, we'll be back in a few minutes. Just remember, keep the lid on tight. I want all your notes when you're done." He grabbed Jim and headed for the Pontiac.

"Please tell me what the fuck's goin on?" Jim demanded, sounding more tired than desperate. "We were just talking to him this morning. He must have seen or heard *something* about Salaam. This bar's the only connection I can make. What are you thinking?"

"I know we've only known Nates for a few years, but I'm willing to give him the benefit of the doubt. I can't see him linked to Salaam."

Jim thought about that for a second. "Dishonesty at City Hall? Who'd believe it?" he said dryly. "But the man didn't have a mean bone in his body--no pun intended."

"Yeah, well, even Hitler had a maid."

The distance from the West Village to Nates' East Village apartment was well under a mile. They were crossing Sixth Avenue when Jim asked, "What is it you wanted to tell me back at the bar?"

"You're gonna' love this. Remember, back at Sciaffa's club, my pager went off?"

Jim shrugged. "So what?"

"Ten minutes later, it went off again. This time it was a different number. When we got to the precinct, I called the first number, and no one answered. That was probably me calling when the uniform on the street heard it ring. What? Maybe a minute goes by and I call the other number? I heard one of the other patrolmen yelling at some guy for picking up the phone."

"Where's all this heading?"

"The first call--which I failed to mention--came from inside the bar. The second came from the pay phone, about ten minutes later. What does that mean to *you*?"

"You're a popular guy?"

"The practical thing would be to say that Nates called from both inside and outside the bar. But from what the bartender said, that was impossible, since he left in a huff. The only one left was…"

"The *killer*!" Jim blurted, staring in disbelief. "Holy shit! How'd the killer get your pager number? Through Nates?"

"Possibly. But why would Nates give it to somebody and go outside? He heard what information we had. Why didn't he run? Obviously, he felt confident enough that he hung around even after the killer allowed him to leave."

"Maybe they were friends and he was going to turn her in."

Pausing, Bill replied, "Possible. Anything else?"

"Yeah. Why the lag time? Why'd it take so long for Nates to

call us from outside the bar when the killer was inside using the ladies room? He only called us once."

"Maybe the phone was being used. Or maybe he was talking to someone else, a third party, a mutual friend...one that was late?"

CHAPTER 14

The tired detectives pulled up to the front of an old eight-story brownstone, its entranceway covered by a short maroon canopy. As they got out of the car, a tall elderly woman with a long, thin cane dangling from her forearm moved slowly out of the building, carrying a small shopping bag.

When they reached the door, an intercom awaited them with a list of tenants. Nates had lived on the third floor, apartment 305. Jim pressed the button and studied the painfully short strides of the old woman carry her into the dark.

There was no answer. They waited another moment and pushed it again. No response. Jim rang the super's bell. "This is a pretty dark street," observed Bill. "Old lady has some balls."

"No shit."

Someone finally answered. The accent was out of place: The beaches of California were three thousand miles away.

"Chill, bra! Can't a dude pinch a loaf?"

"Too much television, eh?" Jim joked, as he listened to the strange voice.

"Yes, good evening," Bill said into the speaker. "We're here from the city and county inspector's office. There's been complaints of vermin and foul odors coming from your building. We'd like permission to take a look around."

They heard rustling and movement from within. "Ahhh. . .*shit.* One minute."

Jim, hands cupped around his eyes, his nose pushed up against the glass, spotted the manager coming out of a ground floor apartment, and stepped away from the glass.

"Here he comes, and you're gonna *love* him."

The super was no more than thirty years old. Complementing short, matted, dreadlocks pulled back in a ponytail, a multicolored Rasta hat hiding the lion's share of his natty locks, he wore a black T-shirt adorned with a big green marijuana leaf. The beads swinging from his neck supported a large wooden crucifix. He was noshing on an open bag of chips, whose chewed remains had decorated his tie-dye sweatpants and brown, open-toed sandals. He opened the door slowly.

The two detectives were greeted by the odor of marijuana clinging to his body like a parasite. His eyes, glazed and bloodshot, shined like a sill of ripe tomatoes.

He made little eye contact with either of them, as he licked the last bit of moisture from his lips. Nothing milk and an Oreo couldn't cure. He looked like Bill felt.

"Uh. . .uh, sorry man, I didn't hear the buzzer. . .I was crankin' tunes," he said, staring nervously at his feet. He preferred the predictability of his sofa.

"Hey. . .we didn't come to hassle you, ya know. Everything's groovy, really." Bill tried to contain himself. "We've had reports of huge rats on the premises."

"Hey, bro, dig your threads," added Jim, feigning interest. "By the way, what's your name?"

The manager began to relax, as he extended an offering from his bag of chips.

The two declined. "I told my mother--the lady who owns this building--that the rats would come if she didn't do something about the garbage. And you know what? She said adios and went to Egypt. I have a little rendezvous scheduled for Monday."

Bill hadn't seen an individual that high on grass since college. "Listen carefully," he said. "We're not inspectors. That's just our cover, dude. We're police detectives on a stakeout. One of our snitches told us that someone was dealing drugs out of this building. Notice anything suspicious?"

The super averted his eyes, instantly withdrawing into his mental cocoon. After some quick miscalculations, he mumbled under his breath. "Yeah, I have." Looking around, he leaned farther out the door. "People've been goin' in and out of the apartment on the third floor. Wait'll my mom finds out."

"Which apartment?" Bill asked in amazement.

"Three oh . . . uh . . . three-o-five, I think. You should go up there and bust 'em, pronto. Careful, though, the one guy's a tough hombre." He swung his arm back behind him and pointed with his thumb. "I'll hang in my apartment."

He let them in and disappeared, littering chips in his haste. Bill and Jim headed for the stairs.

The hallway was well lit. The wide carpet on the steps looked like it had just been replaced or recently shampooed. The red looked nice, Jim thought, as he grabbed the thick wooden railing at the base of the landing.

They found the door they were looking for on the far end of the third floor, its fluted jamb sharing space with the half open window of the fire escape that descended into the dark alley below. The doors were illuminated by the soft light of wall sconces housed in frosted glass. Looking back down the hallway, Bill noticed apartment 305 was the only one missing a bulb. "Place's pretty nice," he said. "I'll have to talk to ol' Kravitz about getting myself a raise."

"You ain't kidding," replied Jim, looking around in disbelief. "Stoney's mom really takes care of the place."

Mulling over the missing light, he scratched the top of his head. Bill turned to his partner. "I think the roommate didn't show up because the perp came here first, but Nates wasn't here."

Jim nodded.

"Do me a favor? Head downstairs and get the other kid. I'm sure he has a master key. We won't be needing a warrant on this one."

"You got it."

Bill waited outside the door. A curious neighbor, her gray hair in curls, leaned out to investigate. He flashed her his badge and a manufactured smile. She vanished.

With added scrutiny, he crouched to inspect the bottom of the lamp. There was no logical reason for the bulb to be missing. Pulling on a rubber glove, he gently ran his fingertips along the door and window, looking for signs of forced entry. An examination of the lock-set for signs of tampering was a dead end as well. He dropped to his hands and knees, hoping to get a glimpse under the door. There was little to be seen, but he recognized the familiar smell of incense, and the television seemed overly loud for a Saturday night.

Momentarily, the super, devoid of humor, plodded up the stairs in front of Jim. He pulled a set of keys from a chain attached to his sweatpants and eagerly opened the door.

Tilting his head in the direction of the stairs, he offered a friendly reminder. "Yo, man. . .you don't want to mess with the likes of these dudes. You might want to call for back up."

"Stay here," Bill snapped, dismissing his delusions. "If you hear any commotion, call 911. Got it?"

"No problemo, señor."

Drawing his weapon, Bill entered first, his back pressed against the wall. Inching their way through a dimly lit entrance, their soles squeaking on immaculate tile, they came upon two opposing doors at the end of the short hall. The one on the right appeared to be an entranceway closet, the other, adorned in a small basket of potpourri, the hall bath.

They strained to hear for signs of life but, aside from the excessive volume of the T.V., they heard nothing.

Bill tilted his head to the door on the right. "I'll take the closet," he whispered, "You check the bath. On three."

Gun leveled firmly on the toilet, Jim sighed in relief. Flicking on the light, he checked behind the door.

Bill, his voice rising in distress, came falling out of the closet backwards.

"You little motherfucker!" he screamed, trying desperately to rid himself of the attacker. Alarmed, Jim spun on his heels and leveled his weapon on his partner. "What is it? What is it?"

His eyes located an angry, short-haired tabby, leaving Bill's chest for the suspect safety of the living room.

"Holy shit!" said Bill, leaning against the hallway wall, head back, eyes closed, his hand on his heart. "That thing scared the shit out of me!" he said, gasping for air.

"Gee, Bill, don't get so worked up. When was the last time some pussy jumped in your lap?"

"Very funny. Miss Candy would've loved it. By the way, the

hall light's out on the floor."

The lone clear incandescent bulb looked to match what was in the rest of the fixtures lighting the hallway. Oddly, its filament still intact and it had been wiped clean.

"Looks like Nates' roommate doesn't like soiled light bulbs," said Bill softly, holding it up. "The thing's as clean as a whistle."

"Yeah, right--factory fresh."

They continued towards the living room, guns out, their sliding backs as flush as wallpaper.

The living room was large, with unusually high ceilings trimmed in white plaster. A large chandelier hung from the center on a short chain. The floor, a sizable expanse of spit-shined, bleached oak, was covered by a wide Persian rug. The fireplace, clean from lack of use, was decorated with small blocks of streaked black granite. The room had an elegance inspired by a passion not typically ascribed to men.

The television, corralled by long, smooth drapes of flowery muslin wrapped daintily with wisps of a wine tabaret, sat before a large leather sectional set perpendicular to the bluestone hearth, to the right, a massive bookshelf rose almost to the ceiling.

The art work, stationed at different heights along the walls, regardless of size or medium, suggested a refined eye.

A Picasso litho sat across from a set of Rembrandt etchings. The only thing missing was a length of velvet rope. Although the living arrangements were unorthodox, and this wasn't uptown, he had to wonder which inhabitant had the scratch to indulge such taste.

The blaring, wide-screen television was tuned to a speech on South East Asia and its effects on the psyche of the American veteran today.

"Smell that?" asked Jim, his nose testing the air.

"Yeah. I did when I was waiting in the hallway. It's coming from the back room."

"Did you see a supply of his and his matching towels in the hall bath by any chance?" Bill snickered, peering into an empty kitchen.

"No. But it was decorated pretty nice. I must give poor Nates credit for his tastes, decoratively speaking."

"Let's get this over with. Christ, the guy left on every light and appliance in the whole apartment. The mayor must've been paying him well."

The queen-sized bed was unmade. On the dresser stood pictures of Nates and another man sitting on a couch, cuddling the cat. Bill assumed it was the missing roommate. Abutting the photo, an urn of incense burned in smoky silence. There were two nearly empty long-stemmed glasses, filled with white wine, set out separately on opposing night tables. Small pools of water had condensed at their bases. The sight of the moistened coasters didn't surprise him.

Above, a ceiling fan spun slowly, throwing a comfortable breeze across the bed, at the foot of which lay two small piles of clothes: two pairs of jeans, and two shirts. The sizes were different. Men's briefs were still inside the pants, and it looked as if one of them was in desperate need of a re-wipe.

Jim moved off across the room as Bill opened the top drawer of the night table to his left, uncovering letters, some personal belongings, and a copious supply of red, white, and blue condoms. He was surprised to find a bag of marijuana and a wooden pipe shaped like a scarab.

Fingering the mattress, he turned to Jim. "A queen size bed. How apropos. Looks like there might've been a little hanky panky going on. He was supposed to meet Nates, and there're two relatively fresh glasses of wine. See? You're not the only one with domestic problems. Poor Nates went out not knowing his man was a cheatin' bastard."

"*Please*, fuck off."

Browsing the dresser on his side of the room, Jim noticed a bathroom door partially hidden behind an ornate Oriental blind. Pulling it aside, he took a few steps towards the door, stopped at the threshold, stuck his hand inside the door, and flicked on the light. "Shit!" was all he shouted.

At the same moment, the door to the closet slid open and someone came out. Bill leveled his weapon. "Freeze! On the floor, now!" Adrenaline pumped through his veins, as his darting eyes came to rest on the body of a naked man.

"Hands behind your head!"

The man, sobbing hysterically, complied quickly, his craned neck searched the room.

Handcuffs firmly in place, his face pushed into the carpet, the naked man offered a muffled plea. "Please, help him. . . .*Please*!"

Pulling the man to his feet, Bill draped a robe, with the legend

Nates embroidered neatly on the breast pocket, over his shoulders. The man sat down on the edge of the bed, tears running down his face.

With the sound of his heart still pounding in his ears, Bill demanded, "Who are you and what're you doin' here?"

The man wiped his face with the shoulder of the robe. "M-My name's Russell B-Bloughs. I'm a friend of Bruce and Nates."

"I want you to leave the room and wait for us on the couch," said Bill firmly. "Don't even *think* about leaving, and whatever you do, don't touch a thing. Christ. You're lucky I didn't shoot you!"

Rising, his pale face contorted in fear, the tall man, hands cuffed behind him, headed out of the room. The lifeless body of Nates' roommate, lean and muscular as a middle-weight, lay naked in the tub, his arms draped across his chest. The position of his body, the neatness of his hair, the serenity of his face, suggested that he had been laid gently, carefully in place.

Foul play, unnoticeable except for the thin streams of blood crossing his ribs, puddling in the roundness of the drain, came in the form of a tiny puncture wound at the base of his left breast. At his feet, the murderer left a different calling card—the bloody remains of Nates Johnson's head.

The two left the bathroom in silence. Moving to the night table, Bill removed a handkerchief from his pocket, picked up the phone, and called it in. When he was through, he turned to Jim and said, "The guy in the closet *had* to get a look at this person."

CHAPTER 15

Russell Bloughs, his face a mask of fear and uncertainty, sat on the couch, staring ahead blankly, as if time had ceased to exist. His thin, hairless legs were drawn up in his manacled arms. He was weeping softly.

Bill had him rise to remove the cuffs. "Sir, your friend is dead. I'm truly sorry."

The man put his hand to his mouth, bit into his clenched fist, and nodded. Bill didn't mention Nates' death. The man was held together by a thread.

Jim stood motionless in front of the windows across the room, peering out into the night, thinking about his ex-wife, his children, and what should've been. In the presence of death, the past seemed far away; but that was all that seemed to matter. Off in the distance, he heard the familiar sound of a siren.

Minutes later, whatever manpower the evidence team and the medical examiner had to spare, arrived in an eerie silence. Bill and Jim, talking to the robed man on the couch, paused to point toward the bedroom.

Russell was a tall, fair-haired, thirty-eight-year-old tax account-ant who lived and practiced in the East Village. After a few awkward minutes, he became less a suspect and more a man who held the memory of his departed friend in the highest regard. "What—what happened to Bruce?" he asked, numbed.

"Russ. . .do you mind if we call you Russ?" Bill asked, hoping to allay the man's fear. The man shrugged. "Your friend's been murdered, and we need your help to find out why."

The accountant looked up, his trembling mouth bent in a rainbow of sorrow. "I didn't see a thing, I swear. I just. . .heard things."

Nodding in support, Jim reassured him with a pat on the shoulder, "We believe you, so start from the beginning. This is very important. We need to know the whole story."

"Bruce and Nates were having a rough go of it lately. They were arguing a lot. Nothing they couldn't have worked out. Bruce'd been spending most of his time freelancing after hours. He was a gifted hairstylist, and he had a growing clientele outside the salon. It made for some professional jealousy between them."

That explained the scissors and combs around the bedroom and the boxes of supplies in the hall closet.

"Bruce had asked me to come over before he met Nates for a drink at the Backdoor. It's off Bleecker. He wanted to talk, ask my advice, considering their situation. I got here early, about 7:00. We were watching television and chatting over a bottle of wine." He paused to dry his eyes. "I don't think Bruce was aware of how fond I am. . .I mean, was, of him. Both of them, actually. They never hid their sexuality. Everyone respected that. After a while, knowing that Bruce needed to leave, I made a pass at him, and he seemed to respond. One thing led to another, and we made our way to the bedroom." Noticing the shift in Jim's posture, he added, "Are you two all right with this?"

"We're not here to judge you," said Bill. "It's been a long day for all of us. Please--as you were saying?"

Russell sat up straight, took a deep breath, uncrossed his legs, and pulled together the lapels of his robe. "We took off our clothes and got into the bed. We talked briefly and had some more wine. The phone began to ring over and over, but Bruce refused to answer because he thought it might be Nates. Ten minutes later, there was a knock at the door. Bruce almost had a bird. He was convinced Nates had misplaced his keys and begged me to get into the closet. . .which I did. The next thing I know, the television's blasting and Bruce is pleading with someone."

Jim interrupted. "Then how could you've not seen or heard anything?"

"I could barely hear over the T.V. And, may I add, scared shitless."

"Did you happen to look out the door?" asked Bill.

"I peeked a bit, but this person, this *monster*, had already taken Bruce into the bathroom. I heard him pleading, begging for this person to leave. Then he let out a short scream."

"What did you do?" asked Bill, writing quickly.

Russell began to squirm. He hesitated as tears welled.

"I. . .I closed my eyes and prayed. I didn't know what else to do. I was frozen."

"Why'd you stay in the closet for so long?"

"So *long*? You missed everything by no more than a few *minutes*."

"Are you serious?" said Bill, rising. "Jim, you hear what he just said?"

Jim pulled Bill aside. "Well, Nates' head was in there."

Moving to a Van Gogh print in the corner, Jim was amazed to see a stream of blood running from an ear. "Bill, come check this out."

He moved a high-backed loveseat from the corner. Behind it sat an easel, a small tarp neatly folded, and a wooden box of paints leaning against the frame of an unfinished painting. To its right lay a blood-stained eyedropper.

From over his shoulder, Bill concluded with a shake of his head, "If this person was five minutes ahead of us, it was that old lady we saw as we pulled up. We practically held the fuckin' door for her!"

Working a kink out of his neck, he barked at the disinterested patrolman guarding the door, "Bring over the old lady from 304."

"The one with her head stuck out of her door?"

"That's the one. And when you're done, retrieve the super from the first floor."

Mayor Kravitz was going to want answers. They had few. He turned back to the robed man.

"You mentioned Bruce worked after hours. What did he do, *exactly*?"

"He moonlighted for certain customers, after he was done at the salon."

"People wanted him to come to their homes?"

"Sure. Rich people, struggling actors and actresses, sick friends who were confined. . . . He was a very charitable man."

Jim returned from the corner carrying the canvas and the wooden box.

Holding up the incomplete portrait of a nude male, Jim asked, "Whose is this?"

"I believe it's the work of Bruce's old roommate. He was a photographer and a painter."

Inside the case, Jim found an assortment of oil-based paints, and a fresh spool of wire--the kind that coiled easily.

"Where's he now?"

"He left months ago but Bruce hasn't heard from him in weeks."

"Where'd he go?" asked Jim, testing the strength of the wire.

"Don't have the foggiest. I know Nates didn't care as long as he had Bruce to himself."

"And Bruce?"

"He seemed scared most of the time. Like he was waiting for some unseen axe to fall. He said Victor--that was his name, Victor Lawrence, was insanely jealous."

"Would anybody know his whereabouts?" asked Jim, taking down the name.

"He's a freelance photographer. Could be anywhere. Where do you think these furnishings came from? Victor brought them back from his assignments."

"Who'd he work for?"

"The *Post*, I think, and some wire services."

Pulling a picture of Salaam from his breast pocket, Jim asked, "Ever see this guy?"

Russell inspected it briefly. "Not sure, maybe he's been around. But the haircut does look a little like Bruce's style."

Bill returned dissatisfied from the bedroom, as Jim filled him in on the ex-roommate.

"Did Bruce have an appointment book," Bill asked, "something to keep track of his clients?"

"I'm sure. But salons covet their client lists. Stealing's unethical. It would have pissed a few people off. I can't see him leaving it around."

"Angry enough to kill?"

"*Please*, detective--they're hairdressers, not *terrorists!*"

Bill had to agree--it wasn't worth getting killed over. But maybe knowing one of the clients was.

"Does he own a car?"

"Not that I know of."

"Great. What do you know about this old roommate Victor Lawrence?"

"Well, he said he was forty-eight. I think he's a bit older, but that's me. And he's *very* butch. Rugged, well built, physically strong. A real specimen, if you know what I mean. Liked to work out— sometimes two, three times a day, like he was training for something."

"Was he in the military?"

"Who knows? He once showed us pictures he'd taken of soldiers in Vietnam."

"As a soldier or a photographer?"

"I'm sorry, detective, I really don't know. Nates knows a *lot* about Victor, of course--you should ask him. Enemies are like that, you know."

"Enemies? How so?"

"I'm told Nates met Bruce after Victor had kicked his ass for being with another guy. After the fight, Nates took Bruce in, cleaned him up, and they became good friends. Victor's hated him ever since."

"Did Bruce sleep around a lot?" asked Bill.

"Well . . .Bruce was handsome. Rich men liked his style. He never had problems finding men. It drove Nates crazy."

"Did these rich men pay him?"

"I'm not at liberty to say. The man is dead."

With a nod, Bill gave up his seat and headed for the book case.

"You're telling me Victor kicks Bruce's ass," Jim asked, stepping forward unconvinced, "and Nates takes them both in? Doesn't exactly sound like a match made in heaven."

"After the beating, Victor disappeared for a while. Probably on another one of his assignments. Six months later, he returns to find Bruce and his apartment gone. Since the community down here is so small. . . ."

"Go on."

"Um, yes. . .Victor finds out Bruce was staying with Nates, and he comes looking for a place to crash. Nates wasn't too keen about it, but Bruce convinced him to let him stay. Victor had some

100

invisible power over him. They'd disappear, sometimes for days at a time, returning with nothing but a tan. I think Victor had a place near the ocean. Nates was *constantly* complaining about sand in the couch."

"So you're telling me Nates could live with this guy in his own home?"

"Well, they shared certain interests, and Nates just loved Bruce. He would do *anything* he wanted."

"What kind of interests?"

"Art, poetry, photography, those kinds of things. Victor brought things back, because he knew Nates would let him stay."

Returning from across the room, Bill asked, "I see photographs of Nates, Bruce, and you. Any of Victor Lawrence?"

Pulling the ties of the robe firmly about his waist, Russell sauntered to the bookcase and returned with a small framed photo.

"It's not a very good one."

"Which one's he?"

"The blonde-haired guy in the middle."

The photo contained a small group of men dressed in drag, commemorating Halloween—not a face recognizable, and one man offered only a robed arm and what looked like the corner of a diploma. Victor Lawrence, the indigent, was clad in a sheer tiger suit.

"Who's the missing guy, the one in the blue gown?"

"Some hairy friend of Victor's. I don't remember his name, but once he got drinking, all he talked about was how Victor saved his life."

"Army buddy?"

"Haven't a clue."

At that moment, the neighbor arrived from next door. The patrolman pointed her in the direction of the two detectives, before returning to the stairs.

Bill introduced everyone, as she took a seat next to Russell on the couch.

"Ma'am," asked Bill politely. "You opened your door when you heard us before. Did you happen to see anyone else tonight?"

The old woman, rosary beads in hand, replied in a wavering voice, her head moving with a slight tick. "Yes, I saw an old woman with a shopping bag. Couldn't see very well with the light being out in the hallway--violation, you know."

"Did you happen to notice anything about her," asked Jim writing, "something we might use to identify her? She alone?"

"Yes, and her wig was a mess," replied the old women. "Must've been in a hurry."

"How did you know she was wearing a wig?" asked Jim.

"Hey, sonny!" the old women snapped, not happy with his tone, "I started wearing wigs when you were in rubber pants. She *was* wearing a doozy."

As the two detectives traded looks, the patrolman entered with the super in tow. He took a seat next to the old woman.

"Now listen, jerky," Jim barked, putting his foot up between the super's legs, "I know it's late, and you've been up rippin' a few tubes, but you said you saw old ladies going in and out. Did you see only one old lady, or were there more?"

The super shifted in his seat, eyeing the detective with an uncertain contempt. "I want a lawyer!"

Hovering an inch from his ear, Bill murmured, his face a mask of frustration, "You're *not* a suspect. Today, anyway. If you saw an older woman this evening, we'd like to know."

Relieved, the man replied, "Sure. Some old lady buzzed me before you got here. Said she had some clothing for her grandson in 305. I looked out my door, she held up her bag, and I let her in."

"Was she alone?"

"I think so."

"You let a total stranger into the building? Defeats the intercom, doesn't it?" added Jim, amazed at the sad sight before him.

"The last time I read the paper, man, old women were the ones bein' mugged. Old folks come and go all the time around here."

"All right," said Bill cutting in. "Did the woman get buzzed in and you went back to the bong, or did you get a look at her?"

"Yeah, she was tall, looked like old lady Swanson here, but wearing a cool, floppy hat."

With that description, and Nate's head, they could tie the two murder scenes together to the one in the alley. The perp was a pro on a mission, a killing machine who had little use for a clock, and who wasn't going to stop. They had to keep moving, try to get a step ahead.

"Good night, everyone," said Bill, closing his note pad. "Other detectives will meet with you shortly. We'll be in touch." With a head motion, the patrolman escorted the tenants towards the door.

Bill turned back to the man in the robe. "Was the light outside the door operating when you arrived?"

"Yes, I believe it was. If Nates saw a burned out bulb, he'd replace it immediately. He hated loose ends."

They questioned Russell for a few more minutes. They offered him a ride, but his clothes would have to stay.

"Russell," Bill finally said, "I have more bad news for you. Mr. Johnson was murdered too--killed in the Village, outside the Backdoor. I'm very sorry."

Reality took a moment to sink in, as the man dropped his chin to his chest. He looked up with fresh tears running down his cheeks. "I always wondered when the dying would start again." Russell said at last. "I think I'll take you up on that ride."

"Certainly. I just have one question before you go."

"What's that?"

"Think Victor Lawrence's capable of these things?"

"Is there a *more* capable enemy than a friend, detective?"

CHAPTER 16

The body was being wheeled out of the apartment when the captain arrived—an uncommon visit, but the shit had already finished hitting the fan over the mayor's assistant. The captain looked more agitated than usual.

"I just got a call from the mayor with regard to Mr. Johnson. Do we have more terrorists in our city, detective?"

"The murders are connected," Bill confided. "Highly unlikely we'd have two perps in floppy hats, killing all over town. Nates tried to call us today. It might be the old roommate. We don't know, but it's tied to Salaam or the roommate, maybe both. I'm sure of it."

"I thought you said the roommate is dead," said the captain, lowering his eyes to the cat purring against his leg.

"He is. I'm talking about a third guy, a photographer, who hasn't been seen in a few weeks. One Victor Lawrence. We're running the name. We believe the killer met with Nates briefly, sometime between seven-thirty and eight, then ambushed him while he was on the phone calling us. We think he left in a cab. After some lag time—probably to change costumes—he came here and killed the roommate, leaving the head of Mr. Johnson at his feet. It's possible he was looking for something, but only the master bath and the picture have been disturbed."

He handed the captain the small Halloween photo and pointed out the man in the tiger dress. "Looks like our killer had a soft spot for the deceased. He was spared the deliberate brutality inflicted upon the others. Victor Lawrence, past lover and documented cross-dresser, is now our main suspect."

"The mayor's going to want more than speculation, detective."

"Captain, this person, male or female, is a professional. Two men are butchered, one glows in the dark, and no one's seen or heard a thing. Nuclear materials mean national security. I was under the impression the spooks were pros, real neat freaks."

The captain nodded. Bill continued, "Well, maybe this person is a loose cannon, looking to get weapons-grade materials into the country for money, maybe a little payback. What was once CIA's jurisdiction became the FBI's as soon as it crossed the border. You saw Willard's concern--the CIA may have fucked up. Look around you—these men are harmless, nothin' but loose ends." He turned to face the captain directly. "Sir, I never thought I'd say this, but the feds have the facilities and the resources. We should meet with the mayor again."

"Works for me. You've got your hands full. I'll hammer out the details with the feds in the morning. Our new problem's the media. I can't wait to see the morning papers. We should leave dealing with *that* up to the commissioner. Where are you going to go from here?"

Although he hadn't discussed it with his partner, Bill replied, "We thought we'd head over to Salaam's apartment and see what we can dig up." He shrugged, looking for Jim's consent, which came in the form of an eyebrow raised in displeasure.

The three men stood before the bloody painting as lab men collected samples from the ear. The captain rocked back on his heels and shook his head. The two detectives left the scene in silence.

In the Pontiac, with another bent Tiparillo wrapper lost to the wind, Jim said, "You think we're in over our heads, don't you?"

Bill forced a weak smile.

"I'm serious," said the other, digging for his lighter.

"What's with Salaam's apartment? Willard's probably cleaned it out already."

Pulling the car lighter from the center console, Bill replied, as he handed it to his partner, "I doubt it. Willard's going to let us do the leg work. Detectives investigating a local murder don't alarm the masses as much as starched collars and stiff ties. Feds poking around would send Salaam's friends packing. Besides, the killer seems to want to deal with *us*. I just don't know *why*."

"You should've told the captain," Jim said, exhaling like a coyote courting the moon.

"*What*—that they dropped a page, lookin' to turn themselves in? No way, they're just fuckin' with us, thinking we'll focus on something that'll play no part in bringing them in."

"Why's that?" Jim was still waiting for an answer.

"Like I said--they're pros and the more variables there are the harder the equation becomes. Simple mathematics."

After a very long pause, Jim asked, changing the subject, "You and Kath havin' problems?"

"No, it really has nothing to do with her," replied Bill, his immediate reflections broken by a drunken cyclist with a death wish. "We live in a time when we need, more than ever, someone to come and save us from ourselves."

"Ah, dry your eyes, Billy boy," teased Jim, leaning over, administering a slap on the knee. "Nothin's gonna happen. We get to see the darkest outlets of mankind--*every* fuckin' day. It grows on you, numbs you, until it steals your humanity. I'd say that entitles *us* to any outlet that we see fit."

Turning the corner, Jim gazed into the wet darkness, his eyes glued to the Budweiser sign blinking in the window of the corner bar.

As he inched the car forward, Bill rolled his hands on the steering wheel, trying to find the address. "What entitles *them* to seek such an outlet?" He hit the brakes abruptly. "Shit-holes like these?"

"Got that right," replied Jim, eyeing the decaying edifice.

The conversation ended as the two pulled to the curb a few car lengths shy of the red brick tenement streaked black by decades of exhaust. A rusting fire escape, cluttered with dying plants, snaked skyward, stopping at a window that was pumping a heavy Rap beat into the night air.

In the lobby, they were greeted by a man sprawled face down, unconscious on the floor, with a bagged bottle of malt liquor clutched tightly in his hand.

"Effective doorman. I can't wait to meet the super." Jim stepped carefully over the man and the yellow puddle between his legs.

"Second floor," added Bill, flipping through his notebook.

The building was a crack addict's match away from being condemned. The lobby walls were covered with grime and graffiti, the tan apartment doors a symphony of peeling paint. Angry voices bellowed from above.

The second-floor landing contained shredded garbage bags, discarded cigarettes, and the stench of soiled diapers. Apartment numbers were missing on a few of the doors as they proceeded down the hall.

Seizing the doorknob of Salaam's locked apartment, Bill heard a noise from within. With a nod from Jim, he drew his weapon and kicked in the door, splintering the jamb.

A young punk in a Yankee hat stood straddling the shattered window fronting the fire escape. "Freeze! Don't move!" Bill screamed, his gun leveled on the kid's chest. The boy froze, dropping his eyes to the item in his hand. "Definitely ain't worth dying over, kid! Step back inside and hand it over."

Moving forward, his own weapon trained on the Yankee fan, Jim slowly pulled him and the black notebook back in the window.

Bill flipped through the contents of the binder, while Jim handcuffed the kid and sat him on the floor.

Bill pulled his partner aside. He spoke softly. "From what I can tell, there are symbols for plutonium and uranium here." There was another symbol he had never seen before. "The rest looks like Arabic. Listen—the mayor mentioned important people coming to visit. Do you have any idea who was he talking about?"

"From what I understand, there's going to be some formal acknowledgment of the new Vietnamese government at the U.N. this week. The President, CIA Director Stevenson, FBI Director Sterling, and a long list of foreign dignitaries are supposed to be there."

"The plot thickens."

With all the excitement, a small group of tenants had gathered in the hallway. Catching sight of the two investigators and their prisoner, they scattered like roaches at dawn.

A few apartments down, an old woman stood solidly outside

her door, smoothing the front of her blue dress, her ebony skin, wrinkled by years, aglow with a welcoming warmth. Small wire spectacles hung from a length of beads strung around her thin neck.

"Do you know where we might find the super?" asked Bill politely.

"Don't patronize an ol' woman," she replied in a smooth Appalachian drawl. "Neva known a badge to ask a question he really wanted answered. Ya'll be wantin' to know about the man whose door you kicked in."

"Yes, ma'am," replied Jim with a disconcerted smile. "Seems we weren't the only ones breaking in. You won't mind if we stop by in a few minutes to ask you a few questions?"

"Course not. I'll make us some tea." She turned and headed inside.

In the rush to arrest the burglar, they hadn't noticed the decor or the tight quarters of the deceased. The bathtub shared space with the kitchen, neither looking as if they got much use. And, opposed to the rest of the apartments, the place was *spotless*.

Religious icons dotted the shelves along the wall. Two small prayer rugs sat rolled up under the window facing the street. Remains of map corners, held in place by worn colored thumbtacks, were stuck firmly to the wall over the bed, suggesting the map had been removed in haste. Judging from the number of holes left behind, the map had been used often.

In the corner sat a simple wooden dresser; its open top drawer contained socks, men's briefs, and an old cigar box with photographs secured by a rubber band. One of the pictures, dated 10/31, caught Bill's attention. Wearing a blue graduation gown, and carrying a diploma, Salaam had his arm around another man. They were in front of a gated mansion, the address of which was barely visible on the stone pillar behind them.

"Jim, check this out."

"What's up?"

"I know I've seen this building before, but does this look like the same arm that was wrapped around our naked accountant on Halloween? *Blue* gown, *same* date. Maybe Victor Lawrence knew Salaam. 'Good friends,' I think was the term used."

"Yeah, but it looks like he's celebrating a graduation, not Halloween. Besides, why would Victor kill a man whose life he'd allegedly saved--and in such a brutal way? Not to mention, Bloughs didn't recognize him in the mug shot."

"You have a point, but he *did* have a beard, and right now I'm not worried so much about the photos. It's the journal—obviously, this guy's a scientist of some sort." Bill had seen such a framed diploma before. He knew just the person to see.

He handed Jim the photo, pulled a small folding magnifying glass from his back pocket, and turned to inspect what was left of the map.

"Where'd you get that?" asked Jim, admiring the metal case.

"I've always had it. My old man gave it to me the night before he left." Jim let it go.

"What do you make of this?" Bill asked, holding up the corner behind the lens with an odd, bluish hue. "It says *New Jersey*!"

"The kid said he was always getting lost," said Jim, bending to check the cupboard under the sink.

"But why would a cab driver, trying not to get lost in New York, need a map of Jersey?"

"Maybe he doesn't want to get lost there either?"

"Fine work, Sherlock," Bill replied, looking about. "Apparently, Willard *has* left this place alone. It's high time our boys come clean it out for him. Have a blue-and-white pick up the kid. We'll give him the night to think about his situation. Get in touch with Rico and see how things are panning out at Nates' apartment. When you get back, we'll speak to the old lady and see what she knows about her neighbors. I'm gonna take another quick look around."

Both of their pagers went off within seconds of each other.

"I wonder what's up now?"

Bill checked the number on his pager. It was the M.E.'s office.

"Excellent," said Bill. "Maybe the good doctor has some answers for us."

Bill looked around the room for a phone; oddly, there wasn't any. He checked outside the broken window. Across the street was a payphone. He made a mental note of it. Their pagers went off again. The two headed for the hall.

"Unload that kid and meet me across the hall," ordered Bill, scribbling in his pad. "She'll let us use her phone."

"Sure. One question."

"Shoot."

"Why the blue lens?"

Bill shrugged. "Not really sure but my old man used to say, 'Blue is the color of truth'." Bill turned and headed back into Salaam's apartment.

CHAPTER 17

The old tenant answered the door with a smile and welcomed them in. Her neatly manicured apartment, although low in light, was awash in old photographs that dotted the short walls and doily-covered tables. The smell was a cross between an incontinent cat and chipped cedar. It made Bill think of another time, another place.

The two detectives took seats on the shawl-covered couch, the host on a high-backed chair worn ragged by the claws of a cat. Offering a hand, she said politely, "My mamma always told me introductions were important. Name's Annabel Perkins."

"Detective Bill Masters, ma'am," he said, surprised at the firmness and duration of her grip. "This is my partner, Jim Lackey."

"Pleasure to meet you both. I'm sure you men are stretched for time, so let's get busy."

Unlike the don, Jim liked her style. "What can you tell us about the man who lived down the other end of the hall?"

"What do y'all mean by *lived*? He go somewhere?" she asked, concerned.

"Yes, ma'am. He was murdered," replied Jim.

"My *Lord*!" she exclaimed, her hands moving slowly to her face.

"Poor man. Murdered right across the hall." She paused for a moment, adding, her head cocked in thought, "I didn't see them take anyone out."

"Who's *they*, and *when*?" asked Bill, as he fumbled for his notes.

"Friday night, late. Strange men in funny suits. They looked like aliens."

Bill recalled the observation Jim's suit-wearin' bum had made. Willard had been flat out lying. That was bad.

"Were they alone?" asked Bill, catching Jim's stares.

"Two men lingered outside. That was all I cared to see. I know when to mind my own business."

"Were they carrying anything?" asked Bill, sounding almost desperate. "The men in the funny suits--I mean?"

"Looked like those little boxes I've seen the Con Ed men carry."

"What can you tell us about Mr. Salaam himself?" asked Bill, trying to slow the conversation down. He knew Con-Ed men didn't carry Geiger counters.

"I know a crackhead when I see one. Damn fool!" she replied, sipping tea. "Would you like some?"

"No, thank you," replied Jim.

"Stop your squirming, son," chimed the old woman. "I know it ain't that comfy. Man your size'll soften it up in no time."

Through an impish grin, Bill asked, "Mr. Salaam, ma'am?"

"You want to know if he's a crackhead? I've seen generations of hookers, pimps, pushers, drug addicts, murderers, and rapists pass my door. Mr. Salaam, bad seed that he was, was one-- homosexual, too. Seen them doing their thing right outside my door."

"Anything else you can think of? Something he might have said?"

She nodded. "I talked to him about the weather, mostly. Man knew more about the weather than I would have expected from a cabbie. Must've studied science or something. Told me, if one could get out into the Atlantic a few hundred miles, winds would jus' sweep me up an' take me back to Africa."

"Anything else?" asked Jim, who wanted to go back to the garage.

"A religious man who'd drop and face the East no matter where he was. He'd do it on the sidewalk, if it pleased him. But some religions plow an evil path to righteousness, their wicked roves pulled by the yokes of martyred souls." She smiled politely, as her teacup returned slowly to her lips.

"Did you happen to see a lady with a floppy hat, dressed real nice? European look?" asked Bill, sifting through his notes.

"I'm no fashion plate, but I think I know who you're talking about. They left together on Friday, about eleven."

"Had you ever seen her before?" Bill asked.

"Understand, detective," she said softly, "I'm no window hawk. I mind my own business. She may've been here, she may've not."

"If you don't want to get involved, why are you talking to us now?" asked Jim, glancing at his watch.

The woman thought for a moment. "Do you think I *like* this neighborhood? They're just a bunch of Black folk chasin' ghosts, blamin' their troubles on the White man. They'd rather put their future in the hands of big mouths and small brains, when all we have to do is believe in ourselves. Folks *ain't* eva coming togetha' if they dwell on the things that keep em' apart."

Bill looked at his watch. It was close to midnight. "Mind if I use your phone, ma'am?"

"Certainly. Right there on the wall." She pointed to the kitchen, her long, bony arm stretched out like the limb of an old tree.

Bill headed off, leaving his partner to wrap things up.

"Mrs. Perkins," asked Jim, leaning back on the sofa, trying to make some small talk. "Why are you *really* helping us. . .religious reasons?"

"Honey, I raised eleven children on my own--the Lord's awaitin' *me* with open arms." Turning her head to the wall, she eyed the framed remains of an old sales receipt, dated *May 18, 1839*, the name *Perkins* scrawled on the "owner" line of the receipt. "No, detective. I do it knowing someday we may no longer be free."

Jim was digesting her words as Bill returned from the kitchen, motioning for him to move. Rising with his business card extended, Jim added, "If you can think of anything else, give us a call. We wish we'd more time, but we must be going."

As the two headed for the door, she rose from her chair and followed. Leaning against the jamb, she said her goodbyes. "Now, you gentlemen enjoy the rest of your evening."

The mood in the front seat was upbeat, as the two detectives headed back to the precinct to lean on the Yankee fan. They had stumbled upon a piece of evidence that could talk. The old woman had given them information they could use and uncovered a few things that the two needed to understand. One of which Jim was dying to know.

"What's up with the call?"

"Talked to the M.E.," said Bill, eyeing a throng of teens who milled on the corner, passing a joint. "Get this. The preliminary tests show Salaam was exposed to radiation. It entered through his nose, like he snorted it. Unfortunately, the guys from Langley barged in and took him away. Hopefully, we'll know a lot more when they're through. The tests came back on the urine, too—two different types, both male. And—get this--the M.E. said the lipstick stain on the collar turned up antibodies indicative of tuberculosis."

"Really? With the urine, that puts another person in the alley, probably lying in ambush, waiting for the broad to bring him in."

"Either that or the chick *is* Victor Lawrence," said Bill, raising and lowering his brow.

"Makes sense to me. What kind of woman would do those kinds of things anyway?"

"What do you think about the Martians roaming around Salaam's apartment?" Bill asked.

"Willard's a lying sack of shit. If he doesn't know the whole story, I'll eat my hat."

"Do you think they knew all along Salaam was dirty and used him as bait?"

Jim, rubbing his eyes asked, "Who knows? What does anybody *really* know about Salaam? *He* could've been using *them*. So far, he's only guilty of being dead."

"If our alleged cross-dresser was with him earlier, then they were associates in this. There's got to be clues in that apartment— hair, fibers, semen, blood, rank panties. . .something. We need to find out the connection between Salaam and the killer. Did you talk to Diaz?"

"Sure did. Captain thought it'd be a good idea if we lean on a few of Salaam's cronies coolin' off upstate. Only one has potential. Their fearless leader with the hair problem."

"Why would any of those scumbags want to help us?" asked Bill, closing in on the precinct.

"This guy's got two hundred and fifty-five consecutive reasons."

"Which one's that?"

"Our buddy from the Liberty bombing. Tarik Hassan Afreet."

"The blind guy?"

"Half blind. You're thinking of the *deaf* guy," Jim pointed out with a laugh.

"Right. Anything with Hicks?"

"He's running Salaam's name through Interpol, and the INS is contacting all foreign embassies willing to lend a hand. They're also researching all past arrests for arms smuggling over the last ten years. An evidence team is on the way over to Salaam's apartment, as we speak." Jim paused. "What if there's radiation in that apartment?"

"My guess, any traces and the FBI would've sealed off the building, if not the entire block."

"Who said they were feds?" asked Jim.

"That's just great."

CHAPTER 18

They pulled up to the precinct with a few tangibles: The earring and the binder, both small and circumstantial, brought them one step closer to the killer. They also had a living piece of the puzzle-- it was time to see where he fit.

They met with the captain, who had returned to the precinct to deal with the impact the story would have if any of the facts leaked to the press.

He was on the phone, briefing the chief on the men in yellow suits.

Meanwhile, the victim had *not* spent his entire evening in a back alley. He had been dressed for a night on the town, and his clothes reeked of smoke and the scent of a woman. Where had he been?

Their latest catch sat nervously behind the two-way mirror of the interrogation room, clad in handcuffs, his only comforts the worn Yankee hat on the table and a half-smoked cigarette in his shaking hand.

Bill followed his partner into the room. The officer in charge rose from the metal heater and left with a nod. Bill straddled the chair and locked eyes with the suspect. The only sound was the annoying drone of the clock above the door.

Guilt, he had learned, transcended race, or creed, or gender.

Guilt was shy, preferring not to look into the face of blame until the high-priced lawyers crawled out of the woodwork.

Bored with the standoff, Jim withdrew a camera from behind his back and snapped a Polaroid of the culprit. Pulling the picture from the camera, he moved behind him and took a seat on the heater.

For ten minutes, they continued to eye the young man without a word. His ruffled head of black hair, body odor, and otherwise unctuous looks, made Bill want to cringe. His goatee was unkept and the skin under his neck had more visible pores than a plucked hen.

After a few more minutes of ominous silence, the suspect sprang to life. He raised his manacled hands. "Could you take these fuckin' things off?" Jim obliged.

Bill didn't like the guy's tone. "Apparently," he said quietly, "you're unaware of your present situation, or you wouldn't be playing asshole. Being an accomplice to a federal murder rap is a tough way to go down. Upstate, that goatee'll make a purdy piece of prison pussy, while your shit gets tossed more times than a salad bar at Sizzler."

Embraced by a rising fear, the kid slammed his knuckles on the table, sending his Marlboros to the floor. "What the fuck are you *talking* about? *Murder?* That's complete *bullshit!*" Desperate, his eyes turned to Jim, who'd bent to retrieve the cigarettes.

"Let's face it, son. This isn't new to us." He slid the smokes gently onto the table. "We've seen your kind before. Our biggest problem is that your rap sheet's as long as my leg and you're over eighteen. That apartment you broke into *was* the home of a federally protected witness. Friday night, said witness turned up dead in an alley down on Eighth, brutally strangled and carved up like a Thanksgiving turkey."

"You think I. . .I. . .I did it?" he asked, pointing to his chest.

Bill watched his wheels begin to turn. "You got that right, my boy. Now if, by chance, you can convince us otherwise, you won't have to get raped every day."

The suspect's gaze narrowed. Jim leaned into his line of sight. "*C'mon*, you know how it works. Tell us what we need to know, and we help you out." He pointed to Bill. "Your buddy here bangs the assistant to the DA. You'll be on the street in no time. Promise."

"You're gonna' help *me*?" the kid asked in disbelief, his fingers running nervous laps through his greasy hair.

"Sure," said Jim. "Personally, I think you're innocent, but try convincing a jury. They're just *dyin'* to put away a white boy, hoping to balance things out. Innocence or guilt really isn't the issue, provided everyone's happy. It's great politics."

"I ain't killed nobody! Some transvestite-lookin' thing—"

"Stop right there!" barked Bill, rising quickly from the chair.

Moving to the lower cabinets along the wall, he returned with a tape recorder and a free-standing mike. "Now, continue. Start with your name."

The boy adjusted himself in his seat and talked into the microphone. "Name's Blake Wheatley. I'm from Staten Island. I'm nineteen years old. My buddies and I were cruisin' Times Square, lookin' for some action."

"What night was that?" asked Jim, failing to contain a yawn.

"Friday, around twelve or so. I tell my boys, I gotta take a leak, so I jump out and run into an alley to drain my potatoes. Out of nowhere comes this tall chick in a tiger dress. She's just standing there in the dark, checking me out. Asks if I'd like to earn a grand. I'm thinking she wants me to bang her. But she says she wants me to get something from her friend's apartment. The downside bein' the cops might be watchin'. I asked for two hundred up front. She gives me two bills right there. Zing, bang."

"You wouldn't happen to have any of it left?" Bill asked, scribbling on a pad.

"Nah. We found what we were looking for down at the docks. A few beers, and some other essentials, the girls gobbled up what was left. Know what I mean?" he asked, ending with a wink and a quarter smile.

"Yeah, we know what you mean," said Jim, "but I think we've gotten a bit ahead of ourselves. What was she wearin' again?"

He thought for a moment, dragging on the filter of his cigarette. "Blondish hair, a funky hat, a striped dress, and long white gloves up to her elbows."

"What did her face look like?" asked Bill, crossing his fingers.

"Her *face*? Looked old and pretty busted. I couldn't see much with the hat on. She smelled nice, though. Besides, I was looking at the Franklins, not her fuckin' face."

"Which alley was this?" asked Jim, disappointed.

"Some shithole next to a drug store. Bought some smokes 'n' took a piss."

"You got a good eye for detail. Where did you happen to take that leak?"

"I don't know, couple feet, inside the shadows?"

"What happened after she gave you the money?"

"She told me about the binder and how to get it. I zip to the apartment, it's not there. I start looking around, checking closets and drawers. I checked under the bed, the mattress, places like that. Didn't find much, just a lot of fag mags and chump change."

"Where *was* the binder, then?" Jim asked, scribbling on his pad.

"Call it experience, but I happened to notice a loose floorboard under the bed. There was the binder and some funny money I'd never seen before. I left it, because I wanted to collect the rest of the grand. Then you two heroes showed up."

"Where were you supposed to deliver the binder?" asked Bill, pulling his knee up to his chest.

"That's the weird part. She said *she'd* find me."

"Did she give you the address of the apartment?"

"You found me there, didn't ya?" he replied, stabbing his butt into the tray as if it was Bill's face.

"I meant written down, jerkoff! You know, so we could see the handwriting? I figured a little rat like you would've taken the loot and run."

"No, she didn't give me a thing." He had answered with restraint, realizing he was low on smokes. "For a thousand bucks, yo, I could do that with my eyes closed."

"Yeah? Your planning and timing were top notch. Jail's a great place to plan a heist."

"You were supposed to go Friday night," Bill observed. "Why the delay?"

"I went there, but it wasn't right. The cops she told me about were a bunch of guineas hangin' out in a black Cadillac."

"Where were you?"

The guy pulled his last cigarette from the pack. "I was on the fire escape outside the window. Some fat fuck was stompin' around, pissed off." Jim offered a light.

"They're hanging out front and *you* climb the fire escape without being noticed?" asked Jim, unconvinced.

"I still had some of the money left," the suspect replied, talking through the smoke. "There was a five-dollar whore on the corner, drunk as a skunk. Gave her a ten spot to hang her nasty ole titties in their window." A tarnished smile appeared. "Those greaseballs were so grossed out, they drove off like madmen. I waited 'till they were out of sight and jumped onto the fire escape. They rounded the block and were back like two seconds later."

Bill nodded. The kid was coming around. "How long were they in the apartment?"

"About twenty minutes or so."

"Hear anything they said?"

"Some shit about a missing cab, blah, blah, blah. How their boss' was gonna' want answers. The fat guy was saying they'd kept their side of the bargain. Delivery was on time. . .how he almost died of a heart attack digging some hole. The rest I couldn't understand."

Jim produced a mug shot of the world's biggest dispatcher, Salvatore "Fats" Mancini. "Is this the guy?"

"*That's* him."

"What did you do then?" continued Jim, his blood pressure rising, eager to return to the garage.

"Seeing that these guys were not meant to be fucked with, I climbed to the roof, jumped to the next building, and climbed down the fire escape on the other side."

"Naturally." Bill paused and looked over at Jim, who nodded at the door. "You've done well. . .*so far*. We're gunna leave you alone for a few minutes. Somebody will ask you for a urine sample. I suggest you buck up." He stopped the tape and headed for the door. The kid had come clean, but he was providing more questions than answers.

They left to find the captain. The don and Fats had lied, which surprised neither of them. They wouldn't be so cooperative next time around. Turning the corner, they found their boss coming up the stairs as Bill's pager went off. He didn't recognize the number. It would have to wait.

"Put that kid on ice," the captain ordered. "Somebody just blew up your mob pal's taxi company. Prelims rolling in from the bomb squad are calling it a surgical explosion. Back of a cab."

Bill nodded, thinking, "Salaam's, I bet." He paused to check his notes. "Did they say what kind of explosive was used?"

"Not a clue, but we're all still breathin'," said the captain with a sigh. "Get everybody down there. Just have Diaz and Hicks bring me up to speed before they leave. I'll handle this end for now. Commissioner'll be sending us reinforcements—even *he* can't ignore three homicides and one explosion."

"Sir, before we go, you should know about the kid. Someone matching our perp's description hired him to grab Salaam's journal from his apartment on the night of his murder."

"What journal?"

"Salaam, we think, was a scientist whose work he kept hidden in a journal at his apartment. The killer wanted this kid to retrieve it. Guess who was there?"

The captain shrugged. "Willard?"

"No. Sciaffa's men, and that slob from the cab company. Talking about 'keeping their end of the bargain.' I guess they really wanted that cab back."

"Just go down there and get back as soon as possible. Chief's going to call another meeting with the mayor in the morning. Forget about his assistant, Kravitz almost had a coronary when he heard about yellow men running around his city."

"Hey," said Bill, "Willard's boy Salaam was dirty. Can't blame him for trying to keep this thing quiet. It's his ass if this goes south, and right now he's on the border."

CHAPTER 19

Worn from the lack of sleep, Masters and Lackey reached the bomb scene, surrounded by the sound of horns and crackling timber as three fire companies waged a frantic campaign to contain the blaze. Rain, combined with the intense heat and steam, produced a plume of thick smoke that poured from what was left of the upper windows. Towering flames licked at the night sky as men, suspended in a bucket, hosed the roof and what was left of the smoldering parapet.

On the street below, two firefighters, water streaming from their helmets, their faces black with soot, wrestled a hose that had slipped from their grasp. The explosion had torn a section off the front of the building and shot the missing cab across the street like a cannon.

The two entered the scene cautiously, hop-scotching over hoses and puddles of water and foam in search of the man in charge. They found him standing below the cab of a big ladder truck, one leg up on the runner board, barking orders in every direction. He had a large cell phone to one ear and the head of his fire axe slung next to the other.

Bill flashed his ID. Listening intently to his call, the stubby, sharp-eyed man nodded and hung up.

"Bill Masters. This's my partner, Detective Lackey. Others'll be rollin' up shortly. What do we got?"

"Sorry, gentlemen. . .my wife needs diapers," he said, holding out his hand. "I'm Captain Ramsey." Pointing to the mangled remains of an axle, he began, "Looks like a car bomb, as you can see from the debris field here. Obviously, it's unsafe to enter, until we get her under control. From what we *can* tell, an above-ground fuel tank went sky high; could be others deeper inside."

"Employees?" asked Bill, half hoping the fat, lying bastard was out sampling a menu somewhere. Jim stared deep into the flames. He didn't look as compassionate.

The fireman pointed toward a partially sleeved arm lying nearby, and the rest of the body under a bloody sheet on the opposing sidewalk.

"That's all that's left of whoever was standing near the entrance when the thing went off. Shot across the street like a missile, head first, into the wall."

"He big and fat?" asked Bill, approaching the remains.

"No, he's a small, skinny guy."

Jim and Bill looked at each other and said simultaneously, "Vinnie!"

Lifting the sheet from the shoeless corpse proved futile--the head and both shoulders were a mass of blood and crushed bone. Physical identification would be impossible.

"Any ID?"

The fireman held up his hands and tucked in his chin. "I'm here to fight fires, detective."

"Any idea when you'll get it under control, captain?" Bill asked, apologetically.

"Unless there are some unforeseen secondary explosions or other accelerants, maybe forty-five minutes. Odd—it seems to be putting *itself* out."

Bill's pager went off again. Same unidentifiable number as before.

"All right then. Gentlemen, let's get ourselves a cup of coffee. Captain, can I use your phone for a sec?"

Shrugging his shoulders, the short man answered, "Certainly. Department's payin'."

Bill dialed. The phone rang a few times, and a man answered.

"Hello," said Bill, disappointed it wasn't Kathy. "This is Detective Bill Masters. I'm returning a page."

"*Un minuto*," replied the other in Italian. Seconds later a new voice came on the line--a very familiar one.

"Detective Masters?"

"Yes."

"Anthony Sciaffa."

With his finger pressed to his ear, Bill said, "Mr. Sciaffa, I don't think it's wise for us to speak, since I'm now knee-deep in the remains of your cab company. You're aware of this?"

"Detective, cut the bullshit! I'll tell you everything I know."

"In return for what?" He never fingered the man as a rat.

"Protection."

Bill made a habit of insulting his friends; he reserved his charm for enemies. "Excuse the skepticism. But, why would a man in your position need protection from a guy like me?"

"I respect your candor in light of the present situation. It tells me many things. But I *insist* you allow me to explain when we meet."

"You *had* your sit-down! But you chose to be a prick!" Bill snapped. "I have a witness that places your men inside Mr. Salaam's residence the night of his murder. *I'd* be insisting on an attorney."

"Excuse me, detective," the other said calmly. "I've grown tired of the pawns of jurisprudence. I've done nothing but run an errand for a stranger. . .so indulge me. No tricks. You have my word."

"Where? The club?" he asked, pacing the length of the ladder truck like a caged tiger.

"No, no. The club is no longer safe. This was a warning to a silent partner--a partner in charge of collections. The only person who needs to worry, I believe, is me."

"Where, then?"

"Your apartment," suggested the Don.

"You're kidding," replied Bill, uneasily.

He hung up with the arrival of the other two detectives and handed the large phone back to the fireman. He'd meet the don later, around noon. He would inform the others.

Breakfast was in full-swing at the greasy spoon on the corner; the smell of fresh coffee welcomed them inside. Eager to sit, they ignored the waitress and piled into a booth across from the kitchen.

Over the tapping of silverware and clanging plates, Bill asked, through a soft haze of burnt toast, "Anything in the apartment, Rico?"

"Some." Rico accepted a menu from a short-haired waitress with dark moons puddling under her eyes. "Muddy boots--fairly new. Mud was more like sandy clay, really--had been dried for days. Some lipstick samples in the bathroom, perfume, tissues in the waste can. The dresser contained foreign and domestic currencies, some methamphetamine, and four ticket stubs from Great Adventure. Under the floor boards we found phone bills, electric bills, a few airline boarding passes, and a small ledger full of numbers." He had a puzzled look on his face.

"Something else?" asked Bill, browsing the menu and motioning for a round of coffee.

"Who keeps, let alone *hides*, old utility bills? They weren't even his. And, *why* wasn't the FBI all over that place?"

"That's been botherin' me too, but a man *is* what he hides, Rico." Bill checked his notes. "Where'd he fly?"

"All over. Domestically, D.C., Chicago, L.A. Abroad, he'd been to Paris, Prague, Russia, and, oddly, South East Asia."

"When?"

"Over the last year."

"The name on the utility bills?"

Diaz, fumbling through his notes, leaned over for better light under the grease covered lamp hanging from the wall. "Victor Lawrence--682 Christopher Street."

Before Jim had a chance to react, Bill said, "First off, it's probably an old address, but get over there and check it out anyway. Get a list of all incoming and outgoing calls made from that pay phone outside Salaam's apartment over the last two months. Cross reference them with the bills found under the bed. *No one* goes without a phone."

"No problem, Bill. Bet you're right."

The waitress returned with their coffee, accidentally spilling some on Jim's shoe. She didn't bother to apologize.

"How about the map corners?" Bill asked, grinning.

"We picked one up from the service station down the block. As you expected, it was the same. That one cluster of holes you pointed out is around Great Adventure, a place called Herodsville. Explains the ticket stubs."

"South Jersey. Plenty of sandy soil down there," said Jim, sipping his coffee. "I wonder what it's all about?"

"Maybe he wanted a tan." Bill was staring out the window. "One with a half-life of a hundred thousand years."

Hicks paid the check, while Diaz headed for the can. Bill pulled Jim aside, avoiding a couple near the door pawing each other good-bye.

"Other than the fact that they're all gay, we need to concentrate on Victor Lawrence and his connections to the others. Gut tells me he's our guy."

"Unless, like everyone else, he's dead," replied Jim, shrugging his broad shoulders, as he headed out the door.

CHAPTER 20

Rounding the corner adjacent to the scene, they could see that the frantic pace of the firemen had slowed. Water and foam covered everything; a persistent cloud of smoke hung in the air. Except for the men in matching black raincoats, holding umbrellas, nothing was dry.

"Agent Willard," said Bill, approaching from behind. "Funny how you always arrive after the fact."

Willard, in the only tan trench coat, spoke over his shoulder. "Shoo, detective. Go fix a traffic ticket." He turned his attention back to his call.

"Cut the crap, Willard! You know damn well this is all tied in with Salaam."

Willard, his beady eyes squinting to hear, waved him off.

The deceased on the street, and whatever was left of the driver in the cab, had been hastily removed. Bill assumed it was on a chopper headed for a slab next to Salaam. Agent Patterson, stepping cautiously among the ruins, was the only fed who seemed to have interest in the job at hand.

Bill didn't know why, but he loathed most of the agents he came in contact with. Yet, Patterson he liked, or at least respected him. He was humble and preferred silence to substance, a rarity in his line of work. He reminded Bill of his father—at least the one he could remember.

With clear plastic bags spilling from his pockets, the affable agent combed the ramp, looking for evidence among the thick hoses and streams of running water and foam. He bent over to pick up something as Bill turned to address Jim who, just moments before, had been right behind him.

"Listen to me, Willard!" Jim said very loudly, "I'm *tired* of this hocus-pocus *secrecy* bullshit."

He went for the lapels of Willard's suit.

"Call off your dog, Masters!" warned Willard.

"We have a witness that places *known* underworld figures at your boy's apartment," said Bill. "He's been jet-settin' around, which means Salaam was either workin' for you or against you. So no more fuckin' around! What were you doing here earlier today?"

"Correct me if I'm wrong, detective. One of my informants had been murdered. I, like you, was just getting started with my investigation. Was there a better place to start than his place of employment?"

"I'm so relieved by your sense of diligence. Just the same, I smell a rat." Patterson approached out of the corner of his eye, holding something under the beam of his flashlight.

Willard stepped forward, lifting his glasses from his nose. "What have *we* found?"

Patterson, his jaw firm, offered it to his boss. Taking a quick look, Willard handed it to Bill.

"As expected, detective," explained the quiet man, pointing for accuracy. "Gravity switch. Pros at work. This isn't found in your local hobby shop. Offset, too. Configured to blow near the fuel tanks, at the steepest angle of attack." He turned his head in the direction of the entrance. "Down the ramp and boom! Tanks ignite, no more taxi. Bomb had to explode adjacent to the fuel tanks to achieve these results. They'd been here before."

"Agent Willard," asked Bill, rolling the piece of detonator in his hand, "wouldn't you agree, under the circumstances, there's a connection between your boy and Sciaffa?"

"It's too early to tell. But if there is, I'm sure his union lawyers are working on his defense as we speak." Turning his back, Willard returned to his cellular and his investigation.

The bombing was federal: they were guests of Willard. But Bill was going to make things happen; whatever Willard expected didn't matter.

More FBI personnel arrived as Patterson returned to poking around the ramp, stopping occasionally to drop pieces of debris into plastic bags.

Bill took advantage of the commotion, pulling Jim in the direction of the ramp.

Armed with flashlights, they walked along the damp wall, steering clear of the hoses being dragged out by the tired firemen, knowing the remains of the dispatcher's cage awaited them at the bottom. A lone fireman, his axe flung over his shoulder, was leaving its interior. "We're safe," he muttered, his voice unusually high-pitched and raspy. "Fire killed it." He didn't stick around for a reaction.

"There's something strange about this," Bill said, probing the darkness, his own voice rising an octave.

"Like what?" asked Jim as he stepped over a puddle.

"I don't know. Something's different. Your voice, my voice, they sound a little squeaky. Don't ya think?"

Slumped, smoldering over the wooden desk, lay the charred remains of the underworld's heaviest henchman. The bloated enormity reeked of burnt hair and flesh; wisps of smoke rose slowly, like spent candles on a birthday cake. Although he wanted to ream the fat bastard, Jim figured, any soldier, whatever his cause, deserved a better end.

The unmistakable size, the chunk of charred Stromboli still clutched in his bloated hand, left little doubt to his identity. Although he was cooked as well as any dinner entree, Fats and his chair hadn't budged an inch.

Delving deeper into the garage, the sounds of dripping water echoing like an urban grotto, they soon discovered the remains of two other drivers, their charred bodies, still behind the wheel, having fused with their dashboards. Livery had become a hazardous occupation, Bill thought, as he pulled a handkerchief from his pants pocket and covered his nose. He hoped the don was ready to open up.

After sharing a few uncontrollable gags, the two had seen enough. Fats and Vinnie were dead, the remains of the first cab driver could have fit in a thimble, and federal agents were now entering the scene with enough portable lighting to illuminate all of Manhattan.

Two hours elapsed as the FBI's bomb squad, a montage of blue windbreakers and baseball caps, had been busy collecting samples from the various surfaces about the scene. Explosives, like humans, leave fingerprints behind, residues that can lead to a point of origin.

Bill was curious about the preliminary results. First hunches were always the best. They took solace in the fact that no one was wearing a protective suit. He eyed a heavy-set, short-haired blonde whose every step tested the in-seam stitching of her dark blue pants. As the two approached, she looked more and more like a crossing guard than an FBI agent.

"Excuse me, Agent--" Bill eyed her identification as she turned-- "Pursy? This here's Detective Lackey, and I'm Detective Masters. We were both assigned to this case by the mayor. We hoped to ask you a few questions."

Aside from her sagging breasts and wide ass, she was no different from any other agent. Playing to her emotions was like pouring water on a duck's back.

With a hint of eye contact and loads of attitude, she said to neither one in particular, "Gentlemen, please. We're conducting an investigation!"

Jim muttered out of the corner of his mouth. "Of all the feds to talk to, *you* pick Dickless Tracey herself."

"I resent that!" she spat, dropping her clipboard to her side.

"*Yeah?* Well, I resent your attitude, agent," he said, looking down. "Why monopolize the truth? Do we have to call the mayor? I realize, on the federal level, 'redundancy' and 'waste' are words worthy of promotion and praise, but I assure you, we are motivated solely by the interests of the people of New York." He motioned to Bill.

"Listen, detective," she said, retreating a step out of Jim's saliva range. "I could lose my job just for talking to you. But I'll tell you this. I've been to over two hundred bomb scenes in my career. This is the first one where there's no trace of a bomb. Sure, the gasoline's highly volatile, but look at the tanks. They were detonated from a short distance as a result of some primary blast. I place that source in the trunk of the cab, or what's left of it.

"But there are absolutely no signs of an explosive. No dynamite, no TNT, cordite, thermite, fertilizers, C4--*nothing*. Aside from the gravity switch and the petroleum-based residues we found on the remains of the cab, this place is as clean as a whistle." The two detectives looked at her wide-eyed. "Take a look around you, gentlemen. Notice or smell anything odd?" Sensing a small victory, she continued, "It's nice to see that you two don't know it all. Did you notice the two in the back were melted right into their dashboards? Ever see that? I haven't. They didn't shatter from a shock wave. But they fused from a heat *so* intense, it's like nothing we've ever seen. If you combined the contents of those fuel tanks with whatever was left in the car, in the absence of some other explosive, at that distance, it wouldn't be hot enough to melt a candle. But we can't find a thing. Small traces of aluminum and another element we have yet to identify. It's certainly not an explosive."

She crossed her arms and stared, holding back. Bill couldn't tell if she was mad, nervous, or just plain scared. "Is there anything else, Agent Pursy?"

Glancing around, she leaned back on her heels and began to speak. "Aside from the melted glass, there's the utter disintegration of the fire system that runs from here back to where the others were found."

She had hoped they would understand. They didn't. "Gentlemen. Those pipes are made of hardened steel an eighth of an inch thick, wrapped in a blanket of asbestos. From ground zero above the tanks, back about ninety feet, the piping has completely evaporated. Asbestos can withstand temperatures well above four thousand degrees, and for extended periods of time. The wrapping and the pipes were gone in an instant."

She pointed to the steel feet of the gas tanks, which were bolted to a thick slab of concrete. "You feel there's anything missing from the scene, something obvious?" No answer. "We're told those gas tanks had been filled yesterday. You'd figure a place this size would burn, what? Maybe twenty percent of it, leaving behind enough fuel for a tremendous blast.

"Take a deep breath, Detectives." They inhaled in unison. "It smells clean, like a forest. Aside from burnt flesh, there are no heavy vapors, yet we can't find a single trace of petroleum within a ten foot radius of those tanks. Hundreds of gallons of high octane fuel were *completely* combusted," she said, snapping her fingers, "in the blink of an eye. Heat of that magnitude is found only under controlled conditions or on the surface of the sun, *not* in the trunk of a New York cab."

Bill felt his sense of security begin to wane. "This may be the wrong time, but. . .have you ruled out the possibility of a nuclear device?"

The reaction of the agent was not exactly what he had expected. "No offense, detective. We would hardly enter an environment like this without testing the radiation levels first. What we found was negligible to humans."

He shook his head. "None taken. One more thing. Why the high voices?"

"Helium's my guess. But where it came from, we haven't a clue."

Before she was finished, the stabbing voice of Agent Willard rose from behind. "What do we have here, Agent Pursy? New York's finest obstructing justice once again?"

"No, sir. Detective Masters here was merely demonstrating some of his boyish charm."

"Very good. Then I imagine you won't mind getting back to work?"

"Yes, sir!" she replied, picking up her things and moving quickly to another location.

Willard trained his attention on the two detectives. "You two gentlemen seen enough?" he asked, pointing to the ramp.

"Give us a break," answered Jim. "As always, we haven't seen dick. What's Quantico got on Salaam?"

"I just got off the phone with Washington, and they'll be faxing the results within the hour. If you'd like, I'll see to it your department gets a copy in the morning."

"Thanks, Willard," said Bill. "You're a real team player." He wanted to puke.

"I've done everything in my power to accommodate you two," the agent replied, "but my patience has worn thin. You'll have a chance for further questions at the next meeting with the mayor. I'll ask you once more to leave this investigation to my people. Utter one more word and I'll have you arrested for evidence tampering."

Bill knew Willard, a man who led by fear, was testing them. To question his resolve in front of his people would force him to follow through, and being detained would serve no purpose.

He looked at Willard, smiled, spat on the ground at the man's feet, grabbed the arm of his stubborn partner, and jerked him towards the ramp.

CHAPTER 21

Jim returned to re-canvas the area of Salaam's demise, leaving Rico and Hicks back at the precinct to sift through the evidence. Bill was across town, entering an ivy-covered brick building that housed the NYU physics department. He was looking for its chairman, and his godfather, Dr. Samuel Groves.

The professor, a life-long friend and mentor of Bill's father at Berkeley during the late thirties and forties, had been instrumental in bringing Bill's parents together. A perennial contender for a Nobel Prize, he had participated in the Manhattan Project during the war.

He was an unassuming man in his late eighties, both humble and quiet, slight in posture, with a balding head deep as a cul-de-sac. His white trowel-shaped goatee reminded Bill of Lenin, his omnipresent pipe of Douglas MacArthur. He had dined with presidents, rubbed elbows with royalty, and for a moment, danced with the atom. At his age, his work was still his passion.

Bill roamed the long corridors, trying to find his office. A fellow faculty member, leaving the ladies room, pointed towards an office at the opposite end of the hall.

The unmistakable aroma of Prince Albert, Grove's trademark

tobacco, led Bill to his door. The man himself, his back barely visible through the small window, sat quietly beside his desk, bent over, leafing through an old brown leather valise.

Bill knocked softly.

"Enter!" Groves barked from his wooden chair. As always, a hand-carved meerschaum was dangling from his lips, a gift from a man he had adored in another age. The polished representation of the god Vulcan was far from attractive, but, Bill knew first-hand, bad memories rarely were.

Time had treated him well, Bill thought, stepping over a puddle left behind by an umbrella leaning against the stack of bookshelves guarding the door. Ahead sat a row of red leather chairs around an old cherry desk. To the left, a matching red couch and a small refrigerator crowded the far wall, fighting a treadmill for space. A large blackboard and a set of folding chairs laid claim to the area to his right. With his hands on the back of the middle chair, looking past the large wooden desk piled high with papers and framed photographs, he could see the view of the courtyard below.

The weather had, again, turned foul. Rain was pouring heavily from the lower gutters, and a rumbling groan of thunder threatened from a distance.

The old man, in a thin v-neck sweater, green corduroy pants, and brown Cole-Haans, swiveled in his chair, eyeing his uninvited guest through the bottom of silver framed bifocals. A warm smile spread across his face. "William, my good man! Isn't this a pleasant surprise! How are you?" Putting down the pipe, he made an effort to rise. Bill gestured for him not to bother.

"Just fine, sir. And how, may I ask, are you?" He grinned, as his eyes fell upon the detached wires of the smoke alarm above the window.

"Well. . .physically?" the other laughed, realizing his pun. "I'm just great. Mentally, I'm a bit exhausted. I've graded thirty papers for my summer mid-terms, and I'm not done yet. My eyes can barely focus, not to mention the effects this weather's havin' on these old bones."

Without a thought, he touched a match to his pipe. His hand, rough and mottled with liver spots, held steady above the bowl as thick plumes of aromatic smoke rose, filling the void between them.

Removing the pipe from his lips, he continued, "Did you

happen to catch any of my lectures?"

"No. Too advanced for me, professor."

"Never too young to be taught what one doesn't understand, my dear friend," the man said, jabbing the stem of the pipe in Bill's direction. "Meaning is not lost in words, you understand, but in our failing desire, our willingness to learn from them. We have become a fast-food society hell-bent on cramming our children's minds with useless fodder."

He rose slowly, moving to the high-backed chair behind his desk and relit his pipe, mumbling a soft complaint about damp tobacco. "To what do I owe this unexpected visit?" he finally asked, seeing his guest was not smiling.

Bill took a seat in the middle chair. "I'm presently working on a murder that involves a victim who was exposed, at some point, to high levels of radiation. We haven't gotten the results back, but the coroner fears the worst."

"Who was he?" asked the old man, whose good humor had also vanished.

"I'd prefer not to tell you, if that's all right."

The professor puffed slowly. "William, if you have any doubts of my loyalty to you, your father, or our country, that will be acceptable. If not, I'd prefer to hear the whole story. That's where the truth will lie."

Bill nodded. ". . . His name was Malik Abdul Salaam, an Iranian cab driver who, according to the feds, had loose ties to known terrorists, here and abroad. He was found brutally murdered in an alley Friday night." He was surprised at the immediate effect the information had on the professor. "Is there something wrong?" he asked.

"Please. . .continue."

"We were assured by federal authorities that the deceased wasn't involved in, or responsible for, the Statue bombing, but was rather a conduit into the organization--basically a federal mole."

"He was my student," said the old man sadly.

Salaam's diploma had been no prop. Things were getting more complicated. If he'd been studying with the professor, he'd known a lot.

"The case is branching out into areas that I can't seem to connect together."

"The mayor's assistant?" asked the older man with an insightful shrug. Noticing Bill's reaction, he added, "I've become quite the media whore, in my old age."

"Exactly. But we've no idea how the two are related. If you knew the man, what can you tell me about him?"

"William," the other replied, "I deal with *hundreds* of students a year. I certainly can't get to know them *all*."

"Hours ago there was a bombing, the details of which have left the FBI technicians scratching their heads."

"And you think I may be of some help?"

"Yes. I believe this student of yours may have been part of a new plot to harm the city. At this point, we have many more questions than answers. I was wondering what background information you could give me on nuclear weaponry."

The professor tilted in his chair, blew a smoke ring, as he pondered the request. He set down the meerschaum. "I'll sum it up as simply as possible. Bear with me. I haven't discussed this topic in a very long time." Opening the top drawer of his desk, he fumbled before popping something in his mouth. He took a sip from a water bottle and picked up his pipe.

"Nuclear weapons are no different in design than your average bomb. The technology, although more advanced, meets the basic criteria. An explosion occurs. Death and destruction soon follow. The differences lie in the materials used, the level of damage, and the added effects of radioactivity. Nuclear bombs are unique. Escaping the explosion *won't* prevent your death."

Bill had resisted giving the professor the Arab's notebook. He hadn't booked it into evidence. "Could the average person, given the right materials, construct such a device?"

"On the upside, I'd have to say no. The calculations required for such an undertaking are beyond the comprehension of any garden-variety physics student. An extensive background in nuclear physics, mathematics, and explosives would be a necessity. Not to mention the primary elements of the equation—the fissible materials needed to construct such a device. *That* would require tremendous financing and political connection--a rogue government, perhaps some other wealthy benefactor.

"On the downside, the major theoretical obstacles have been overcome and the rest has been since de-classified. Just log onto the Net."

Rising from the chair, pipe in hand, the professor turned to the blackboard, erasing the mass of equations left from an earlier discussion. He noticed Bill moving to one of the metal chairs, admiring a framed version of the periodic table mounted on the wall above his head.

"A gift from my graduate students."

As the tapping of chalk grew silent, the old man unveiled a collection of concentric circles representing an atom.

"This is the basic molecular make-up of a uranium atom. It's shy a few protons, but I assure you you'll get the picture. "Uranium is an element--more succinctly, a substance that can no longer be broken down by chemical means. It's found in nature and mined in various places around the globe."

"I thought the bombs were made with plutonium."

"You are absolutely right, my dear boy. But plutonium is a by-product of uranium. During the war, the production of pure plutonium became the largest single construction project ever undertaken by the United States. Two tons of irradiated uranium ore will produce an amount of plutonium equal to the size of a dime. For the sake of simplicity, let's stick to the uranium atom. Uranium 235, an isotope, is what is required, and its supply makes up less than one percent of all the uranium reserves worldwide.

"The instability of the uranium isotope is the very essence of radioactivity and manifests itself in the form of alpha or beta rays, which are not part of the visible spectrum of light. As in the case of your victim, they're highly destructive when exposed to human tissue."

Bill held up his hand. "Not to be rude, professor, but the coroner went into the subject in great detail."

"Splendid. Then I can skip that tedious discussion," the old man said, tapping the bottom of his pipe. "Uranium atoms are relatively stable in nature. It's when you put large amounts of refined material together that an explosion can occur. This amount is called the 'critical mass'. The breaking of nuclear bonds creates a chain reaction, resulting in massive amounts of energy being released.

"The ferocity of the release will, however, be less than that of a large scale nuclear explosion, which requires an assembly of atoms at high speeds and higher temperatures. This is where the knowledge of explosives becomes very important."

"Well, how much uranium would you need to go critical?"

"Approximately sixteen kilograms, or thirty-five pounds."

"A significant amount to be toting around," Bill replied satisfied.

"Keep in mind, my dear boy, that uranium is one of the denser elements known to man. A kilo of uranium is about the size of a golf ball."

Bill rose from the chair to get a drink from the water dispenser in the corner. "Is it possible they could be producing a hydrogen bomb, something less crude and primitive, one that could produce a large, catastrophic explosion?"

"William, you always seem ready to tread the path others choose to avoid. I imagine that's what makes you such a great detective-- not to mention your luck with the ladies." The professor laughed, turning his attention back to the board. "A hydrogen bomb is not practical for someone interested in a simple act of terror. A hydrogen bomb is a fusion reaction using isotopes of hydrogen-- deuterium or tritium, the first found in sea water, the latter virtually non-existent in nature. Both need to be heated to temperatures found in only two places--the surface of the sun, and the heart of a nuclear explosion. You need a fission reaction first to achieve the second."

"So there's really no need to go beyond the first to achieve the second."

"Exactly."

The professor returned to his seat and relit his pipe, allowing Bill time to recall the scene at the garage and the chilling words of Agent Pursey. "You mentioned the extensive knowledge of explosives. Do you mean like dynamite or TNT?"

"Originally," he said through a renewed cloud of smoke, "we'd hoped to fire a bullet of plutonium into a stationary mass of plutonium. We concluded the velocity required would melt the projectile. The problem was solved by shaping TNT charges into explosive lenses, each timed to explode a few billionths of a second after the reaction started."

"Is there *any* way to induce a reaction, detonate it, without major explosives or temperatures of that magnitude?"

"William, there are always scientists, companies, and especially countries looking for better ways to kill. It's where the big money lies."

"The agents at the bomb scene were amazed at the damage."

"What was the explosive?"

"That's the kicker. Aside from the fuel tanks, they found nothing but petroleum-based residues, minor traces of aluminum, and some other metal they couldn't readily identify."

Bill sensed the professor was growing uncomfortable with the subject. "Gasoline is volatile, when its vapors have a chance to accumulate," he reasoned.

"I thought the same thing. But evaporating asbestos-covered pipes and *melting* glass and human beings from well over thirty yards seems extreme. An explosion without a shock wave, one that was all heat. On scene, everyone sounded like a mouse. The technician said we were breathing helium." The expression on the old man's face had him worried. "What is it? Please tell me."

"I'm sorry if the petulant moods of an old man have startled you, my boy. Understand, we're discussing a subject whose mental images are as indelible as death."

"We may be in over our heads, professor. You were my first and only choice for advice on this matter. You're an important man with many powerful friends. Years back I found some of my mother's old letters describing you to my father as 'a man who'd extinguished the fires of his passions for the sake of his country, a man worthy of uncompromising trust.' I'm told he didn't trust many."

"I owe your father much. His spirituality showed me how to rekindle those passions." Forcing a smile, the professor added through the clenched teeth supporting his pipe. "I understand perfectly, William. What kind of detective would you be, if you did not seek my advice in this matter?

"Historically, the scientific communities shared their discoveries with each other, keeping everyone honest and the competitive juices flowing. With the arrival of conflicting political views and corporate greed, our ideas no longer our own, we became targeted by those who had the most to lose from progress. They would stop at *nothing* to silence us." Lost in thought, his attention was drawn to the row of pictures on his desk.

Eyes still staring, he unconsciously lit his pipe and continued. "The Russians had been experimenting with uranium-fluoride plasma inducers--the means by which uranium-fluoride, controlled by pulses of an argon laser, produces a stream of highly excited electrons capable of sustained thermonuclear temperatures for a billionth of a second. The idea, extremely technical, costly, and inefficient, never really interested me. The cold war ended their research. I haven't heard much on the subject in years."

Bill checked his watch. He needed to get home and change before Don Sciaffa arrived. He rose from his chair.

"I thank you for your time, professor. Before I go, take a look at this notebook we found in the dead man's apartment. Let me know what you think. This is unbooked evidence that belongs in the hands of the F.B.I., but I felt it would serve us better in yours. I'll need it back as quickly as possible. Everything's in Arabic, but from what I can tell, the calculations and formulas appear to be in English. If there's anything in here that can help us, please call me immediately."

"You know I will," said the old man, offering his hand. He pulled Bill in close. "William," he whispered, the lines on his face darker, his tone more serious. "I pray you bring an end to this predicament. I'm one of the reasons it exists. Be very careful. Don't trust or underestimate anyone."

"I'll keep that in mind." The door closed behind him as he flipped up the collar of his coat and headed down the hall, burdened by the suspicion that the professor was hiding something -- something very important -- and he didn't know why.

Alone in his office, his weight against the door, the professor stared uneasily out the window into the rainy morning. Dragging his palms down his face, he took a few breaths and covered the short distance to the window to draw the blinds. Taking a seat at his desk, the shaken octogenarian leaned forward, picking up the wooden-framed photo of a close friend, the man's wife, and three young sons standing in front of the family's prized '59 Corvette.

Slowly, he dragged his finger across the face of the beaming mother--a brilliant scientist, a sister and daughter rolled into one. Her cruel and unexpected passing had created a vacuum that sucked the very marrow from the lives of those who adored her most.

Beneath a tear, her contagious smile beamed brighter than the mid-day sun that cast a shadow on the old New Jersey license plate that spelled out a simple five-letter word--JANIS.

Reaching for a tissue, he dabbed his eyes, placed the pipe on its stand and pulled a dusty brown bottle and a glass from the bottom drawer. He had an eerie feeling, one he hadn't felt in a very long time.

The once familiar drink, now warm in his belly, did little to calm his nerves. Settling further into the depths of his chair, he turned his attention to the notebook.

The neatness of the Arabic, the clarity of the numbers and equations, pointed to someone who knew the importance of the notebook. To a scientist, that meant one thing--replicability. The professor remembered Salaam's writing and his attention to detail.

The author of the document, one of the three brightest theoretical minds he had ever known, had been trying to construct some device. It wasn't until Grove's came across a symbol rarely used in physics that his breath was taken away. These symbols were reserved for late nights, when men of vision, giddy from lack of sleep, found it necessary to argue over theories that were at the moment impossible to prove. The diagrams and calculations caused his skin to crawl. He realized, with a gnawing sense of jealousy, that his student, the cab driver, had made a reality of the impossible. If what he was seeing was true, time had, once again, come up for sale.

He picked up the phone and, with an unsteady hand, began to punch in a number, but, thinking better of it, he returned the receiver to its cradle. Relax, his instincts told him--be patient and find a secure phone.

CHAPTER 22

Certain little could be gained by returning to the scene, Jim drove through Times Square, cursing Bill and his wealth of great ideas. In his estimation, re-canvassing the edges of a crime scene was best left to those looking to make grade.

Passing Eighth Avenue, he skipped the u-turn, pulled the shitmobile to the curb, climbed out, and checked his weapon. A steady drizzle had resumed.

Halfway up the block, a lanky man, impeccably dressed in a bright blue silk jacket and black cotton pants, was standing under a long awning, shielding himself from the rain.

Jim flashed his badge. The man said nothing. Too tired to engage, Lackey pulled open the door and stepped inside.

The bar had been open long enough to attract a few patrons to the line of stools in the back. Two tourists in matching Izods, their collars fully furled, talked quietly as they sipped colorful drinks through paper straws. On the far end, twirling a sailor's hat, sat a man staring sadly into the abyss.

Aside from two men embracing on the dance floor, Jim noticed the odd underlying chemical smell of a doctor's office. He crossed the parquet floor and quickly found a slim, pale bartender with green, short-cropped hair standing behind the bar with a wrist as limp as a Dali clock.

"Hey, Toodles, you own this fuckin' place?"

Moving his wrists to his hips, the sight of Jim pulled at his heart strings. "My heavens. . .a lost Shar-Pei," he said wryly, drawing a few chuckles from the two out-of-towners sharing a cherry.

Dropping his chin, Jim moved his thumb and forefinger to the bridge of his nose, gently placing his shield on the bar. "Look," he said, calmly, "we got off to a bad start. Let's try again." He tossed down the police photo of Salaam like a dealer in Vegas. "You seen this mutt?"

The bartender's eyes widened. He too had read the papers; panic set in. "Officer, I--I don't want to get involved."

Jim squinted. "*Detective*, my friend--and who mentioned anything about getting *involved*? I'm interested in yes and no answers, that's all."

"Forgive me. But--"

"But *nothin*'! Seen 'em or not?"

Jim's heavy gaze was all the grease the other needed. Leaning in cautiously, he relented with a nod. "Mmmm, not sure. Seems like something of a brute, doesn't he?" He paused in thought, puckering his lips as if to kiss. "Yeah, I've seen him before--the other night. Nasty cuss, too. Smoked like a chimney and smelled like a *locker* room."

"What can you tell me about him? Was he alone?"

The man on shore leave held up his hand, motioning for another drink. The bartender reacted quickly. When he returned, the out-of-towners started to kiss, sharing the remaining cherry.

"Would you *please* give us some space?" Jim asked politely. They were too slow. ". . . Now!" Mumbling their objections, they moved toward the privacy of the coat room.

"All right," said Jim to the green-haired man, "What can you tell me about the guy?"

"Comes in every once in a while. Think he drives a cab. Most of the time he's alone, ya know, just cruisin', lookin' for a date. I hadn't seen him for a while--'til the other night, when he came in for a beer. He looked horrible, acted nervous, like he was high on *something*. Mentioned he was running late. Asked if I'd seen a woman waiting. I told him no. Like *I'd* be looking?" he added, forcing a breath through his tight lips.

Jim looked up from his notepad. "Then what happened?"

"Things got busy, so I left him alone and went about my business."

"Did he leave after the beer?"

The man shrugged. "Never served him another one."

Jim thanked him and left. Standing beneath the awning, hand out to the rain, he scanned the block and turned his dampened collar toward the sky. Without warning, he turned abruptly to his left, grabbed the well-dressed guy with the sunglasses by the lapels, and forced him against the building. "In business for yourself, are you?" he asked.

"*Yo*," the man exclaimed, startled, his hands rising defensively. "What da *haps*, man?"

In one motion, Jim flicked his shield and spun him forcibly like a top. "Strike a pose!"

"Who's you, Madonna-five-o?" he quipped, angering the detective further. "I ain't dealin'—just standin' here, yo." Jim reached for his cuffs.

"Aw, this is *bullshit*!"

"Yeah? Well, bullshit says, standing more than fifteen minutes' makes you a loiterer."

The other jumped back and angled his head to beg. "But I jus' been standin' here, my man, mindin' my own biness."

Jim, weighing the additional paperwork, eased his grip. "You stand here all the time, eh?"

"Zackly," replied the man as he turned, his large hands smoothing out his suit.

Considering his French lacking, Jim continued, head nodding, his lower lip frowning in acceptance. "Saturday night. . .late?"

Pulling his sunglasses to the edge of his nose revealed a set of jaundiced eyes full of caution. "Mos' of my biness associates ask for an appointment."

"Label this a cold call," insisted Jim, his cuffs spinning on the end of his finger. "Were you here or *not*?"

"Yo, chill. I'm like the mailman--rain, sleet or snow, you dig?" he said with a certain pride. "I gots ta keep an eye on my in-vestments."

"What in-vestments are those?"

The man lifted his shades from his nose to the top of his head and looked across the street at the two well-dressed women on the corner toting designer shopping bags.

"Oh, you're a *pimp*?" asked Jim sarcastically, looking up at the name *Trinity's* pulsing in lights above his head. "I got the impression you were out trollin' for colon."

The man's voice rose a shade. "Damn, Jake, why you sweatin' *me*? The only thing need impressin' is that fly suit of yours. Besides, I ain't the guy jus' walked outta the joint." Jim's jaw tightened, and his cuffs reappeared.

"Okay--yo, no need to get excited. I's here Saturday...mos' the night. Know what I'm sayin'? That help you out?"

Returning his cuffs to his pocket, Jim produced the photo of Salaam.

"Seen this guy?"

"Sho nuff. Motherfucka done near burned my threads. If my bitches weren't so busy stealin' my *money*, I'd a sang him a lullaby." He threw a few quick jabs at the air around him.

"See anything else?" asked Jim, unimpressed.

Shaking his head with a laugh, the man replied, "Yeah, Aladdin liked a little steak wit his po-ta-toes."

Jim looked confused.

"C'mon dog, dude wuz gettin' up 'n one of dem he-bitches."

"Wearin' a tiger print dress?" Jim asked, raising a tired hand to his forehead. They had taken the bait—hook, line, and sinker.

"Man, his Adam's apple close nuf take a bite outta, you dig? Ole Sweetness' in the pussy biness. If he tell you it was a *man*. . .you best believe."

"Get a good look at his face?" Jim's pencil was moving quickly down his pad, as he spoke.

"Bitch had a big ole floppy hat covering his face...'sides, ol Sweetness don't swing that way. . .you hear what I'm sayin'?"

Sweetness turned to the reflection in the glow of the bar's front window for a second opinion. Satisfied with his appearance, he turned back to Jim, eyeing his gilded hands as if something was missing. "His earring...big tiger dangling down. Never saw nuthin' like it."

"Did you hear anything they said?" asked Jim, eyeing his pad, pleased with the progress.

"Arab dude sayin' how he was sorry...and some shit about Tuesday. Or was it Monday? When I gave 'em a dose of stink eye, they stopped talkin' and moved on, the blonde's hand on his ass, jus' carryin' on.

"Yo--it true the trannie jacked that dude's tongue 'n' ear? Cus' *damn*. . .that's some *cold* shit."

Jim squinted. "How'd you know that?"

Sweetness winced in disbelief. "Where you been, man? Nothin' has wider eyes, sharper ears, or bigger mouth than the street. She's tellin' ol' Sweetness Whitey's at work."

"We never discussed race, and you never saw his face--what makes you so sure he's white?"

"Oh, I'm sure y'all downtown're eager to pin this rap on one of the brothas...nice and tidy'n'all. You axe me," he asked, as philosophically as a sixth-grade education would allow, "This one of dem serial psychos...you know, the ones you see on cable 'n' shit? Black folk might stab ya a few hundred times, shoot ya'n'all, but they ain't gunna cut you up like that. Naw, Whitey's your man, and he is lookin' to settle an old score."

CHAPTER 23

Before Bill had a chance to kick off his shoes, rid himself of his smoke-infested clothes, and make it to the bathroom, his beeper sprang to life with yet another number he didn't recognize.

Returning from the hall closet, towel in hand, he dropped on the couch, his feet up on the glass coffee table, and returned the call.

"Good morning. Plaza Hotel. How can I help you?" asked a young woman, her sultry voice competing with the robotic drone of a nearby printer.

"Good morning, miss. This is Detective Bill Masters of the NYPD," he said, drying his head with the towel. "Someone just paged me from this number?"

"Oh, I'm very sorry, sir. This is the lobby pay phone. I just happened to be passing by on my way back to the front desk. There's no one here at the moment."

Pulling a pad from the end table, Bill wrote the number down. "Thank you. Maybe they'll try again later."

The Plaza was a stylish haven for foreign dignitaries, the rich, and anyone famous, who came to New York looking for privacy and a good masseuse. Since she was nowhere to be found, maybe

Kathleen was finishing another one of her power lunches he thought, heading toward the bedroom.

As he stood before the mirror, running a comb through his damp brown hair, he leaned down in his towel and pulled back the curtain to check the weather. Across the street, hanging out the window of an oversized black Cadillac, he noticed a thick tattooed arm clutching a cigar. The don had arrived.

Opening the door, he was shocked to see the neatly dressed don accompanied by nine-lives Vinnie, who, noticing Bill's confused look, chuckled, "Sorry to disappoint you, detective, but. . .wasn't me on the sidewalk."

"Rat bastards didn't get Vincenzo here," said the don, playfully slapping his nephew's cheek. "God bless 'em."

Bill found it difficult to picture Vinnie as anyone's nephew, or one to brag about. Beside the fact that his press-on hair was listing like the Titanic, he had a tired, has-been look—a feral type who had cruised the eighties singles scene decked out in synthetic fibers, flattened collars, and pelts of chest hair covered in gold.

Offering them a seat on the sofa, Bill pulled a high-backed embroidered loveseat from the corner. Bent at the waist, tossing some old newspapers to the floor, he asked, "Get you anything to drink?"

The don settled into the couch, slowly drawing his spit-shined Armani loafer up over his knee, swatting at the lint occupying the crease of his black Versace suit. His graying hair, slick with gel, sat perfectly on his head. Gold rings covered his manicured fingers like a set of brass knuckles. Onyx stones graced his cuffs and the small pin that held his paisley tie in a perfect square with his round shoulders, both pinned to the back of the sofa with the understated air of a rutting peacock. Pulling back the cuff of his suit, he replied, eyeing his watch, "No time for drinks, detective. We need to keep movin'."

"By all means...proceed--I'm all ears." Bill didn't expect much.

Crows' feet appeared in the corner of the don's narrowing eyes, as wary finger tips drummed the side of his loafer. He needed to trust *someone*. "First off, for the record," he said, waving a finger. "I had *nothin'*...I mean *nothin'*, to do with Mr. Salaam's death. If I could get my hands on that sandnigger now—*marone*! It'd be a different story. He *did* owe me money, but his method of payment's what started this whole fuckin' mess."

Riled, he reached into the breast pocket of his jacket and withdrew a leather cigar case and a diamond studded Vuitton lighter. "Do you mind?"

"If it'll help, by all means."

Rolling the cigar around in his mouth, the don pulled a shred of the thin Cohiba from the tip of his tongue and put it back inside the case. "What I'm about to say, off the record of course, *may* implicate me in a number of illegal activities. With your guidance, I hope it'll benefit the people of New York, *not* those Ivy League pricks from the prosecutor's office. I can't have it used against me in court. I want your word, *capisce?*"

Masters was a cop, not a *consigliere*. "Excuse me, Mr. Sciaffa," Bill replied, cocking his head with a confused smile, straining to recall the last time he had given a known felon his word. "How can I promise anything, before I've heard your story? How do I know, once you're finished, *my* life won't be in jeopardy?"

"Why would I go to all this trouble, just to have you whacked?"

"I'm not talking about *you.*"

The point well taken, Sciaffa shrugged off its significance and continued. "A few weeks back, I was informed by one of my associates that Mr. Salaam was behind on payments arising from his failure to make good on a bet. Ten large seemed a little steep for a man on Mr. Salaam's income. I blame myself. Fats, God bless 'em, knew food, not money.

"Naturally, being that he was from Iran and spoke Arabic or some shit, I attributed his tardiness to a communications problem and gave him an extra week. A rare gesture -- once news like that hits the street, everyone thinks I've gone soft. But broken bones are messy, and I need reliable drivers."

Shifting uneasily in his chair, Bill asked, "Did he come up with the money?"

"No. Not exactly." The don paused to drop his growing ash in a dirty ice-cream bowl Kathleen had left behind on the table. "As you may or may not know," he went on, sitting back, his arm draped over the back of the couch, "I own a few firms that deal with the preparation and burial of the dead."

"Funeral homes."

The irony hung in the air. "Exactly," Sciaffa replied with a flick of his chin, continuing, through a cloud of smoke, "Collection time came, and he doesn't have the money. But, if we would run an errand for an unnamed third party, he'd gladly pay us fifty grand in *cash*. Immediately, I smelled a rat. The feds will go to any length to put me behind bars."

"Can you really blame them?"

"Detective, I know who I am. I just like it if there's some *rules* to the game."

"There's your problem."

"How so?"

"It's not a game."

"Skip the dramatics. Life *is* a game that's played to win. Whatever doesn't kill you makes you stronger and whatever tries and fails will always try again. That's the world I live in."

"So what *did* you tell Salaam?"

"I said *no*! Next day, he hands one of my associates a briefcase containing twenty-five g's in small bills."

Bill raised his brow. They'd checked Salaam's financials. He didn't have that kind of scratch. It had to be the rich benefactor the professor had spoken of.

"Do you know the source?"

"Salaam was a junkie and a fag. He could've been dealin' or usin' my cab to mule around town, but movin' that amount of junk makes you a player, and I would've known the source." Sciaffa offered Bill a wry smile. "But, I must admit, detective," he said, nodding through a puff of smoke, "money. . .money's *my* narcotic."

"That's good to know, Mr. Sciaffa," responded Bill, checking his own watch, "but we need to move along. So Salaam offered you the money?"

Slowly working a kink out of his neck, the other said, "The A-rab wanted us to grab an incoming casket at the airport, process it, and bury it in Jersey."

"Which airport, and where in Jersey?"

"Kennedy. . .some jerkwater town called Herodsville."

Bill's reaction must have been visible, because the don narrowed his probing glance and asked, "You've heard of it, Detective?"

"Yes. The name's surfaced in our investigation. We weren't sure of its significance. Please...keep going."

The don paused, pulling a lighter from his pocket. Cupping the collection of diamonds, he cocked his head to place the flame beneath the ailing cigar. "Being that customs at Kennedy is a fuckin' joke," he mumbled, through rising smoke, the stoked ember soon casting a glow on his face, "we brought the coffin in the front door and right out the back."

"Where did the coffin originate?" asked Bill, leaning slightly to see around the cloud now shrouding the man.

"Russia."

"Where?"

"Mur--maid. . .mur--minks or some shit. I don't know."

Bill pursed his lips. "Did you take the coffin directly to Herodsville?"

"What, do I look like an idiot to you? At that point, I still got no fuckin' idea who the hell I'm doing this for or why." Moving forward to make room for his livening hands, he continued uneasily, "The only other addiction I hold dear is breathing, detective. I cross my T's and dot my I's. Loose ends always spell trouble." His point made, he leaned back to his original position on the couch.

"So you opened it?"

"Damn thing was sealed shut. Weighed three, four hundred pounds, *easy*. Kept looking to see if fuckin' Fats was sitting on it, God rest his soul."

"Get it open?" Bill asked, sensing the obvious.

"Any wise guy who can't pick a fuckin' lock ain't no wise guy. *Capisce*?"

Bill nodded.

"We get the thing open, we find a regular-size stiff. It was the coffin that weighed a ton. Fuckin' thing hadda be made of lead."

"What can you tell me about the body?" Bill asked. "Decomposed, or was it preserved? Male or female?"

"The only thing I know about the dead, they can keep a secret. Taking a guess, I'd say he was deceased about a week. Smelled like hell."

"What did *he* look like?"

"Dirty blonde hair, decent build. He was covered with tattoos and it was odd--his ring finger was gone and he was missin' half his forearm. Thing was filleted like a friggin' mackerel."

Bill paused. "Any particular tattoo come to mind?"

"Yeah, a tiger or a cat across his chest and some other military shit on his arms."

"Like what?" asked Bill, moving forward in his chair.

"I don't know. A red parachute that was upside down. What

does it matter?"

"Any other things you might have noticed?" asked Bill more forcefully.

"Well, it may be of no importance to you, but one thing I found odd was the suit the guy was wearing."

"Suit? I thought you just said he had a tattoo on his chest."

Grinning, the don removed a small black comb from his breast pocket and ran it through his thick hair. "As you may know, I collect vintage clothing."

"What the hell does *that* have to do with anything?"

"All you law enforcement hacks are the same. You're like women. You always talk when you should listen." The don took a long puff on his nearly spent cigar and looked to his nephew for corroboration.

"Black silk, double-breasted, at *least* twenty years old, made to measure by a tailor in Milan. The stitching was unmistakable. I've been waiting over a year for his latest line, but the man is old and slowed by arthritis."

"Then what happened?" Bill asked, with measured disbelief.

"Well, as I told you, I'm a collector of suits, but I must admit, I'm a thief at heart."

"You *stole* the stiff's suit?"

"With a few minor alterations, it would've fit me like a glove. But I got to thinkin'. . .someone who buries a ten-thousand-dollar suit in the middle of nowhere returns to claim it. I know I would."

"So you buried it. . .as agreed?"

"Not exactly. I wouldn't pay forty grand for a suit and a week-old stiff neither. There had to be something else of value inside the coffin."

"What was it?" Bill asked, already sensing the answer to his question.

"For you and *me*? The suit was it. Popping the buttons on the jacket and shirt revealed stitching that closed a wound in his chest. The incision was messy and, given the smell, it was not the work of any undertaker I know. Loosening the threads, we found a heavily reinforced container hidden inside the rib cage. Lower in the abdomen was a thick, transparent container filled with a clear liquid containing a hundred or so black balls, each the size of a marble."

"Any labels?"

"There was the symbol for radioactivity, followed by the letters

U, F and L."

"What did you do then?"

"We may be hoods, but we aren't retarded. We put everything back and buried it as instructed."

"Where?"

"A mile or two outside of town, along a big chain-link fence. We buried it under some tree."

"*Where?*"

"In the ground," replied the don, reaching the outskirts of his confession. He had a worried look on his face.

"When did this take place?" asked Bill, not pressing the issue.

"About a week or so ago."

"Did Salaam ever pay you the rest of the money?" Bill asked, scribbling more notes.

"No!" the other spat, reaching to adjust the knot of his tie. "Probably spent it on drugs before he got what was coming to him."

"Why do you think someone's out to target *you* now?"

"I looked inside the body, Detective. So did Fats, Salaam, and the guy you thought was Vincenzo. Every one of 'em are dead. Now *you* know. I suggest we keep movin', or we'll be next."

Bill knew the man would never take such an intrusion into his personal life sitting down. Unless of course, he was scared, which was unlikely. But he was in Bill's apartment, and that, at least, showed concern.

"Have you tried to find out who this person is?"

"My contacts in Milan came up with a name through the tailor. But 'Mr. Smith' didn't sound too promising. The only thing odd was, the man brought the suit in to be refitted."

"So?"

"It was brought in eighteen years ago," snapped the don.

"You're shittin' me." With renewed interest, Bill shifted in his chair, leaning back, putting his legs up on the glass-topped table.

"A request for a cleaning and an alteration were made, but Mr. Smith never returned to pick it up."

"When *was* it picked up?"

"About a month ago."

"Why hadn't the tailor sold it by then?"

"Mr. Smith, I'm told, had a habit of leaving his suits in the tailor's care for extended lengths of time. He stored them and forgot about em."

"Who waits that long to pick up a suit?" Bill asked.

The don shook his head wryly, surprised New York's finest had trouble understanding the obvious. "Guys who get pinched."

Tailors in Milan and ten-thousand-dollar suits meant privilege and a plea-bargain. Out in eighteen meant sentenced to at least twenty-five. He couldn't remember an American blue blood or Wall Street type who'd drawn a sentence like that in the last twenty years. But that didn't mean it'd never happened.

And if the don was lying? In the vast universe of crime, the dead always made the best patsies. "Maybe your associates are setting you up," Bill pointed out, "looking to muscle in on your turf. The racial landscape of the underworld's been changing. Russian, Chinese, Korean mobs are getting stronger. You get caught, it's open season."

The don nodded, vaguely concerned. "Yes. That's always a possibility. But, like you hinted to earlier at the club, only governments and mobsters choose to get rid of their friends." Smiling, he looked at his aging nephew. "I've got nothing left but enemies." He pointed his finger with conviction. "And the Russians? *Please*. They'll never last. They don't know the politics. . .they don't know the fuckin' *law*."

Surprised and grateful for the don's unusual candor, Bill nevertheless felt unfulfilled, as he had when he left the professor.

CHAPTER 24

Back at the precinct, Jim, sitting at his partner's desk, feet up, hips rocking nervously in his chair, was mulling over the morass of information forwarded by Willard and the FBI. Pictures, documents, reports, rap sheets, all piled high and in no semblance of order.

Willard had deliberately sent it in disarray, hoping to delay them further. Jim grabbed a file full of pictures from the scene at Nate Johnson's apartment--compliments of his own crime lab. Itching for a cocktail, he'd been away from a mattress for over twenty-four hours, racing blindly through a haystack for a needle without a name or a face, and sleep was now nipping voraciously at his heels.

Rising slowly, he stretched his long arms, tossed the heavy file contemptuously on the desk, and headed for the coffee maker.

When he returned, fresh cup in hand, he plopped in Bill's chair with a lifeless thud, set his elbows on the desk and cast a tired gaze at the pile of pictures scattered about. When he realized he wasn't dreaming, his heart jumped and his eyes grew as wide as saucers. He could feel the sweat on his palms as he shot up in his chair, pulling a single picture from the pile. Labeled in blue pen, it read: jewelry(location-bedroom dresser).

He took a series of deep breaths, pushed himself away from the desk, and reached for the handle to the bottom drawer, selecting a thick folder from the rear. Sifting through the report, he selected an old, grainy black-and-white photo of a diamond ring taken for insurance purposes over thirty years before.

According to the few specifics available, the pink diamond had been hacked from the finger of the victim, and not been seen since—until now. Jim held the two pictures next to each other. The words inscribed inside the band were the same--"Blood and Faith".

The mayor's assistant had had in his possession the missing link from Bill's oldest case—the brutal slaying of his own mother.

Jim couldn't recall the last time his partner had spoken of his past—of her death, his father's disappearance and the deep paternal relationship that had vanished with him. Recently, he'd learned from Kathleen that Bill's mother had been a federal scientist working for Airmont Chemical, a corporate player subsidized heavily by the U.S. government during the Vietnam War and the patent holder for the toxic defoliant widely known as Agent Orange.

One afternoon, in May of '70, she left home to mail a letter. She was found in the local post office parking lot, slumped over the wheel of her Corvette, a single, small-caliber wound behind the left ear. The letter, the ring, and accompanying finger were missing. Jim knew from Bill's past frustrations that, as a federal employee with top-secret clearance, national security interests prevented anyone outside of the FBI from entering the investigation into her death.

Bill's father, a local politician, church elder, and a vocal opponent of the Vietnam War, had withdrawn from public life after her death, distancing himself from his community and family.

Then, one day, he disappeared. Without Bill's faith in a few blank postcards, his father would have already been declared legally dead. Regardless, Jim knew the effects of Bill's past would pale in comparison to the news of his mother's ring.

When the phone rang, he lurched forward. At the sound of his partner's voice, he fell silent and listened.

"Any developments on your end?" asked Bill, after he had sketched his talk with the professor. He was standing in his doorway, eyeing the don and his nephew entering the elevator at the end of the hall. After a lengthy pause, he added, "Are you awake?"

"Uh, sorry," Jim said, leaning back, covering his face with a forearm. "Few things. *Mainly*, the chief informed Willard the journal was in the hands of your professor friend and he blew a *major* gasket. You should see this cluster fuck he sent us. Are you coming in? I'm ready to keel over."

"I don't know," Bill said, moving towards the kitchen for a cup of coffee, "but we've just had a *major* breakthrough."

"What's up?" asked Jim, grinning uneasily amidst the irony.

"Salaam had the materials in his possession and Sciaffa brought it in. The big question is—who has it now?"

"Sciaffa actually *told* you that?"

"Right on my couch," Bill replied, sipping his coffee.

"Aren't we gonna arrest him?"

"Not yet. We may need him."

"How'd he pull it off?"

"Through one of his funeral parlors, smuggled inside some stiff. Salaam was supposed to pay him fifty large—ten to square a gambling debt, the rest for bypassing customs and putting it in the ground."

"Where?"

"Guess."

"Herodsville."

"Bingo! A lead-lined coffin containing a stiff wearing a ten-thousand-dollar suit, stuffed with two containers, one filled with little black balls suspended in a liquid, the other labeled radioactive. They intended to make something, but for what purpose?"

"Are you sitting down?" interjected Jim, changing the subject. He could wait no longer.

Bill didn't like his tone nor the fact that he wasn't really listening. "What's wrong. . .not another victim?"

"The lab sent over the photos from Johnson's apartment. They found something, a. . .pretty remarkable."

"What?" Bill asked, unaware that he was holding his breath.

"Your mother's diamond ring. It was in the drawer where you found the dope."

The silence that followed was as immediate as it was deafening.

Seated on the floor, his back resting against the couch, Bill fumbled for a reply that never came. His powers of speech and thought were checked by blinding thunderbolts of rage that tore at the scars that had insulated him from himself and his past. Still-born tears welled up like a long-awaited rain, his lips trembled, as he stared motionless into space, the nails of his free hand clawed at the rug beneath him.

The ring couldn't be real, he thought, having learned early that crimes of such magnitude build an impenetrable wall between the present and the past. He *couldn't* go back.

Bill had lost both his parents in 1970, although only one had stopped breathing. His mother had been a victim of a killer no one could find, his father, as it seemed, a casualty of a conscience he could no longer contain.

Lost for over thirty years, the pink stone she had worn so proudly, a burden of love and blame, had been found. The case had now become personal.

Startled by a knock at his door, Bill wiped his face with his sleeve, hoping to pull his shit together. "Jim, I want it *out* of evidence."

"Bill. . .I. . .I. . .it's *illegal*, man. We already have a big enough problem with the *journal.* C'mon, don't *do* this to me."

"Jim, *please*. Because of what happened to her, I haven't spoken an entire sentence to my father in nearly thirty years."

The knock grew louder. Cradling the phone on his neck, Bill turned to the door. "All right, already!. . .Listen," he said, "someone's at the door. Get the guys moving."

"I think we may need to give up on Victor Lawrence," Jim quickly interjected.

"Why? He's the only one left."

"I called the *Post*. Lawrence spent five years in Nam as an infantryman from 1966 to 1970. That's an awful long time. Get this—he was with Calley at My Lai."

"Sounds like our man. When was that?"

"Let me see," Jim said, sifting through his notes. "March 16, 1968."

"There's a catch," Jim added. "Six months ago, after a quick fashion shoot in Milan, he went to cover the fighting in Chechnya. His last contact with management was three weeks ago."

"Great. He's probably the stiff in the coffin. I'll call you later. Remember, get it *out of evidence*. And let's start avidly investigating *all* the deceased."

The chase, one for which Bill had waited a lifetime, had finally begun. He rose from the floor, shaken and numb. His bones ached. Pulling his gun as a precaution, he headed slowly, and unsteadily, for the door.

Looking through the murky lens of the peep hole, he was greeted with a fish eye's view of a tiny man's head with thinning gray hair.

"Who is it?" Bill asked, looking for signs of a weapon.

The greeting was returned with a muffled reply that he could not understand. When the detective heard coughing, he put his eye back to the hole.

An old Asian man, dressed in a black tuxedo, came into view. His angular face and bony chin, a round copse of wire-thin whiskers, seemed small in contrast to the barnacle-sized mole running along the left crease of his wide, flat nose. His peasant face, wrinkled by time and sun, looked stern, almost fierce, his attire impeccable, except for one thing--his right ear was missing.

Bill flung open the door and trained his weapon on the old man's bow tie. "Freeze!" The gun shook embarrassingly in his hand.

Raising his arms slowly and without fear, the other responded with soothing clarity, "Calm yourself, detective. You've nothing to fear from me. Perhaps I should return at a better time."

Running his left hand down the front of his shirt, Bill muttered sheepishly, "No. . .eh, forgive me. I've—I've had a rough day." Holstering the gun, he added, easing the tension, "Nice suit."

"Bad days begin with long nights, no?"

Extending his hand, squinting questioningly, Bill said, "Excuse me, but I didn't get your name."

The other replied through a toothless, third world smile, "Names are unimportant, detective, but if you feel it an obligation, I will gladly tell you in another place." After a short pause he added, sniffing the air, "I see you are a connoisseur of fine cigars, detective. Castro's favorite, if I'm not mistaken." He leaned across the threshold for a better look.

Bill replied dryly, his thoughts still stuck on the diamond ring, "I felt an urge to celebrate. . . . Pardon my manners. Please, come in." He turned back, his arm cocked over his shoulder, towards the phone. "I need to make a call. Then we can step out for some fresh air and a little privacy."

"Certainly." Bowing slightly, the Asian entered.

Bill sat him on the couch and offered a drink, which was declined graciously with a soft wave of his palm. The detective flipped through a mini-Rolodex in the top drawer of the end table, and dialed a number.

The professor's wife, Bill's godmother, answered as the Asian settled comfortably into the couch, gazing about the room in a benign silence, his polished shoes barely touching the carpet.

"Hello, Gigi," Bill said affectionately, cupping the phone, rolling around the short wall into the kitchen for added privacy, "it's Bill Masters. How's everything?"

"Good evening, William. What *is* the purpose of your call?" she snapped bitterly.

"I—I hope I'm not interrupting anything?" asked Bill, treading lightly, sensing something was very wrong.

"You're not."

"Can I speak to the professor? It's important."

Her initial edge softened as she eased back in her recliner, clutching the stem of a neat martini in one hand, and a dampened tissue in the other. "I'm very sorry, William. Please forgive my insolence. He. . .he stopped by earlier, spoke briefly of your visit, then left without a word."

Bill could sense her composure waning as each utterance sounded, more and more, like a sob.

With some difficulty she added, her glass trembling, "Since then, I've received numerous calls from men to whom he swore he'd never speak with again. Men with secrets. Do you have any *idea* what that means?" Her wavering poise teetered like a wire walker in a stiff breeze. She began to cry.

"I'm truly sorry," said Bill deeply, "but it's imperative that I speak to him."

"For over fifty years," she replied, her quaking voice distant, as if she hadn't heard a word, "he's never spoken of the pain he endured at the hands of his own government—men who took his innocence, his genius, and *forced* it into obscurity.

"Tonight, with an excitement I haven't seen in years, he rambled on about redemption. He'd been drinking, something else I haven't seen in *years*. . . . What in heaven's name did you *say*?"

Palming the receiver, Bill leaned back into the hallway. Motioning to the bearded man, he held up his index finger and mouthed, "I'll be with you shortly."

The old man, content with waiting, continued looking about, paying close attention to the teal green lamp on the end table.

Without warning, Bill heard a muffled scream from the other end of the phone, accompanied by the onset of an argument, and the line falling deathly silent.

Stifling an urge to panic, he called back. The line was busy. When he hung up, the phone rang almost immediately. "Hello!" Bill exclaimed. It was the professor.

"Sir, I was just talking to—"

"Not another word, William," he instructed calmly. "*Listen. Closely.* Think back to our meeting today, about my grad students and what they've created to honor me?"

"Yes?"

"Give me a few minutes, then go outside for some air. First, let your fingers do the walking. New York, LIFEO. When you can find the time," he added cryptically.

"What. . .who's LIFEO?" Bill hurried to the end table for a piece of paper.

"You're the detective. Figure it out."

Bill was too tired for games. "C'mon professor. . . ." The line went dead.

Trailed by the attentive gaze of his guest, Bill quickly found what he was looking for in the low lying bookcase in the far corner behind the couch. The binder of the old science book crackled as he flipped slowly through the pages until he found the Periodic Table.

He slid his finger back and forth until he found what he was looking for: Lithium's atomic weight was 3, Iron's 26, and Oxygen's 8. The professor wanted him to call a New York number with the last four digits corresponding to symbols in the table. One of the three prefixes closest to the professor's house was 652.

"Excuse me," Bill said, closing the book and returning it to the shelf. "A friend wants me to use another phone."

"A man of great wisdom, detective," said the old man, rising slowly from the couch.

"And little trust."

"In your business, faith in one is a sign of the other. I believe we are leaving?"

"Yes, we are." Bill eyed the old man's suit. "I hope you don't have other engagements--it might take a few minutes."

"Time binds those in a hurry," he said. "I've already waited a lifetime."

CHAPTER 25

The two men left the apartment and headed into the rain-soaked streets. The sun had pushed through the heavy mid-day clouds, producing an oily steam that warmed the pigeons as they silently scavenged amid shuffling feet and honking horns.

Bill noticed his Asian companion searching the doorways and stairwells as if he had lived in New York all his life. Was it a set up? Lacking an ear didn't necessarily make him a victim. He seized the man's shoulder. "Who the hell are you, and what do you want with me?"

"Please, detective, remain calm," requested the old man, as he pivoted slightly, twisting Bill's wrist like an auger, stealing his balance, then returning it quickly, satisfied with the imminency of the threat. "There's no need for confrontation. I come in peace, as a guest of your country."

"*What?*" Bill asked, still amazed at the ease with which he was just man-handled.

"My name is Thi Ga Vu. I am the head of security for the Vietnamese delegation meeting at the U.N. this week."

"What *else* do you do?" asked Bill suspiciously, rubbing life back into his forearm, his eyes glued to the hole where his guest's ear had been.

"I'm in the intelligence business," the other explained. "This scar, which you find so attractive, was a gift from one of your countrymen."

"What is it you *want*?" asked Bill, irritated. He didn't want to keep the professor waiting a minute longer.

"My sole interest lies in the man you seek. Nothing more."

"And just *who* might that be?"

The old man's eyes narrowed in anger, and his stance became firm. "Please, detective. Stare if you must, but please refrain from insulting an old man. There is no mistake. You know of whom I speak. This is his handiwork—a butcher who spares none but the dead."

"You know what our man *looks* like?"

The Asian stared through him, as if in a trance. "I remember a young man ranting aimlessly as he set about my torture, shrouded in a glaze of blood. . .the very blood of my only brother."

"You're saying he's a psychopath?" Bill chided.

"This is more than just a man in need of a padded cell!" barked the other, hammering his fist into his palm. "He is a demon, spawned from the souls of our children, whose depravity has become that of legend as his stench settled upon us like a fog. A murderous being--half-man, half-tiger--who awaits those who cross his path."

"No offense, sir, but, are we talking fact or fiction?"

Bill tensed as the foreigner, in his haste to convince, stepped closer for his final rant. "*Please* do not comment on things you know nothing about. Politics are the collective ideals of men, detective. When impressed upon the sovereignties of others, *that* is called war. This man had *nothing* to do with either."

Consulting his watch, Bill said anxiously, "Listen--Mr. Vu--is it? I'm *really* pressed for time. If you can't identify this individual, then we've *zero* to discuss. You speak of something that happened over thirty years ago, twenty thousand miles away."

"Thirty one years, six months, two weeks, and two days, to be exact. I, like you, will never rest until I find this man."

"I gotta go," said Bill, angling towards the corner.

The foreigner was astonished. "Detective, do you intend to dismiss my claims?" the old man asked, following closely on his heels. "I have taken great risks, waited many years, for this day. I want to help you *capture* this man."

"I'm sorry to disappoint you, but I can't do that. You've given me nothing but old war stories. Why should I help, or believe, a spook, foreign or domestic? Lies and cover-ups are your specialty."

The old man, again, caught Bill off guard as he grabbed his shoulder, spinning him around, as he quickly reached into the breast pocket of his tux.

"*Easy*--you don't want to do that!"

"My only wish is to make you a believer." The foreigner pulled something from the pocket and held it up to the light.

It left little doubt to the authenticity of the old man's claim. Bill had seen it the day before.

"Ever see something so beautiful?" boasted the man, holding up a match to the earring found in the alleyway. "Fear not, detective," he said, calculating Bill's response. "This little treasure is *mine*. Like my ear, it too is a reminder of what once was. They were an anniversary gift to my mother before she was mercilessly raped and murdered by French forces setting fire to a fleeing village. My father gave one to my brother and one to me, to protect us when the Americans came. My brother wore his around his neck. He made the mistake of taking it off. It cost him his life."

"How'd you know about the earring?" Bill asked, distracted by certain personal parallels he had drawn from the man's story. But now those lines had converged.

"I'm in the intelligence business," quipped the old-timer, cupping his fingers around the hole on the side of his head. "I hear things and the fact that you have the match tells me this *is* the man we both seek."

Bill thought of his mother and the heirloom he longed to possess.

"Do you want to know what I did?" asked the old operative. "Before I became involved in the war?"

Bill nodded, yawned and checked his watch for the third time. His wrist hurt.

"I taught psychology at the University of Hanoi," the other continued, "called upon by my comrades to analyze American personnel in order to disrupt their morale. Regardless of their hatred, they all left with mementos of their experiences; a paddy-hat, jewelry, or the hand of a wife. I think we, men of experience, can tell much from what killers fail to leave behind."

"The fact that our suspect has struck again," said Bill, "taking nothing, leaving nothing, challenges your theory."

"No, detective. It solidifies it."

"How so?"

The old man waited for a group of people to pass. "Why would a man who kills with such fury suddenly kill with such grace?"

Bill had picked up on certain character traits over the years--scars, tattoos, choice of firearm--that distinguished one criminal from another. Because evil spent more time around the sane, he left the psycho mumbo-jumbo to others.

"There are two killers?"

The response, more question than answer, generated a mixed reaction from the mini tuxedo. "A meritable guess, detective. But I doubt it. This person is an outcast, a loner, someone with no ties. Like a predator, he is silent, prefers his independence, and has an overwhelming eye for detail. This person has a simple existence, yet yearns for the finer things life has to offer."

Bill immediately thought of rare gems, ten-thousand-dollar suits, and a set of solid gold earrings. He thought of Victor Lawrence, Nates, and an apartment full of expensive furniture. Souvenirs were gifts from those who wished to share an experience. He needed to get in touch with Jim. "Mr. Vu," he said emphatically, "I appreciate and sympathize with your situation. But I can't help you."

"Detective, repetition tires the soul. I must insist--we are seeking the *same man*!"

"Every murder involves a loved one. And tomorrow there will be more. But--"

"But this one is *special*," interrupted the man with the hairy mole. "Is it not?" He had captured Bill's attention.

"What the fuck is *that* supposed to mean? How do you know so much about me? You think I can be compromised because our countries are shaking hands and you're dressed like a *yakuza* pimp? Do not underestimate me, Mr. Vu. I, myself, find that particularly insulting."

"Look at you, detective. Your anger blinds you, weakens you, makes you easy prey. Sacrifice is the *truest* measure of a man. I pray you'll reconsider."

Bill held his breath for a moment, feeling the weight of the man's words. "I'd love to help you," he said sincerely, locking eyes in a way the other would understand, "I really would, but I'm sorry, I can't."

"I too am sorry, Detective Masters," said the old man, acknowledging the end of the conversation. "Trust in the unknown begs no one for answers."

"Trust rests on honor, Mr. Vu. My allegiances make that determination difficult."

Irked and unsatisfied by his efforts, the old security officer raised his right arm, summoning a large black sedan that was idling across the street. It pulled out with a screech, turned, and stopped abruptly beside him. He turned to Bill one last time.

"Allegiances outside of blood are as fleeting as the whims of a child. We both share an emptiness that has seeped into the very fabric of our souls."

He tossed something that Bill caught at his waist, and added, "Realities can be as fleeting as allegiances, detective. I recommend a new decorator."

Bill raised a brow to the apparent listening device now resting in his palm. Where had the man found it?

A large Vietnamese chauffeur emerged from the car to man the door, allowing the old man to settle-in next to another anonymous, well-dressed, man sitting cross-legged in the rear.

"War's over Mr. Vu. It's time to move on," Bill said, bending to see the passenger.

"On the contrary, detective," the man replied, deliberately obstructing his view. "It's only just begun." His door slammed and they were gone.

CHAPTER 26

"Hello. . .professor?" Bill asked, cradling the phone on his shoulder, leaning further into the enclosure.

"I was beginning to question your talents, William," said the old man anxiously. He was sitting in the shadow of a colleague's study, puffing softly on his pipe.

"Sir, we're in grave danger."

"The powers-that-be have shown great interest in the journal, yes?" posed the professor, his eyes steadied on the row of cars moving slowly up the drive.

"You've got that right." said Bill, looking cautiously over his shoulder.

"Salaam's theories are quite remarkable, William. Sheer genius." The professor welcomed his guests with a wave.

"Remarkable enough for murder?"

"It's a form of energy whose existence goes *beyond* money or motive," the professor assured him, holding out his hand, motioning his guests to their seats.

"How so?"

"Besides its obvious destructive forces, the means by which to power entire regions of the globe. . .or to propel mankind into unknown depths of space."

Rolling the device in his pocket, Bill surveyed the nearby doorways and dark recesses along the street. He couldn't help but sense, he was being watched. "What's the catch, professor?" he asked, with renewed urgency. He wanted to get off the street.

"This energy. . .lies in the heart of the Siberian wilderness--in a place so remote, it was once impossible to reach by foot."

The Russians were smart, Bill thought. Desperate for money, they would find a way. . .if they hadn't already. Then it dawned on him. "With this technology, the Russians could tip the balance of power back in their favor."

"*Exactly*. Oil, the currency of kings, will be nothing more than desert waste. This source has no lingering half-life, no pollutants, just energy--expressed in its purest form. Astronomers have discovered geysers of it deep in space, generated by the same elements the FBI found at the garage."

"What's the source?"

"Salaam found a way to harness the powers of antimatter."

"Antimatter?" It was so far-fetched, Bill felt like hanging up.

"Please, William, don't disappoint me. Certainly you've heard the term before? The opposite of matter. The yang of sub-atomic physics."

"But you just said it exists only in the depths of space."

"Ever heard of a place called Tunguska?"

"No."

"In June of 1908, a giant fireball erupted above Tunguska, leveling 850 square miles of the Siberian forest and everything within it."

"Meteor?"

"An asteroid of substantial size, equivalent to a thousand Hiroshima bombs."

"Go on."

"Leonid Prosk, a Russian geologist, and the first to examine the site, led four expeditions into the region over a sixteen-year period, exhausting millions of rubles and the lives of twenty men. Reported to have found nothing, he and his team languished away in a *gulag*, their true discoveries silenced by death.

"With the downing of Gary Power's U2 and satellite technology still in its infancy stages, intelligence remained pretty thin until the Vietnam War."

As his attention returned to the pain in his wrist, Bill nibbled anxiously on his lip. "Did the North Vietnamese play a role in these developments?"

"In the spring of '68, the military brass began receiving intelligence reports of unexplained seismic detonations throughout the lower provinces of North Vietnam. The defense community was in an uproar. Time and again, they probed. Operation Dead End, turned out to be just that. Things remained quiet until the collapse of the Soviet Union."

"Any names with that operation?"

"William, these people don't *have* names. Besides, an operation of that magnitude would require a large network of individuals, capable of many things. Rumor had it the CIA was close to getting their hands on some information. Then we heard nothing. Someone has always been a step ahead."

"C'mon, professor," Bill prodded skeptically, "that's all a twenty-billion-dollar intelligence budget could come up with? Sounds pretty important to me."

"You must understand, without documentation or a sighting, this was nothing but conjecture--a wild goose chase."

"How can a falling meteorite solve the world's energy problems?" asked Bill, as he wrestled with the feeling like he was wasting his time.

"Some years ago, an American scientist proposed the theory that once an earthbound asteroid composed of antimatter has broken up, it is possible for pieces to become embedded in the carbonized resins of trees. These resins, providing their chemical makeup didn't induce further explosions, could house the pieces indefinitely. This field was the cutting edge of quantum physics during the cold war.

"Reviewing Salaam's notes, I noticed a chemical equation that produces a clear, inert gelatin designed to keep space cargoes intact in case of another Challenger disaster. The CIA stole it from the Russian space program twenty years ago. How *he* got his hands on it is another concern. Our nuclear facilities use something similar when transporting tritium pellets from one reactor sight to another."

Bill tried to stay focused on the realities of the case. "Have the Russians created energy from this, or is Salaam's work the missing link? It would certainly provide a number of motives for his death."

The professor paused to relight his pipe. "We believe the early stages of Soviet testing led to the Chernobyl disaster. Kremlin reports indicated their number four reactor had melted down. Satellite photos, though, revealed that the fire started in the number two unit."

"And that would mean *what*?" Bill asked confused.

"Only the number four reactor was sealed when they should have done *both*. They were either short on concrete or they *knew* the reaction was going to stop."

"Professor, you've made your calls. Does our government know the perpetrators behind this?"

"We'll know soon enough."

"I'm prayin' you're right." Bill checked his watch. "Listen, I'd like to swing by and pick up the journal." He was not at all pleased with the reply.

"Please don't be angry, William," protested the professor, eyeing the row of concerned looks seated around him. "We. . . ." He coughed. "Excuse me. . .*I'm* one of a few left who shoulders the guilt of what we, as scientists, have both created and destroyed."

He sensed the added urgency in Bill's silence. "William, *please*," begged the old man, his eyes coming to rest upon the now seated man holding a cane; its pewter grip cast in the shape of a two-sided head. "This discovery is unparalleled in the history of mankind, William. It is my duty, it is my *fate*, to ensure this discovery does not fall into the wrong hands."

Bill had listened long enough. Everyone associated with the investigation wanted to give a little, they just didn't want to give it all. Tired of the bullshit, emotionally hung-over, he snapped. "Professor, as it seems, we're both victims of fate. Two men consumed. . .paralyzed by losses *way* beyond our control." He paused, closing his eyes, hoping to control his anger. "My mother's ring. . ." he said, his emotions getting the best of him. "You remember, professor. . .the one, hacked from her hand. . .it's turned up in the apartment of the mayor's assistant!" Oblivious to the heads turning on the sidewalk around him, Bill continued, his accusatory-tone rising as he spoke. "I suspect my father's in town, your wife's in hysterics, and powerful people are on the move within my department. Now you tell *me*, what's going on?!"

"William, calm yourself! I'd no idea!" replied the professor, moving uncomfortably in his seat.

"Yeah. . .that's right, professor. Redemption awaits us both. The power's all yours--I want the revenge. I've waited a long time to get to the bottom of this, and I'll need the bait."

"William," the professor said hesitantly, his eyes locked with the gentleman seated across from him, his tone as ominous as the returning gaze, "sometimes the bottom is deeper than you ever imagined. . . . I cannot, in good conscience, surrender the journal. But I've a solution—one, I'm certain'll benefit everyone."

Bill listened fitfully, but, soon enough, he forced a smile. Old theorems, penned by Salaam, would keep Willard at bay. The professor had one more thing to add, drawing permissive nods from those around him. "William," he said nervously, clearing his throat, "it's quite possible the garage bombing was a test to resolve any sequencing anomalies, molecular timing difficulties, or temperature fluctuation that would adversely affect their efforts. . . you need to hurry."

"Is this *really* possible?" Bill asked.

"I'm afraid so. The induction of pure oxygen, combined and pressurized with other spectral gases, will create a dense, highly accelerated quantum-vortex that could theoretically, if gone uncontrolled, create a black hole--bringing time, as *we* know it, to a screeching halt. The *key* is the amount of heat needed to excite the gases, dividing them along molecular lines, enabling them to catalyze into a form of matter that's exactly opposite of what lies within the balls. Heat, in this case, in the form of electrical energy--and lots of it."

"What about the material that killed Salaam?"

"It's a failsafe, a memento from the past. Without the journal, and a tremendous supply of electricity, fissionable materials become the only option. Either way, we as New Yorkers have a big problem. I'll be in touch."

"Where will you be?" asked Bill, unnerved by the professor's sudden understanding of a subject of which he claimed earlier to know little about.

The professor nodded at the latest arrival standing at the door and replied, "In the wind."

CHAPTER 27

Responding to a page, Bill dialed his partner, who answered on the first ring.

"Lackey," answered Jim through a sip of cold coffee.

"I'm sure your page's important, but my apartment's been bugged. I've no idea *why*, but chances are yours has been too," he added, looking about. "Stay off the phones, if you can help it."

"What're you *talkin'* about?"

"Just go to the pay phone out front and call me at this number."

"You're the boss." Jim jotted down the number, hung up, and hurried to the dwindling line of phones out front.

"What's the scoop?" he asked, winded, his big hand sweeping garbage off the metal ledge mounted below the phone.

"We're being watched."

Jim was skeptical. "C'mon, by whom?" He leaned back and rolled his head from one corner of the block to the other.

"Somebody. . .I don't know. I just got a visit from some fossilized shrink, with the grip of a mason, who moonlights for the Vietnamese security detail covering the meetings at the U.N. meetings tomorrow. He had in his possession, *the* match to the earring we found near Salaam."

"Did you arrest *him*, at least?"

"Hardly, take too much time. Probably has immunity and, besides, he said the one we have was his brother's, allegedly taken by some sick murderous fuck who stalked the Vietnamese countryside killing innocent civilians during the war."

"You believe him?" He gave the two corners another glance.

"The guy *was* missing an ear."

Jim whistled slowly. "Sounds like our perp's been at it for a while."

"After talking to this guy--" Bill began paying close attention to a dark, obscenely clean van rolling to the curb across the street -- "I'm confident we're looking for those responsible for...ya know... the death of my mom. We'll need to cross-reference the apartment's contents with every homicide committed over the last thirty years. Jewelry, furniture, artwork, rugs, you name it. Unfortunately, that'll mean the FBI database."

The lines on Jim's forehead deepened. "Might be a problem," he said, tossing a futile wave at a blonde in a passing patrol car. "That's the reason I called."

"What *now?*" Bill fumed, realizing the van, now parked, had yet to yield a passenger; its tinted windows prevented him from seeing any of the occupants. If he wasn't mistaken, the van had diplomatic plates.

"Willard's boy--Special Agent Patterson--is missing. They're bringing reinforcements up from Washington. It's a full court press."

"You're joking?" Running his hand down his face, Bill turned his back to the van.

"He wasn't returning calls, so Willard stopped by, found signs of a struggle and plenty of blood. Patterson and his weapon were missing."

"Patterson's blood?"

"There were reports of gunfire. When I'm through here, I'll be taking a spin over there with Rico to check things out."

Surprised, Bill asked, "Willard *invited* you?"

"Yeah. Can you *believe* that shit? Called it a 'new era' of cooperation between divisions of law enforcement."

"Man must be desperate." Bill said, turning back to the street. The van, and his sense of security, had departed.

The kidnapping or murder of a federal agent was not the act of a person wishing to remain anonymous. He hoped it wasn't the closing act. "Did you get the ring?" he asked, staring at the back of his hand.

"I put it in your drawer."

"Thanks, partner. Anything else?" Bill asked, changing the subject. He couldn't wait to get his hands on the ring.

"Willard's pretty adamant about getting his claws on the journal. Fucker's been making threats of evidence tampering."

"Cocktail talk. I bet the professor's got a higher security clearance than Willard. . .and he knows it." Wary of the time, Bill changed the subject. "Any luck with the background checks?"

Scratching the stubble on his chin, Jim suppressed the tempting thoughts of alcohol and replied stoically, "Still waitin' on the military requests. Captain thinks that's gonna present a problem."

"Expected as much. Why can't Willard just cough up what we need?"

"Probably, the same reason you haven't given him the journal," accused Jim.

His partner had a point, Bill mused, dismissing any further thoughts of Willard. "There have to be newspaper articles on My Lai, though, something with a picture. Is there *anything* useful in the information Willard sent us?"

"The lab work done on the pictures from Salaam's apartment, the one with the cap and gown, concluded it was taken in front of the old Iranian embassy. The building is now owned by some heir to a Persian rug empire—one Ari Man...the third. Guess the closing date?"

"Halloween."

"Absolutely. But it gets better. I had Russell Bloughs, our friend from the closet, come down and look at the photo. Guess who's the other turd burglar posing with Salaam?"

"Ari Man. . .heir to a Persian rug empire?"

"You got it! The friggin guy's loaded. Jets, limos, body-guards, the whole nine yards."

"Sounds like our bank. Know of his whereabouts?"

"Hicks is looking into it, as we speak. So far, all we have on the guy is suspicion of tax evasion...the IRS has been up his ass for years."

"What else did Willard offer on Salaam?"

"Not a whole hell of a lot. Prison files, school transcripts, some *ridiculously* censored copies of his FBI and INS files. From the two lines I could read, he did his undergraduate work at the American University in Beirut. Postgrad at the University of. . .get this, *Stalingrad.* Also, before I forget, that nutcase up in Sing Sing, Afreet, the one who bombed the Statue of Liberty, was a member of his American University graduating class in Beirut. Majored in political science."

Without warning, rain began to fall. Feet shuffled, umbrellas shot skyward, the sudden squall precipitated by a flash of heat lightning.

"Listen, partner," said Bill, spreading a *Daily News* pulled from a nearby garbage can. It was a long shot, but he had an idea. "I'm gonna head up-state. Somehow, the Liberty Island conspirators fit into the equation. Salaam, first and foremost, was a drug-addicted scientist, *not* a politician, nor a very successful bagman. Someone pulled his strings, and that someone had to be a person, or persons, he trusted. Men with a common cause. And according to Willard's sermon earlier, they only seem to place trust in one another." Bill pulled a pen from the ashtray. "What's that degenerates name again?"

"Tarik Hassan Afreet?" replied Jim, recalling the short time he spent in Afreet's presence and the long cleansing shower that followed.

"Thanks," Bill replied, tossing the pen aside. "What's the quickest route to Sing Sing?" he asked, checking his watch.

Jim did his best to overcome the loud deluge that now cascaded around him. "The President's arriving sometime today to do a little shopping and snarl traffic. Radio reports the Deegan's a mess and the thruway's a construction site. It'll take longer, but I'd try one of the tunnels and get outta dodge."

"Sounds like a plan. Remember--keep specifics off the phone. I'll be in touch."

CHAPTER 28

The steady flow of traffic was beginning to wane as early afternoon approached. Emerging from the Lincoln Tunnel, napkin in hand, Bill wiped away a thin film of moisture obstructing his view. Through the polarized portion of the windshield, he craned his neck to see the scattered billboards perched like vultures over the windpipe of the city.

Ahead, beyond the seedy hotels, a string of aircraft descended toward the runways of Newark Airport to the south. With the Meadowlands' swamps to the west, he planned to swing north and hit Ossining by four o'clock at the latest.

The quiet wooded town of thirty thousand was located on a scenic stretch of the Hudson just north of the City, where they'd once made plumbing and electrical supplies, and which now housed some of the worst miscreants America had to offer.

Tarik Hassan Afreet was a self-proclaimed warrior of the people of Palestine, who, at the impressionable age of ten, had looked on helplessly as the butt of an Israeli rifle crushed his father's skull--at which point, he traded his pencil for a rock, joining a local cell of Hezbollah.

After the gavel had fallen for the Liberty bombing, sentenced to a life of solitude, he had settled uncomfortably into the role of a living martyr, something men of his calling lived to die for.

The two detectives had questioned Afreet briefly during the early stages of the Statue investigation, before Willard and his crew took reign and turned the whole thing into a media-circus. He hoped Afreet wouldn't recognize him.

The weather had cleared a bit as the Pontiac crossed the length of the Tappan Zee Bridge. Whitecaps covered the choppy water beneath heavy clouds as hungry gulls, battling the wind, dropped like rocks into the salty mist.

The horn of a passing train labored against the gusts as he pulled down the lane that led to the prison, perched by itself above a long, low rise of green and brown that descended to the river's murky edge.

The old, white dolomite of the original building peeked out from behind a series of elms, presenting to the world a sense of learning rather than reform.

That feeling ended with the first guard tower--a tall, dark-eyed minaret that loomed high above thick walls topped by coils of razor wire that glistened like the skin of a snake.

Pulling into a parking space in the far corner of the lot, he spotted a row of crows rocking on a length of barbed wire, their loud caws mocking the small group of prisoners smoking in the yard. Above them hung a sign--*One Foot Up, Six Feet Under.*

Bill didn't have a prepared list of questions; he knew the visit in itself was a long shot. Communicating with a prisoner in solitary confinement without prior approval was going to be tough. Tucking his weapon under the seat, he checked his appearance in the rear view mirror and hauled himself out.

Beyond the main doors, behind a long reception desk, sat a thin, square-faced, guard of middle years whose suspicious eyes took him in briefly before inquiring about the nature of his business.

Bill flipped his badge, dropped his keys in a tray, went through the detector, and paused, stopping in front of a thick Black woman holding out the keys.

"Destination?"

"I'm here to see a prisoner," Bill replied, still holding up his badge.

Irritated, she exhaled, put out her heavy arm, and pointed through lidded eyes in the direction of the metal doors at the end of the corridor.

The silence gave way to a lively crowd of visitors waiting impatiently inside. Although there were no cells, the room itself felt like a prison, as guards, wary of contraband that fueled the pen's black market, circulated, assisting those with questions, cautiously eyeing an unseasonable coat or heavy bag.

The request form that Bill handed in was an immediate source of entertainment for the receiving guard whose initial reaction was audible enough to catch the attention of a second guard looming nearby. Scanning the paper work, his laughter left the guard, stationed behind the glass, reaching for the red phone on the wall beside him. Bill drew little humor from his request nor the surroundings. The room was hot and issued a morbid smell that fell a phylum shy of death. Despair was the closest thing he could associate with such a stench.

After a long twenty minutes, he checked his watch, and looked around for the guard. If he wasn't mistaken, the man approaching with the waxed handle-bar mustache, rounded collar, and bow tie was the warden. He was in the company of a short aide carrying a clipboard, whose uniform was different from that of the other guards, and on his right shoulder, inches from his mouth, he had a mike for his radio.

Bill rose, stifling the urge to laugh, as he pictured the older man in a striped, one-piece bathing suit atop a tall bicycle with a big wheel. He bit his lip and stuck out his hand.

The warden smiled coolly. Looking at the name on the clipboard given to him by the smaller man, he held out his hand and said, "I'm Warden Fox."

"Pleasure. . .name's Bill Masters--NYPD." Holding up his shield, the detective got his first whiff of Old Spice. "I'm sorry about the short notice, but I'm here at the request of Mayor Kravitz concerning a sensitive investigation we're conducting within the department."

"Ah, yes, Detective Masters," the other said, grabbing Bill's hand, recalling the bombing and the brief notoriety of both his guests.

"Pardon the delay, detective, but I'm concerned about the man you wish to visit. We've a certain protocol here, rules that need to be followed, when dealing with the likes of Mr. Afreet."

"How's that?"

"As you know, he's a very dangerous inmate--one we prefer to keep under lock and key. Bringing him here would only serve to endanger the lives of the other inmates as well as your own."

"I understand. Then take me where it *is* safe."

"You don't seem to understand. There is no safe place. I must decline your request. I'm dreadfully sorry."

"Do you have any children, Mr. Fox?" Bill asked, trying to keep his Irish in check.

"Yes, two little girls. Why do you ask?" the warden replied, visibly uncomfortable with the line of questioning.

"What you just said brought back memories."

"What? That I'm dreadfully sorry?"

"I said those very same words to the father of a twelve-year-old girl whose head'd been blown off by your boy Afreet. This is about the *victims*, Warden, not the privacy and comfort of some fuckin' zealot."

The warden's determined look seemed to soften. He paused, slowly turning to his aide. "Prep Afreet for a face-to-face. Chain him to the table in interview five. Tell him a reporter wishes to speak with him, and that good behavior'll earn him an extra half hour of prayer. Got it?"

"Certainly, sir," said the assistant, moving off to the set of metal doors behind them, head cocked, relaying the warden's instructions into his mike.

Bill stopped him as he passed. "Is Afreet's last known address in that file?"

Flipping through the paperwork, the other replied, "Six eighty-two Christopher Street."

"Thank you." Finally, a link between the three victims--Afreet and Victor Lawrence: relationships with no relations.

"Okay, detective, if you would, please follow me, we'll take the short-cut. I'll give you a half-hour and the guided tour. Stay on your side of the table and do *not* approach Mr. Afreet. He's manipulative, argumentative, and extremely dangerous. Killed one inmate already. Don't underestimate him. You're here for answers, but I suspect you may not like what you hear."

Bill followed him through another series of well-guarded doors into a long, clean hallway split evenly by a thick yellow line. The sound of human voices grew louder, as they approached the next set of doors at the opposite end.

The warden showed his face to the guard, turned to Bill before pushing himself through, and said, "Chow time!"

With a turn of the key and the last guard behind them, Bill found himself in a massive mess hall.

As they passed, he saw armed guards stalking the catwalk above, their rifles pointed at men in matching jumpsuits, hunched warily over orange trays, separated into groups according to race.

At the far exit, the warden turned with a sense of urgency, waiting for the door to open. "It's when the whispers *stop* that I know my time's up."

Their destination, up a flight of stairs, was a quiet hallway with a few numbered doors. "Do you plan on accompanying me?" asked Bill, coming to a stop in front of the last one.

The warden leveled his sagging tie. "No. Unfortunately, I've a fund-raiser with the board of freeholders in about five minutes. Rest assured, detective, the guards will be there."

The door before them had a black number five staring them in the face. "They'll be bringing him in shortly," said the warden, checking his watch, as he held out his hand. "*Remember*, stay on your side of the table. When you're through, a guard will escort you out. Good luck."

Bill entered and closed the door behind him. The room, white, rectangular, had the sterile feel of a morgue. It was quiet, except for the low hum of fluorescent lights and the distant rumble of the air conditioning. In the middle of the room stood a solid metal table supporting a thick steel ring bolted about a foot from the far side, and two opposing chairs. The wall to his left was bare; the right contained his tired, stubble-faced reflection in the frame of a large one-way mirror.

Breaking the silence, a guard entered from the opposite side. Large, clean-cut, with the face of a boxer, he checked the room before taking up a position next to the door. Scars dotted his overhanging brow; his nose, bulging in the middle, was flat as a pancake. His look, and firmly crossed arms, meant Afreet was near.

Again the door opened, and the entrance filled with one of the largest human beings the detective had ever seen out of a football uniform. The guard, his skin as dark and smooth as lamp-black, made Bill's scrappy partner look like a midget. He was younger than the other guard, but Warden Fox had entrusted him with the trophy of Sing Sing. That, and his sheer size, said enough.

Bill barely noticed the Arab in the orange jumpsuit, whose devilish smile vanished the instant their eyes locked, and whose face returned to its eerie calm.

Dangerous men have a way of commanding respect from their captors, regardless of their size. His senses heightened, thinking he had been made, Bill stared at the black patch that covered the man's right eye.

Odd, he thought, for a man known amongst his peers as "The Wolf" to be so well shaven. The hair, beard, mustache, and body hair, once heavy and aggressively exploited by the media, were all but gone. He'd once read forced shaving demoralized the psyche and bent prisoners to the will of their captors. The feel of a beard would be enough for Afreet to remember who and what he was—something America, and the warden, wanted him to forget.

Moving the man like a puppet, the guard ushered him quickly to the chair and locked his wrist restraints to the eye-bolt on the table. The confined turned and spat at his keeper, muttering expletives in Arabic that went ignored as the guard resumed his position beside the door.

Throwing his arms out of his sleeves, Afreet moved his head back and forth, adjusting his neck like a prize fighter. After a few breaths, he withdrew a pack of Camels from the breast pocket of his jumpsuit. Arms crossed, he peered down his arched nose at Bill. "You look like the weary balls of a camel!" he spat wryly.

The comment would usually have struck a nerve in the detective, but he was dealing with people not far removed from his mother's death. There was no time for smiles or emotions fueled by fatigue. And he didn't need a map to read the man across from him.

"There's a certain freedom in it," Bill said, nibbling the bait. "How about you?"

As if drawing a sword, Afreet pulled a cigarette from the pack and placed it between his lips. "Ah, yes, another American--a calculated sense of humor, a mask of true intent." Without a word, the large guard bent, producing a plastic lighter.

The man's mask hardened. "Are you a Jew?" he asked quickly, his head back, a stream of smoke billowing from his lips.

"No, but this camel's circumcised," replied Bill, staring at the man's Adam's apple. "That going to be a problem?" He noticed a pair of grins on the two bookends manning the door.

"Who are you? What is it you seek?" asked the Arab, tired of the humor, his head bobbing in the direction of the guards. "The demons say you are a writer." He bobbed his nose towards the ceiling, and added, "I say you are a friend of the head devil, Warden Fox."

Bill took a moment to respond, eyeing in detail the outline of the man whose demeanor, tone, and attitude were all wrong. Afreet had served two years of a triple life sentence, locked away in isolation, and here he was enjoying a smoke, acting like parole was a day away.

After another long moment, Bill looked at the two men guarding the door and summoned the larger one.

Leaning down, a look of concern on his face, the big man listened, nodded, and with a grin motioned for Bill to rise, allowing himself to be frisked. After a brief exchange, the two guards checked Afreet's restraints one last time and left the room.

It caused the prisoner brief initial concern. Bill had counted on it—break the routine, so goes his concentration.

When they were alone, with nothing but the metal table between them, the look of intrigue on the Arab's face convinced the detective he would talk.

Folding his hands, Bill began to speak. "What kind of man does it take to blow up innocent men, women, and children?"

With a short laugh, the Arab fell back, tilting his chair. "You disturb my prayers for *politics*? Ask the wife of your president."

Bill should have listened to the warden. "You're comparing apples to oranges." He turned to his reflection in the mirror, angered at how lame he probably sounded.

"Regardless of what the world sees, both fruits start with seeds of similar size." With his manacled hands raised to his face, Afreet lifted the shiny black patch that covered his right eye, revealing a hideous, blood-red sphincter encircled by tangled lashes pointed in every direction of the compass.

"Do you see *this*?" he snarled. "*Do* you?"

"Vividly," Bill replied with tempered disgust, planting his feet firmly on the floor, waiting for the rebuttal.

"*My* legacy of Israeli peace efforts. The American press prefers the term 'rubber bullet' suggesting some invisible degree of compassion as it is fired upon a crowd of children throwing rocks. Americans will never understand that in the desert, war is the womb from which all politics are born."

"You're at war—boys with rocks?" challenged Bill.

"Never question the resolve of those forced to witness the mortality of those they love. I would not be here, if rocks were the only arm of vengeance. We are homeless nomads at war with those who occupy our land, fighting with whatever means we have at our disposal--real or perceived."

"The United States isn't occupying your land," objected Bill.

"Yes, but it lends legitimacy to those who do, supplying funds and technology, interfering with the delicate balances of the region."

"What would you have the Israelis do, allow themselves to be annihilated?"

"Do not be an *idiot*!" barked the Arab, flicking an ash to the floor. "The people of the Middle East, Arab and Jew alike, have been living together for over three thousand years. The *al nakba* of 1947 was a direct result of Western outsiders, swayed by Zionist guilt, drawing new lines in the sand, placing the future of Palestine in the hands of those who would rather see us dead. It is over these grave injustices that we still fight and die."

Bill looked deep into the man's eye. "What can you hope to accomplish—boys with rocks?"

"Victory lies solely with one's will to survive. We possess the will, but never the way. We started with rocks, we shall finish with rocks. The power of Allah has come, sent from the heavens, into the hands of the righteous, to rid Palestine of the infidels, once and for all."

Tipping a hand in a game no one was playing seemed foolish, thought Bill, especially for a man like Afreet who had lived and survived on the strength of his secrets. He'd been courting the writer, hoping his words would again escape into the wind, no longer contained by locked doors and metal bars.

"What was the *real* purpose of targeting the Statue of Liberty?"

The Arab shrugged. "Causes as small and meaningless as ours remain in the news as long as the world sees that *we*, those ground under the heel of tyranny, are determined to transcend our repression, no matter the cost." His bloody eye still exposed, Afreet leaned closer. "An eye for an eye, *al nakba* for *al nakba*. *Catastrophe*! Only after this is done will the decree of our intifadeh be lifted. America will finally see a world of darkness through my eye."

"That's a tall order from inside these walls," said Bill, sickened by his arrogance.

"Sometimes, it is necessary to place great distances between yourself and those you love, in order to fulfill your aims. Are you a righteous man?" asked Afreet, moving back in his chair.

"Let's say I have faith," Bill answered, wary of the direction they were headed. He had gone in for the sacraments but left with only the sins.

"Faith in Christ?"

"'Whoever sheds the blood of man, by man shall his blood be shed.'"

Afreet's lipless smile made Bill want to pull out his other eye. "'Say, The lord is my shepherd, I will not fear what men shall do to me. For in my death I am revealed.'"

Bill was impressed, if not a little confused by the Arab's religious sidebar. "I figured you'd vomit at such utterances."

"Better to know thine enemies than thyself. Is it not?" Afreet snapped, rubbing his wrists. Again, he threw them out, adjusting the sleeves of his jumpsuit. Bill's eyes widened, zooming in on the arm still resting on the table.

Tattooed beneath the thin growth of hair on Afreet's left forearm was the symbol that had populated Salaam's journal and forced the professor into hiding—a mark of absolute power, of salvation, and now, as Bill saw it, the key to the deliverance of Afreet and his people.

The cocky Arab was still working his wrists, when Bill, finished with the exchange, went for the jugular and sucked the last drops of hope from Afreet's untenable existence. "Know an Iranian cabbie by the name of Abdul Malik Salaam?" The rubbing ceased.

Caught off-guard, Afreet's cagey eyes narrowed, and an evil caul swept over his face. He said nothing, as his nostrils flared wider with each breath, and his forearms flexed with an anxious determination.

"You read the paper?" added Bill, amused, hoping to elicit a more vocal reaction.

"I have no use for American propaganda," Afreet replied, trying to look disinterested.

"Well, here's a little propaganda you might find useful," said Bill, offering his badge, saving the final stake for the man's heart. "That cab driver you *don't* know? Well, he's good'n'dead — butchered by some sick fuck who had better use for his tongue and ear. Sounds like a little eye-for-an-eye, to me. Anybody you know?. . . How 'bout a Victor Lawrence--ring a bell?" Bill winked, rose, and turned to leave. "Have a nice triple life, scumbag."

The realization struck like a bullet, the moment Afreet recognized the detective. His face turned gray as slate, veins bulged around his temples, as he rose in an uncontrollable anger, his flailing arms still connected to the heavy table.

"By the way, his journal's a great read," Bill said, inching towards the door.

The prisoner, his dark brow now moist with sweat, lashed out like a rabid animal, pulling wildly on his restraints, screaming obscenities at the top of his lungs. The two guards burst through the opposite door, forcing him flat onto the table. Blood flowed from his wrists.

Struggling with the orange jumpsuit, the large guard looked up and said nervously, "Detective, you'd better leave and *fast*." His thirty minutes were up.

Bill nearly bowled over a third guard the warden had posted outside the door, who pointed at the prisoner and asked, "What'd you *say* to him?"

"Nothing, really," offered Bill with a shrug. "Told him I was a writer, doing a story titled 'Prison Life—A Different Type of Harem.' He went ballistic."

"Ungrateful faggot," smirked the guard, closing the door.

"What? The lion of the desert—queer?" asked Bill, amazed.

"As a three-dollar bill."

CHAPTER 29

Once out of the prison, Bill sprinted to his car in search of his phone.

"Lackey," answered Jim after the second ring.

"It's me," Bill barked, out of breath, recoiling from the heat that had accumulated on the seat.

"You're not going to make me go outside again?" Jim asked, rubbing his bloodshot eyes.

Bill thought about it for a second, as he gunned the Pontiac to life and flipped on the A.C. "Ah, fuck it. Any word on Patterson?"

"He has a one-bedroom apartment in Queens. Stuck my head in, viewed the carnage, and left. If that's his blood, he's a dead man. Must say, the guy lived a pretty Spartan existence--black-and-white television, a few pieces of furniture, a bed and half a suit."

"Maybe he lived with someone else. Is he married. . .girlfriend?"

"Not according to Willard."

"Second home?"

"Possibly, but Willard didn't mention it in his initial report. The impression I got was that their relationship was strictly professional. The only other asset of note was a boat Patterson bought on his vacation three weeks ago. It's docked at a marina in Point Pleasant."

"Leave Willard to deal with his own," Bill said, rummaging around the front seat for his pen.

"He didn't seem overly distraught," said Jim.

"You seem surprised. Professionals are like that. What else you got?"

"The phone company coughed up the records on Salaam's pay phone. One call from Herodsville in the last two months, for a total of twenty seconds."

"How many calls in or out during that time?" Bill asked, pulling out of the prison lot.

"About six thousand, give or take a few hundred."

"When and where?"

"Some service station off of route 195, 'bout two weeks ago. A Jeb's Citgo. Any luck with Afreet?"

"Yeah, he's a gay sociopath with a distaste for anything kosher."

"You're shittin' me?" Jim replied, leaning back, tossing his feet onto the desk. "I didn't see *that* comin'."

"No, I'm serious, and--get this—turns out Afreet's last known address matches up with a few of the utility bills found under Salaam's bed. These fuckin' guys all knew each other. Probably through the bars. Initially, I thought Afreet's network might've been Salaam's third party, but he hasn't had a visitor, or communicated with anyone outside law enforcement, in over three years. This caper started as a conspiracy to blow something up, but, instead, as I'm now seeing it, we had a power play for the reclamation of the Palestinian homeland. The symbol from Salaam's journal was tattooed in the *exact* area of the wounds on both Salaam and the body described by the don. For over three years, Afreet's been waiting patiently for someone to set him free. Saw it on his face. Salaam's theories were the key. Someone's altered the agenda. And *that's* who we're looking for." Merging onto the main drag outside the prison, Bill added, "When I told him Salaam was dead and we had his journal, the guy freaked. Mentioned Victor Lawrence and the fucker tried to get a piece of me."

"I'm sure you were dripping with compassion," said Jim, grabbing another pad.

"No doubt," Bill replied, the large phone cradled on his

shoulder, one arm juggling the wheel and a bag of pretzels on the seat. "How 'bout you?"

"A second request's been made for the military files on Lawrence. Diaz just got back from the salon where the dead roommate worked. Salaam was a regular, but he hasn't been there in months, which contradicts the coroner's report that his hair had been recently cut. He wasn't exactly the picture of health, so maybe Nate's roommate went to see him instead."

"Or Salaam went somewhere else."

"No way. They were friends," protested Jim. "Sure, the guy was a drug addicted freak, but he was a creature of habit, organized, neat, and meticulous. He wasn't going to trust that mane to just anyone. He ended up where he didn't belong."

"A possibility. I wish we had the roommate's address book," said Bill, dropping the passenger-side window for some salt air.

"The evidence team's still sifting through their shit. They'll let us know if they find anything." He flipped his notepad. "Also, it seems Afreet, Sciaffa, *and* Ari Man, all share the same attorney. Name's Horowitz. Odd, huh? Presently, his other rug client is out of the country."

"Horowitz, eh? Strange."

"What next?" Jim asked, hoping for a nap.

"I can make it to Herodsville before dark. Give me the address of that gas station. Maybe someone saw something. Any word from our guy at the *Post*?"

"Thanks for reminding me." Jim ran his pen down the lines of his legal pad. "All spies are accounted for. . .but he did find an old Pravda article translated and dated July 25, 1972, which reports the apprehension of two Americans found within the Sevmorput Nuclear Facility, Murmansk, USSR. Sound familiar? One's named Robert Smith."

"No shit! That's the body's point of origin, and the name Sciaffa matched to the person who owned the suit. What's the other guy's name?"

"That's the thing. All State Department press releases admit to only the apprehension and detention of *one* man. He was released on May 16, 1974."

"Please tell me there's a picture of this guy?" Bill asked, moved by the date's proximity to the time of his mother's death. He checked his watch.

"Yeah, there is, but it's old and not too clear," Jim replied, eyeing the small photo.

"If half of what the don said is accurate, then we have to assume their initial mission was a success. The suit was dropped off at a tailor's, under the name Smith. Twenty-seven years later, the suit and nuclear material are shipped together, winding up in Herodsville. We need to find out who was left *behind*."

"Yeah," objected Jim, "but we still can't rule out the possibility this was sponsored by some foreign government. Put aside the two roommates, and assuming cooler heads prevailed, who ends up paying the biggest price for the successes of Salaam and that nut Afreet? United States, Israel?"

"Ultimately, the world economy and *anyone* who pulls oil from the ground and, considering he's Arab, *that* doesn't make a whole lot of sense. But, at this point, I could give a shit," answered Bill, fed up. "I'm through worrying about things I can't control or understand. The question is who's Victor Lawrence and where does he fit? Do we have a photo of him yet?"

"City DMV has no record of a license issued. . .but they *do* have an expired registration for a gray 1987 Buick LeSabre issued to a Mr. Victor Lawrence, whose present address coincides with that of one Nates Johnson; deceased. We're checking other states as well. The *Post* says his picture's missing from their personnel file. For now, we can only hope the military bucks up."

"Don't hold your breath. I'd bet my pension, he's a spook," Bill said, merging onto another featureless ramp. "Now, give me that address. My phone's crappin' out."

Heading back across the Tappan Zee Bridge, barely avoiding a collision with a windblown delivery truck, Bill retraced his steps towards the city and the arteries that would draw him home.

With each mile south, the concrete skyline behind him began to fade, replaced by mega-malls, price clubs, and lung-choking power plants.

It wasn't until he passed the numerous holding tanks of the Airmont refinery, his mother's last employer, that he was overwhelmed by a feeling of emptiness he had longed to forget.

His mother, a part-time housewife and respected scientist, had gone to mail a letter, following a long night of quarreling with his father. As a child he was in the dark, but she'd stood her ground, a rarity in the face of his father's almost fanatical resolve.

It was obvious from the concerned looks, the shouting, and eventual tears, that the contents of the letter bore a heavy price. Whatever it had been, her missing ring tied directly into his present investigation--and that, like her death, was no accident.

It was all Bill could do to keep his eyes on the road, as the Pontiac wove in and out of traffic along the Turnpike. He reached down, turned up the radio, and positioned the air conditioner towards his face.

The cool breeze felt good, a change from the surreal patchwork of inconsistencies, lies, and government agencies in which he found himself immersed. The Wolf, a man with whom he had more in common than he cared to admit, had enabled him to understand the virtue of resolve. There was something to be said about those who, day after day, brought rocks to a gunfight.

There was little fault found in the purity of the man's politics. He hadn't come to the stump with big teeth and vagaries carefully calculated to numb the senses. When Afreet addressed the issues, there had been no pap, no partisanship, just explosive ripples felt from Tel Aviv to the White House.

Yet, beliefs aside, both men had had their lives affected by the actions of outsiders, forcing them to search for whatever it was that would make them whole.

CHAPTER 30

"Something wrong, mister?" asked the man in the toll booth.

"No--um, sorry," replied Bill, dazed, handing him his toll card and change. "Must've been the yellow air of Airmont."

"Color must have changed," joked the other with a wink and a country smile.

Bill reached for the map half open on the seat but thought better of it. "Say, how far's it to Herodsville?"

The toll collector crouched and pointed down the road, his short arm moving slowly back and forth. "This here's Route 195. Make a right at the stop sign. Go 'bout five miles, just past the entrance of Great Adventure. You'll come to a light, and Jeb's Citco'll be on your left. That's Looming Road. It'll take you into Herodsville. Careful, though."

"Why's that?" asked Bill, raising a brow as he noticed the patience running out of the driver in his rearview mirror.

"Animals from the park have been gettin' out along the western fence. Sanitation truck hit an antelope just last week."

"I'll keep my eyes peeled," said Bill. "You have a pleasant day."

It wasn't long before he hit the deluge of busses and cars leaving the amusement park. There was still an hour or so left of daylight and it looked like the weather might be finally breaking. Thin rays of afternoon light were skipping between the gaps in the clouds as flashes of heat lightning burst on the horizon.

After everyone was done stretching their necks at a one-armed man changing a flat, the heavy flow of traffic began to subside. Bill cruised past the park's arched entrance flanked by two tigers with glowing eyes peering through the dense brush of an animated billboard. Over a small rise, past an abandoned drive-in and two strip-malls, he found Jeb's Citco and eased the car into the uneven lot, setting off a bell, the sound of which neither aroused the mangy brown mutt nor the grimy pair of boots sticking out from under a car idling in the garage.

When Bill tapped the horn, the dog barked. He turned off the engine and dragged himself into the afternoon heat. Immediately, the smell of manure surrounded him like a cocoon. He checked the soles of his shoes.

He sensed the garage, its roof-line sagging like the back of an old mare, and quite possibly the mechanic, were on their last legs. A rusting, faded blue tow truck, hood up, sat parked under a large elm off to Bill's left. Slipping between the pumps, anticipating an unseen clump of shit, he eyed the lengths of duct tape that zig-zagged across the broken panes of the office window like overgrown synapses. Somewhere behind the garage, a compressor hose was hissing uncontrollably.

"Excuse me!" he barked, wary of the now attentive mutt and the loud screeches coming from beyond the fence. There was no answer. "Buddy, you breathin'?" he added, nudging the boots.

"Jesus H. Christmas! Can't a fella sleep?" replied a deep, shitkicker voice. In a flash, a man appeared on a rusty four-wheeled metal creeper from under the vehicle, his head tilted in tired disbelief. He was in his mid-twenties, shirtless, wearing a pair of tattered gray overalls. Aside from his distilled odor and matted blonde hair, he was handsome, of medium height, square-jawed, and in excellent physical condition. His biceps, covered in a mixture of sweat and grime, flexed as he rolled a soiled rag in his greasy hands. "What can I do you for?" he asked, his temper easing as he rose, dropping the cloth to the cement floor.

"Name's Bill Masters. I'm a detective from the New York City Homicide Squad. I'd like to ask you a few questions, if I may."

"You greasin' my chassis?" asked the man skeptically, his

thumbs locked around the straps of his overalls.

"Nope," Bill replied with a grin. He flicked his badge and pulled a pad and pen from his rear pocket.

"I'll be. . .a real D-tective' wantin' to talk to ole Gus. Sure, go ahead," the guy added, reaching into the front pocket of his overalls. "Jeb won't be back for 'n hour 'r so."

Unnerved by the man's enthusiasm, Bill waited patiently, as the townie bit off a large chunk of smokeless tobacco and rolled it around in his mouth. Sucking the plug into his cheek, he bent, spit on the ground at Bill's feet, and rose, offering a brown, mucousy smile.

Looking past him, towards the fence, Bill asked, "Do you have a payphone I can use?"

"Nope. The phone company took it away 'bout a month ago. High school kids kept millin' around on the weekends breakin' shit." He pointed to the front window. "So, Jeb had it removed."

It took a moment for Bill to realize that the call received at the payphone outside Salaam's apartment had been placed directly from Jeb's office. He must've asked for permission.

"You remember a group of Italian guys," asked Bill, "stopped by, maybe a few weeks back? One well-dressed, the other big, maybe a cheeseburger away from a heart attack."

"Jus' so happens they did. The beefy one needed the key to the shit'r. The oily one was askin' about a tree with a yellow ribbon 'round it."

"And?" asked Bill, rolling his right hand impatiently.

The young man spat, raised his arm, angled his head, and pointed down the road. "Been there a long time; since before I was born. Some fella went off to Vietnam and never came back."

"Know his name?" Bill asked, hoping for a break.

Running his sleeveless forearm across his lips, the grease-monkey replied, "Haven't a clue. It's about a half mile down the road--least it was."

"What do you mean, *was*?"

"The 'lectric company cut it down for the big substation everyone's been bitchin' about. They're saying the wires'll cause cancer, make ya stupid. I ain't buyin' it."

"What's the station for?" Bill asked, amused, eyeing first-hand the long-term effects of carbon monoxide exposure.

"Paper's been sayin' the park's movin' ahead with a major

expansion. My brother Stu works there as a mechanic. . .says all them new rides need a ton of juice. Personally, I think they're gonna develop the land, but they wanted the infrastructure in place before they'd buy."

The kid didn't seem as dumb as he looked. "Who's the owner?"

"Fuck if I know. Check the paper," the boy suggested, pointing a greasy finger at the rusty yellow box chained to the warped telephone pole leaning on the corner. "I'm sure you'll find somethin'."

"Thanks. I will." Bill turned and moved to the pole for the latest issue of the *Herodsville Gazette*. Back in the car, he was glad the exchange had ended--he had begun to sweat through his shirt.

Pulling out of the station, an uneasy feeling came over him as he eyed the first metal tower that rose out of the trees along the edge of the park. By the time he reached a small clearing a mile down the road, he had counted three, each spanned by four heavy-gauged high-tension wires dropping sharply into a fortified group of transformers that hummed like a hive of bees. He pulled over for a closer look.

Just above the door of the perimeter fence hung a triangular sign that read *Danger High Voltage*. His eyes glued to the warning, Bill got out of the car. Instantly, the drone was broken by the angry shriek of something wild behind the tree line off in the distance.

The smell of damp earth and hewn lumber filled the air as he reached the perimeter fence, disturbing the chorale of crickets at his feet. Along the tree line to his left, he spotted a stack of freshly cut logs beside a large yellow loader, its wide bucket levitating a stack of shredded stumps. Woven through the roots, refusing to be separated from the thickest bole, clung the remains of a yellow ribbon faded and torn by years of exposure.

The project looked to be just getting started as a piece of the chain link fence the don had described lay draped over the side of a metal refuse container. The soil around his feet was a myriad of deep boot prints and excavator tracks filled with mud and puddled water. The spread could have been someone's yard, a field or a pasture, Bill couldn't tell for sure. But, he knew of one certainty-- whatever the intent, they had plenty of juice.

CHAPTER 31

Back at the station house, Jim stared wearily at his reflection in the men's room mirror; the circles under his eyes had grown darker and his hair was pathetic. Tepid coffee, splashes of cold water and swipes of deodorant, no longer helped. He needed a shower, a shave, and a week's worth of sleep. A few cold ones couldn't hurt either.

Besides fatigue, the phones had been ringing nonstop since Willard turned up the heat, creating an unnecessary flap over the missing journal. This, and the pressure from Kravitz, had his captain at the brink of a breakdown, along with word that the White House had considered canceling U.N. ceremonies with the Vietnamese government. The event was no rock concert. Issuing a rain check would blow the lid off of the story.

Jim was concerned about his partner tooling around Jersey without backup. Bill hadn't phoned for a few hours and he needed to know what he was up to. The results of the last twenty-four hours were pissing *everyone* off. Dark suits had taken over the corridors and most of the vacant desks. Willard's boss was being flown in from Washington.

At his desk, fresh cup in hand, Jim studied the news items faxed by the *Post* concerning the capture of an American spy. Odd, he thought, for the State Department to admit to such an embarrassing event, being that the ability to deny had always been their first and best defense. But an admission, even a prevaricated one, always defused a situation faster when angled in different directions, diverting the focus from the things Uncle Sam wanted to keep from the citizenry.

Scanning his notes, Jim found it fascinating that Afreet, the leader of a holy war, *never*, in three years of incarceration, had a single visitor. Pulling Salaam's prison file from the corner of his desk, he wondered who *had* taken an interest in the Iranian during his time at Rikers. The list wasn't long, but two names were rather distinguished. Agent Willard had interviewed Salaam more than a dozen times in sixteen months and, one Sam Groves, no less than ten.

Jim knew credentials were a doctor's stock in trade, rarely overlooked, especially when signing a legal document. Reaching for the phone and a slightly adulterated version of an INS report, he hoped to confirm which of Salaam's buddies was still in the country. Cross-referencing the updated entries with the names in the FBI dossier, Jim was startled to find that *all* of the remaining cell members had left the country Thursday--the day *before* Salaam's murder. Dialing Bill was futile, since the last five calls dumped immediately to voice-mail.

Still cradling the phone, the fax machine, hidden under a stack of files behind him, rang once and hummed to life. The cover page grabbed his attention. He put the phone down.

Uncle Sam had replied. The report, passed on by some nameless clerk, was the usual government mumbo jumbo, but the picture that followed froze Jim in his tracks. Glaring back was a dark and grainy photo from an April '68 issue of *Stars and Stripes* displaying a few of the men of Charlie Company, First Battalion, Twentieth Infantry Regiment, of the American Division's 11th Infantry Brigade—the men responsible for the carnage at My Lai.

Jim quickly examined the photo, hoping to recognize a face. All of the men were young, solid as stone, hair cropped short, faces thin, and wracked with fatigue. He recognized no one except for the two on the end, their arms draped over each other's shoulders, the tattoo of an upside down parachute clearly visible on each of their biceps. The face was a close match to the old Pravda picture the *Post* had sent over. Mr. Smith was Sgt. Victor Lawrence, a handsome man, his youthful brown hair bleached by the sun, his long chiseled frame thinned by years of war. The face of the other equally attractive young man, Lt. Rick Willis, described as Herodsville's "hometown hero", Jim had seen many times before. But that familiar face and the one he was looking at in the picture shared neither the name he was familiar with nor the smile.

Rushing through the remainder of the fax, he came across a list of home towns. Victor Lawrence, of 423 Looming Road, had been president of the photography club at Herodsville High. Overwhelmed, Jim dropped to his chair and yelled for the captain in a voice that rose barely above a whisper. He didn't want to believe it, but his partner was in serious trouble.

Eager to keep moving--Bill had grown up no more than twenty miles from where he was standing--knowing a little of the terrain, he had come prepared. From the trunk of the car, he retrieved a pocket-knife, a few extra clips of ammo, a camouflaged windbreaker, a light-weight bulletproof vest, a pair of boots, and a flashlight.

Sticking the flashlight into the rear of his waistband, he adjusted the Velcro on his vest, finished lacing his boots, snapped the jacket closed at the bottom, and emptied the contents of his pockets into the receptacle between the seats. The listening device, some loose change, and the cell phone no longer in service, would be of little use. He brought along the *Herodsville Gazette*.

Having studied the treeless tract, he checked his weapon a final time and followed the loamy trench that left the rear of the transformers and trailed off into the nearby woods like the tunnel of a giant mole.

When he reached the fallen trees, he inspected the length of yellow ribbon that hung around the tangled roots, the fabric worn and faded. Wiping away a clump of loose dirt, he uncovered the initials *V.L.* carved into the trunk. The coincidence made Bill's skin crawl.

Creeping around the large loader, he discovered the crushed remains of a mailbox wedged between the treads. The door, bent and twisted, bore the numerals *423*. He didn't see a house nearby, or any signs of life, but he did sense a presence--one that drew him to the pile of stones that marked the start of a path at the other end of the field.

As Bill reached the far side, a misty rain had returned, silencing the horde of katydids celebrating the oncoming rush of darkness. The detective pulled his collar up and took another look around.

The site for the park expansion was perfect; the surrounding acreage dense with overgrown thickets and vines that reduced the amount of light, providing security to those animals whose instincts told them to hide.

Moving down the trail, he climbed around a cluster of moss-covered rocks, stumbling upon a few strange animals foraging among the exposed roots of wild blueberry bushes. Their antlers, like corkscrews, and the multi-colored hides, were like nothing he had ever seen. The closest animal, its tail twitching rapidly, let out a quick snort and the group fled. After a few quick leaps, they were over a rise and out of sight.

The detective carefully stepped over a few fallen trees to avoid an area of soggy soil ripe with the stench of skunk cabbage. He had covered about another fifty yards, before he heard the unnatural hum of the first electrical tower.

High overhead, the ceramic insulators, some as large as dinner plates, fought against the tension of the wires as they carried their deadly load deeper into the forest. Bill ran his hand along a thick power line that snaked through the framework and disappeared into the ground at his feet. Dragging his toe over the spot where the thick conduit entered the ground, he felt soft soil. He was no OSHA inspector, but the trench fell a few citations short of code.

He didn't know if it was his close proximity to the tower's magnetic field, or the presence he had felt, but the hair on the back of his neck began to rise.

Suspicious, he thought about heading back to Jeb's to call the locals for some backup. That all changed with the unmistakable sound of a car door slamming somewhere nearby. He paused, crouched down, and scanned the woods behind him before he moved ahead.

He clawed his way up a small rise, around another dense line of dead brush and bramble, and into a clearing. To his left, behind an old barn with blackened windows, sat the rear bumper of a gray Buick Le Sabre parked on an odd angle. Across a crushed gravel driveway full of weeds, set back further onto the property, was the main house. To the right, sticking out from under a worn canvas tarp, sat a rusty, four-wheeled boat trailer. Two of its tires were flat, the other two missing.

The way the house stood, how the shutters had fallen from their anchors, gave it an eerie look of pain. Shingles from the roof and siding were missing too, as if they had been ripped away, one by one, as punishment for resisting time.

Across the circular driveway that separated the house from the trailer, Bill saw light coming from one of the front rooms. Shadows danced along the walls and ceiling, behind the edges of the thick curtains.

Dropping down below the soggy ridge, he moved quietly along the edge of the property towards the back of the barn, on guard for a dog, a sentry, or anything that might reveal his presence.

He crouched beside the Buick and rose on his toes to peer through the driver's side window. The interior was immaculate, as if garage-kept—rugs cleaned, windows, and dashboard washed. The only sign of life were the pink pistachio nuts in the ashtray and a large-brimmed hat resting on the back seat. Moving to the rear of the vehicle, he noticed a piece of clear plastic jutting from beneath the trunk, streaked with traces of blood.

The barn's overhead door was padlocked, but two distinct sets of tire tracks were clearly visible. The tall weeds populating the gravel driveway had been bent away from the barn, and the edges of the imprints were crisp, despite the hours of rain. A large truck had been there recently, towing something behind it--now it was gone.

Training and common sense told Bill to collect as much on-scene intelligence as possible, then retreat for back up. The sheer fact that his mother's killer might be lurking behind the red front door changed that. His whole adult life, he had followed the rules, matching wits with those who did not. But the feelings, the ones stashed away in the bottom drawer of a desk, had started to pound through his veins like a freight train.

Tossing the gorier specifics of the case around in his mind, it was obvious that he wasn't dealing with a run-of-the-mill psychopath, but with someone who had survived a twenty-year career of murder without capture. Any excuse Bill could come up with for knocking on the door--*I'm lost, my car broke down, could I borrow a cup of sugar?*--seemed overly transparent. Barging in, gun drawn, would be a mistake as well; he knew nothing about what dangers lay beyond the red door. He would have to draw whoever it was outside, creating a diversion to provide the advantage he would need.

His options were limited: The barn was locked, the boat trailer seemed rather useless, and he wasn't packing enough ammo if things got heavy. If Victor Lawrence, or any of Afreet's men, were inside, they would most likely be heavily armed. That left the Buick.

A rag in the gas tank. . .but he had no match. Even if he had, he would be blowing up potential evidence.

Mr. Vu had been right--anger was dulling his edges, clouding his judgment. He'd pull back instead, collect intelligence, and return with the troops.

The rocks off to the right of the garage presented an excellent vantage point from which to survey the front of the house. The elm gripping the base of the closest rock would provide ample shelter from the rain. The space beneath it looked fairly dry.

In an effort to find a comfortable position among the rocks, he felt the old magnifying glass dig into the rear of his thigh. Unless the house was an inch from his face, it was going to be of little use.

Swapping the glass for the newspaper inside his jacket, he hadn't gotten further than the front page before he found the story he was looking for. The headline read—JANUS SALE A DONE DEAL.

Despite the efforts of local residents, the sale, as well as the completion of the Looming Road substation, will proceed as planned. Demolition of existing structures will conclude Monday, July 25 . . . .

That meant the house would be razed before sundown the following day. Good-bye, evidence.

According to the *Gazette*, Janus Ltd. was a real-estate conglomerate based in London with branches throughout Europe, India, and the Far East. A recent downturn in European markets had spurred a sell-off of the company's many worldwide real estate holdings.

The electrical infrastructure had been a gift that the park and the cash-strapped town couldn't refuse. *Some* gift, Bill thought as he raised his eyes and turned the page.

Without warning, there was movement on the far reaches of the yard. Ditching the paper, he dropped into a crouch, and peeked over the rock. Twenty yards away, three hooded figures in camouflage fatigues were moving single-file in the shadows along the edge of the driveway, red dots from their laser sights danced a few feet to Bill's left. Seconds later, they were across the driveway onto the porch, their compact automatic weapons raised, barrels sweeping, focusing on the space around them.

Pausing for a moment, they kicked open the door and entered, spilling both light and shadow onto the steps. A quick volley of gunfire ended in a sudden, eerie silence, followed by the sounds of a struggle.

A minute passed.

Suddenly, a man appeared in the doorway waving a bloody rag. Through the haze of gun smoke, Bill sensed he was injured. "Cease fire!" the injured man cried. "Cease fire!"

Before Masters had a chance to react, a fourth man emerged from the recesses of the driveway, his gun trained on the figure in the doorway--Agent Patterson of the FBI.

The masked commando moved cautiously towards the wounded agent, circling, studying his face. From where Bill was hiding, Patterson seemed to be in desperate need of medical attention.

Convinced the hooded man was alone, Bill rose. "Don't *move*!" he ordered, emerging from the shadows, his weapon leveled on the man in black, whose furtive reaction left the detective no choice but to duck and fire, the lethal exchange dropping both men to the ground.

Despite his appearance, Patterson moved quickly for the commando's weapon.

Gasping for air, Bill clawed at the front of his shirt and jacket. His thin vest had been no match for a round from an AK-47. The pain was unbearable, but there was no blood, only a constant ache below his heart. Wincing, he half-whispered, "Patterson, I'm hit."

The agent limped slowly to Bill's side and dropped to one knee. In the shrinking daylight, he pulled opened Bill's jacket to look for an entry wound, but, removing his vest slowly, found only a black, softball-sized hematoma still growing on his chest.

Reaching into the pocket of Bill's jacket, Patterson removed the old magnifying glass his father had given him. Its thick metal case was dented and the blue lens it contained was cracked along its edge.

"Welcome to combat, detective," said the agent, handing back the glass. "Looks like somebody's watchin' you."

"This duel ain't over," Bill said through his teeth. Sitting up, he saw his hooded opponent writhing on the ground.

With some help from the agent, he slowly rose to his feet. Stooped, his left arm numb, he limped towards the wounded man partially hidden among the weeds of the gravel drive and yanked off his mask. "Jesus. Mr. Vu. What are you doing here?" he asked with remorse, realizing immediately that back at his apartment the wily operative had duped him into taking a tracking device, in order to follow him.

"Detective," interrupted the agent, "I'm going to secure the inside."

"Good idea," Bill replied, moving to the colonel's side. From the looks of the bleeding and the sucking sound escaping from the old man's chest, Masters concluded they didn't have much time.

"Go easy. We'll get you out," he said as calmly as he could, wondering why Vu was even there. He was startled by the flash and sound of two additional rounds fired from inside the house and quickly backed away from the downed man. From the rear of the Buick, he waited, gun trained on the front door.

When Patterson emerged moments later, with the muzzle of the old man's weapon smoking at his feet, Bill returned to the injured man.

"Mr. Vu, you didn't come here to avenge your brother," he said, rummaging through the man's field pack for a first-aid kit. "Why are you here?"

The steady rain and severity of the wound inched Vu deeper into shock. Bill removed the sheathed k-bar strapped to Vu's ankle and cut through his fatigues for a better look at the injury. Exposing the skin, he located it and a gold chain from which hung the match to the earring found in the alley.

Closing the gap between them, the detective pulled a dressing from the pack, pressed it over the wound and repeated firmly, "*Why* are you here?"

Its effect was immediate: The man rallied to answer. "The victor coming to retrieve the spoils...stolen...from...us." The long sentence forced a deep cough that spattered his face in blood.

"When?" Bill asked, leaning closer.

"Sixteen...March...1968." He coughed, once more.

"My Lai?"

The old man could no longer speak. Blood was streaming from his lips like water from a spring. A feeble nod was enough.

Darkness had crept upon them as the soothing sound of peeping frogs rose amid the faint glow of fireflies. Bill's eyes finally settled on the quiet FBI agent leaning against the rear of the Buick.

"Is there a phone in the house?" Bill asked, amazed Patterson was still standing.

"No, I don't think so," the agent replied, rubbing his temples.

"You gonna make it?" Bill received another listless nod. There wasn't much time. "What do you wanna do?" he asked, grimacing. "*Someone* had to be communicating with this team. We gotta get help."

"That won't be necessary, detective," said the agent firmly, moving in, the barrel of his gun rising. "Goodbye, Colonel." He fired a short burst that lifted the man off the ground, leaving Bill on his heels, shielding his face from the fiery report. The agent looked down at Bill in disgust. "Dry your fuckin' eyes, detective. I just answered the prayers of hundreds of American mothers. Jus' one more to go."

"He's the *head* of *security* for the Vietnamese contingent meeting at the *U.N.* tomorrow!" Bill pleaded. "You looking to restart the war?"

"I'd say he's a bit underdressed," the agent replied, coldly.

Bill rose, holstered his weapon, and walked gingerly toward the house. The agent followed closely on his heels, shedding the thin ropes still dangling from his wrists.

As he crossed the creaking boards of the front porch, Bill was greeted by the acrid smell of gunpowder that hung motionless in the scant light of the doorway. Over the threshold and across the worn wooden floor was an open closet, bare, except for a few empty pistachio nuts.

Refracting muddled rainbows into the shadows of the adjoining room, two glass doorknobs lay on the floor amid a small pile of spent shell casings.

What little Bill could see, beyond the entranceway, into the two rooms on either side, was a collage of peeling paper and crumbling plaster, the woodwork chipped and in need of care. The furnishings and few wall hangings were covered with dusty sheets and heavy tarps.

He inched deeper into the room on his right and spotted the soles of military boots aimed at the sky. He raised his weapon and moved in for a closer look.

Lifeless, were three men with multiple gunshot wounds, lying in a semi-circle around a chair from which hung short lengths of rope, their tattered ends wicking the blood from the floor.

They were male, dark-skinned, no older than thirty, each wearing faded army fatigues. Clean shaven, all but one wore glasses. Weapons, similar to the dead commando's, were still gripped tightly in their hands. Too tightly, Bill thought, assuming they were Afreet's men. Without their fatigues, they'd have looked like dead librarians.

Wary of his injuries, the detective crouched down to inspect the men in masks. He pulled off the first, surprised to find the face of a middle-aged oriental woman with week-old stubble for hair. Each mask removed revealed another woman, a few years older than the last. Although his inspections were preliminary, they seemed to have been shot in the back.

Turning back, Bill realized the agent was no longer present. The floor creaked above. He could hear pounding feet, running water, and a sudden bang of loose plumbing. Patterson had moved to the steep staircase in the room off to the left.

Bill took a seat on the small, tarp-covered couch that overlooked the carnage. Having never witnessed a murder, his adrenaline was surging, his hands shook, and he couldn't think with any degree of clarity.

Minutes passed to the sound of Patterson's feet pacing the second floor as Bill closed his eyes to gather his wits, his mind racing wildly through the horrors of the last twenty four hours. Regardless of the smorgasbord of players on both sides of the law, their motives, and the snowballing pace of the investigation, they were still no closer to their killer.

A lengthy silence from above summoned Bill's eyes to half-mast. Calmer, his breath returned, he couldn't shed the feeling that his surroundings had been staged, as if the dead were ready for an audience. He was equally troubled by the fact that the women commandos had had the advantage but, judging from the position of their bodies, the element of surprise had been taken from them. . .yet *everyone* was dead.

His concentration was broken by the force of the renewed

footsteps coming from the second-floor. Plaster dust fell from a crack in the ceiling, as Patterson thundered down the stairs. When he entered the room, Bill held out his hand. "Thanks for everything."

Naturally, the agent extended his hand. Bill gripped it tight, turning their hands over. Patterson had been upstairs freshening up, his hands wiped clean, revealing the pink dye that stained his fingertips.

Exposed, the agent quickly took a step backward, raised the weapon, and barked, "Toss your piece, detective, and let me see your ankles!"

With his gaze locked on the agent's hands, Bill lifted the cuff of his pants and dropped his weapon to the floor. His attention moved to the blood-soaked Band-Aid stuck in the crease of Patterson's arm.

"How long you been drawing your own blood?" he asked, his stance widened to avoid the crimson stream moving across the floor, the smell of death churning in its wake.

Patterson pulled another chair from the corner of the cramped room, and set it down backwards on the floor. "A lot less than all the others," he replied cryptically, straddling the seat, the assault-rifle across his lap, his steely gaze focused on Bill.

"You don't really think you can pull this off, do you?" Bill asked, angry at his own fading confidence.

"We already have. Look around you," said the other, with a wave of his arm. "Arab insurgents are the ones to blame."

"Who's *we*?" Bill asked, rubbing his ribs.

"Those dedicated to doing the world's dirty work, detective."

"You call decapitating and butchering innocent people *work*? Who would've thought 'twisted fuck' would go this far on a resume?" Bill knew any mention of his mother would be a mistake. Patterson was an obvious pro.

The agent's eyes went wide with amazement, his head pivoted in disgust. "For a New York City detective, you really *are* naive," he said. "Here's a little eye-opener for you. Ever see a leper? You know, the guys with their noses and dicks fallin' off?....Of course you haven't. Society's weakness has programmed you to shun them, put them out of your mind. The same can be said about other segments of our society, those that provide our enemies with the perfect medium from which to operate. You know why?"

Bill's rage kept him silent.

"Because in Vietnam, *we*, the U.S. military, found that the best places for our enemies to hide were amongst us, right under our fucking noses. But like the sons who died there, we tried desperately to forget the lessons learned.

"Recruited, one by one, over the years, Victor Lawrence, Mr. Johnson, and his roommate were a *single* strand in Afreet's worldwide web of terror. And trust me, there are *many*."

"So this whole openly-gay-lifestyle thing was a *ruse*?" Bill asked, impressed.

"The days of the bombs dropping in other backyards are over, detective. We're facing an ideology, without tangible arenas, that shares no common language, whose sole purpose is the collection of our souls. Mr. Johnson, a.k.a. Akan Mohammad, had access to every shred of intelligence data regarding New York's infra-structure, its communications, its command and control strategies and codes, procedures for evacuation, et cetera. The mayor's fav-orite converted hairstylist--Aziz Bakar--was the courier who pranced around City Hall, trimming hair, gathering intelligence, delivering communiqués. Our enemy is smart and getting smarter, using our laws and technologies against us. Our agencies are top-heavy bureaucracies that are out-gunned, undermanned, and under qualified. I've been snoopin' around FBI field offices for years, and I've yet to meet a single person, domestically, who can speak a lick of Arabic. Now, considering all that has happened, how safe do you feel?"

"Where does Afreet fit in all this?" Bill couldn't imagine his department was this blind.

"When you were bangin' co-eds, Afreet was out spreading the gospel of unrest in the Muslim areas of Azerbaijan. After his arrest, Victor Lawrence was his cell-mate for a year."

"And Salaam? Where was he?"

"Going to school, studying for the top slot in Iran's first nuclear program."

Shifting on the sofa, unable to get comfortable, Bill asked, "As long as were talkin' all friendly, whose side're *you* on Agent Patterson?"

"Real name's Rick Willis, detective. Lived here, in this little town, my whole life. Had a house right up the street. That is, until my country called. But I wasn't the only kid in the neighborhood lookin' to be a hero."

"Victor Lawrence," snapped Bill, fighting off the pain.

The agent nodded, raising his hands to all that was around them. "This was where he grew up, before he and I attended boot camp together. Then we moved on to OCS, Special-Forces, and, as if by design, we were selected for a Black-Ops unit formed specifically for classified missions above the 38th parallel."

"Let me guess? *Dead End.*"

The agent's body tightened, as if stung. "Excuse me?"

Bill ignored him. "Find anything?"

Fatigued, the agent's own crispness had begun to erode. Maybe it was an accumulation of all the lives he had taken, Bill thought, waiting for a reply. His tough, wiry frame looked spent, his shoulders were hunched with a weight few men could fathom or begin to understand. Bill could see his lower lip tremble.

Struggling, to the point of tears, he turned his face to the light. Bill couldn't explain it, but he no longer looked like the man who had occupied the shadows just seconds before. Like a snake, he had shed his scaly exterior, leaving himself exposed.

Patterson collected himself and mustered a reply. "Not until the ambush of Colonel Vu and his men."

"My Lai?"

The turn-coat took another moment to remember, his thoughts swimming aimlessly in the darkest backwaters of his mind. ". . .We had the element of surprise, but Vu had superior numbers," he said, staring into the darkness, his face an eclipse of torment. "After an intense firefight," he recalled, "they quickly outflanked us, putting us on the defensive. Luckily, Calley and his reinforcements arrived, and the hamlet got caught in the crossfire. *Vu* set the tone, *Vu* refused to give quarter to anyone—man, woman, or child. He wanted *no* witnesses."

"To what?"

The agent's lips parted, but again, he struggled to provide the answer. Like Afreet, he had lived a life of secrets, a world where truth was a commodity that needed to be broken down, reduced to conjecture, or swept under the musty rug of conspiracy. But he was still human, and denying the will of truth had finally taken its toll.

Still, he didn't answer. He didn't have to. Bill just came out with it. "You were the guy Uncle Sam left swinging in the breeze, you shipped the body, which means *you* were in cahoots with Salaam and the don."

With obvious deliberation, Willis turned towards the light and smirked. "You're pretty good, detective. Willard should've warned me 'bout you. Usually, I'm history before any local flat-foot'd get a whiff of my trail. But, *cahoots* is certainly not the word I'd use to describe my relationship with either of those men."

"Then your primary mission was a success," Bill said, skipping the debate. "That's why they kept you for so long."

Again, a faint grin. The gunman rose and moved to the window, leaving bloody footprints in his wake. Pulling back the musty drapes, he replied, "Success is relative, detective. Spending years behind bars, being beaten and sodomized by animals, while my country turned a blind eye, was not *my* idea of success."

As darkness continued to fall, so did the barometer, ending the day with a light breeze that took the edge off the stifling heat. The front door remained ajar, leaving the hallway bulb prey to the dalliances of a few wayward moths and a disoriented click-beetle that ricocheted about the ceiling like a bullet.

"Who're you waitin' for?" Bill asked, leaning back to relieve the pressure on his ribs.

"The waiting is over, detective," said Willis, never taking his eyes off the yard.

Bill wasn't ready to bite. "How'd you escape?"

"I didn't," the other said, satisfied, returning to his chair. "One day a man, with the thickest glasses you've ever seen, came to my cell and told me my 'indoctrination' period was complete. I was free to go. Imagine that—my *indoctrination* to freedom was over."

"Somebody paid somebody off," Bill concluded, his ribs now throbbing in unison with his heart. *Or the Russians got what they wanted.*

"After being dumped on the Czech border, a beggar app-roached, handed me a loaf of stale bread and a bottle of vodka. Starving, and suffering from tuberculosis, I gobbled the loaf, nearly swallowing a small envelope that contained money and a new American identity: business cards, passport, a driver's license, social security card, and a key to a hotel room stocked with food and clothing."

"Uncle Sam didn't waste any time takin' ya back."

The agent didn't answer right away. Again, he was struggling with something. "... Wrong, detective," he answered. "*My* savior's outside government influence."

Thinking of the don, Bill asked, "Outside the law?"

"Sorry. I've offered enough already," the other said, shaking his head, angered by this rare lapse in judgment. Suddenly, a rivulet of blood rushed from the agent's nostrils. Acknowledging it with a swipe of his arm, he looked at his sleeve and laughed.

"How many have been exposed?" asked Bill.

The question raised the ire of the older man further. "We've *all* been *exposed*! You. . .me, those we care for every day. Exposed by an assembly of ancient, paranoid, over-weight, finger pointers, whose bi-partisan strings are pulled by those whose interests lay outside our borders...." Eyes darting, ears pricked like a Doberman, the agent stopped suddenly to listen. A moment passed.

Satisfied, he continued, "America has become a junkie, hooked on foreign oil. And, like a junkie, we'll suck *any* dick for a fix. We putt around in our gas-guzzlers, deplete our ozone, pollute our air, *knowing* that we freely support those who would rather see us dead."

He rose, reaching into the seat pocket of his pants. He removed a wrinkled piece of paper which, to Bill, looked like an old folded envelope. Waving it, he declared, "The solution's right here. I found this little memento upstairs in a drawer in Victor's old bedroom. We intend to break the cycle--cold-turkey." Returning it to his pocket, he moved back to the curtain.

"Salaam's formulas?"

Willis faced Bill with a wry grin. "Platitudes, detective, platitudes." He turned his back and slipped to another window for a better view of the barn.

"The Iranian government murdered Salaam's family because he was a thief, or because he was gay?" Bill asked, adjusting himself for added comfort.

"Neither. His father's theft of documentation vital to our national security led to their deaths. . .and others. It was *highly* classified information that would bring the entire region to its knees. The apple didn't fall far from that tree, you might say." He squeezed the envelope a little tighter.

Perked up, his eyes glued to the letter, Bill changed the subject. "How'd Salaam escape?"

"Victor and his team sprung him for his lover, some rich Saudi arms dealer with a soft spot for Persian rugs."

Picturing Ari Mann, his arm slung over Salaam's shoulder, Bill's palms moistened. He knew the answer to his next question as his focus remained on the envelope. "Hadn't the U.S. pursued these theories before?"

There was another long silence as the weary agent hesitated, wrestling with the same unwritten code that had kept him alive through the war, the years of his unspeakable term of capture, and every single day since. His adult existence had become a closed account of accruing secrets held forever in, what Uncle Sam had hoped was, a vault of timeless silence. Staring through his watch, he was ready to blow the hatch.

He started off slowly, staring ahead. "The person in charge of the project was murdered just west of here, killed in a post office parking lot, her work stolen." Willis patted his pocket with a wicked smile as he pulled Bill across the finish line. "... Until now."

A void, thirty-plus years wide, had been filled in less than thirty seconds. If a mid-level mole knew the specifics of his mother's demise, Bill could only imagine who else was in the loop.

Through clenched teeth, Bill swallowed and whispered, "Who killed her?"

Both men held their breath. Patterson looked up and turned his head away from Bill, toward the men sprawled on the ground, clinging to the silence.

Bill snapped, "*C'mon*, Patterson, or Willis, or whatever-the-fuck-your-name is! Cut the Willard act. You're not the only kid to grow up around here. It was in all the papers. *Who* killed her?"

"Victor Lawrence and his team."

"Bullshit! Who hired 'em?"

". . .OPEC."

The answer sent a chill to Bill's core, but he held the line. "What was our response?"

"Do you know who *ran* Airmont Chemical during the oil crisis?"

Bill barely shrugged his right shoulder.

"The CEO was Jack Stanton, the current President of the United States. His *father*, Papa Stanton, is one of Texas's richest oil tycoons." After an unsure pause, he added, "Hell, let's say the Western hemisphere. And with the oil crisis looming, no one was going to 'rock the boat,' as I recall the specific language."

"Where does Willard fit in all this? The lack of cooperation's been treasonous, even for him."

"His father's Airmont's residing Chairman. Given their latest earnings report, and the market tanking, the boat is, again, starting to 'rock'."

All for the love of oil, Bill thought. Or was it just money? Did they *ever* consider the costs to the lives of those they would affect the most?

"Do you remember her name?" Bill asked softly, changing the subject. Emotionally, his fight was nearing its end.

The ex-agent paused. He looked at Bill, not with the eyes of a trained killer, but with those who had, for the first time, sensed embarrassment. "Masters," was all the thick-skinned agent said, before he broke eye contact and returned to the front door. He stood with a hunch in the doorway, as he snuffed the hallway light.

Looking at the agent's back, too tired and sore to move, Bill questioned the man's steely calm and his complete detachment from the realities of his surroundings, regardless of the truth. For a man of his talents, staying put led him to believe the agent was waiting for someone--but he had his sights set on the horizon, not the yard.

Looking at his watch, the agent sighed like a stood-up date. The weather *had* slowed the operation. With the butt of the gun cocked on his hip, he turned, and in one deft move, he emptied the magazine, removed the clip, and caught the ejected cartridge before it hit the ground.

Tossing the weapon onto the couch next to Bill, he straddled the chair in the darkness and leaned in on its front legs, an arm's length from the detective's face. Needing to dispel some more guilt, he had made another serious decision.

Sitting back, his left hand tucked inside his jacket like Napoleon, Bill raised his free hand in a mock surrender. He considered sweeping the chair with his leg, but the man was no longer armed. He'd hear him out.

"Our enemies," Willis began, his stale breath close enough to share, "care little for laws not sent from heaven. They're cowards who sequester their conscience, abandon love, and corrupt their faith, as they detonate the souls of their children."

Scowling, Bill replied, "And this bothers *you*?"

"The world's worn through the veneer of American kindness, detective," he replied, insulted. "We've been taken hostage by our freedoms and our misguided, superior sense of self. When you go head-to-head with a snake, you better be prepared to get on your belly and learn to hiss. The average American male's as soft as a baby's ass."

It was time to get it out in the open. ". . . That would be *Janus's* job?" Bill asked, lowering his chin slowly in self-agreement.

The agent stared for a moment, before he rolled forward on the chair.

"Kudos, detective. Yes. Janus. By ridding itself of media control, budget restraints, and liberal debate, Janus will level the playing field, taking the fight to our enemies in *their* streets, in *their* backyards. Call it our modern day militia."

Bill coughed, bringing blood to his lips. His back arched in panic as he tested the ease of his next breath.

". . . Tastes different, when it's your own, doesn't it?" smirked the agent, offering a slow, I-told-you-so, nod.

Bill felt ashamed, knowing his reaction belittled the lives of those stacked on his desk who had tasted that same bitter fear before they died.

"*Relax*, detective," he jabbed, "your ribs are broken and one probably nicked a lung. Breathe slower."

Heeding the man's advice, he swallowed, took a shallow breath and said firmly, "You sound like terrorists, interested in only anarchy and fear."

Maybe it was the tardy response or the man's manic stare but for Bill the temperature had dropped substantially since the sun had gone, drawing moist cool air through the broken panes, over the couch, and down the back of his coat. Knowing a mere shiver would be enough to start him coughing, the detective pulled the front of his jacket closed and waited for a reply.

"Terror and anarchy end in chaos and disorder," the ex-agent began, "we're not looking for a coup. We're objective observers from all walks of life who donate their time and resources to focus on the affairs our government refuses to address. We've developed a strike-first mentality, setting up our own intelligence cells throughout the world."

Bill wasn't buying it. "Any group with a policy of killing innocent civilians is a terrorist organization and the bombing of the don's garage killed three people whose only crime was drawin' a paycheck!"

"We're *not* mercs lookin' to pad the bottom line or anarchists lookin' for drastic change. Our interests lie solely with *our* blood and *our* faith. We are a country at war, and New York's become the battleground."

Bill shook his head. "You sound just like Afreet."

"We work for what's in the best interest of man-kind," he fired back, "not his *God*." He paused to rub his temples. Bill wasn't getting the picture. Lowering his hand from his face, the agent stared deep into Bill's eyes. "If we hadn't stepped in, I can assure you, by the end of *this* week, *everyone* you ever knew would be dead . . . ." He snapped his fingers. "*Just. . .like. . .that.*"

"All *this*," Bill's arm swept over the carnage in the room, "so you can share a cell with Afreet?"

"Listen to you, detective. You're like the rest of America—buildings are falling down around you, but you don't want to listen, you'd rather waste valuable time burying your head in the quicksand's of accountability and world opinion. Modern laws have become a rich man's folly and where we're headed, only old rules need apply. Americans just love to be liked. Well, guess what? We're *not*." He leaned back, spread his arms. "Janus rises above the mundane inspection."

"Janis was my mother, you sick fuck!" Bill yelled, his eyes swamped with tears. He was coming unglued.

Patterson pulled a single white pistachio nut from the depths of his front pocket and popped it, shell and all, into his mouth. "I know. I've *always* known. She paid the ultimate price for *her* freedoms. What're you willing to do for yours?"

Bill, speechless, just stared in disbelief.

The Agent didn't wait for a reply. "Freedom's *not* the right to an education and a well-paying job, detective" he said, rolling the shell around in his mouth as he spoke. "Nor is it a fancy car or a summer home. No, it's a *privilege* that's been paid for with the blood of millions, a commodity whose present price exceeds that of which most of today's flag wavers on Capitol Hill are willing to pay. Unlike our forefathers, they keep forgetting, freedom matters little, when you're *dead*."

When he was done, a definitive crunch blended with the man's last words. "It's a fact our enemies are counting on."

Still gripping the chair, Willis went limp, his head falling onto his outstretched arms, his bladder streaming to the floor, followed by the watery thud of his lifeless torso.

The top half of the man's face was barely visible as he lay amid the slaughter he had caused. Bill wanted to label it senseless. But, given the man's labored testimony and painful gravity toward evolving truths, he didn't know for sure.

The dead agent's eyes were still open, the brightness of his life fading to a state Bill had begun to see more and more among the living--it had become the reflective inner-eye of those on the street--an uncertain fear; an unwanted look at fate, leaving everyone on the edge as anxious and scared as an unfledged bird.

Sitting back, his chest throbbing, Bill continued staring for a few minutes longer, digesting the scene, wondering what avenue to take, now that he could breathe—like never before.

Rising to his feet, he stood over the dead agent, suppressing the urge to kick him for his part in the charade. Dropping with a wince, Bill felt the lifeless gaze upon him as he rifled through the man's pockets, removing the wrinkled envelope and a small address book, its cover black, the journal's symbol centered in red, like the belly of a black-widow—a warning to all who touched it.

He moved to the hallway and turned on the light. Wiping sweat from his brow, he started with the address book that, from the first entry, read like the social section of the *New York Times*. There were Wall Street executives, religious officials, local politicians--including Kravitz--probable friends, and the rest Bill could only guess.

Toward the end of the alphabet, his head flinched in amazement at the highlighted initials J.S., which summoned to the forefront a recent news story, where Jack Stanton, the residing President of the United States, in all his perverse vanity, shut down the air space over Kennedy International at the insistence of his *local* hairstylist.

Closing the address book, he put it in his pocket, swapping it for the old wrinkled letter without a postmark addressed to Jack Stanton, then President of Airmont Chemical, in response to his decision to scrap, as his mother put it, "*her life's work*," and another unprecedented decree to "lock-down" the lab.

Citing Stanton's smoke-screen of cost over-runs and unseen production delays as the main justifications for the project's demise, she responded with the only thing Bill could recall from the argument that happened so long ago. "The test was a *total* success!" The last paragraph was her proof, or what looked to be the half of it.

The chemical equation took up just six lines. The only thing Bill could understand were the four periods lined up after the last element. She hadn't given it all. The steady hand of the Arabic notations in the margin around the equation returned his blood to its boiling point.

Dropping his eyes to the conclusion of the letter, he saw her signature stabbed defiantly onto the page, its bold trail swirling through the initials of the sole recipient of a carbon copy. In capitals, she'd typed the letters, D.A.D.

It made little sense to Bill, since his mother's parents had died at the hands of a drunk driver five years before he was born. The fact confirmed by her Airmont personnel file; the only shred of evidence the government--Jack Stanton's government--ever offered him.

Tapping the folded letter against his hands, Bill felt the weight of the notebook in his pocket and wondered why Patterson would stress the importance of the letter, only to kill himself, leaving the keys to the kingdom in the hands of a New York City cop.

CHAPTER 32

With the distinctive sound of a helicopter rising in the distance, Bill limped from the hall, recalling Patterson's intense interest in the horizon. Killing the entry light, he picked up his weapon and moved to the front curtain.

Squinting down the barrel of his gun, he aimed for the rotating strobe descending from the sky, its narrow beam combing the far reaches of the property, settling on the body of the dead Vietnamese lying in the drive.

Itching to fire, Bill eased his trigger finger, recognizing both the copter's F.B.I. markings and Agent Willard's leering face aglow in the dim lights of the cockpit as his arm pointed frantically at the man on the ground. Rotating its tail to preserve the scene, the helicopter initiated its landing.

Covering his eyes with his arm, Bill opened the front door and stepped into the storm of flying grass, moisture and dirt. Taking a gentle step down, he sat on the edge of the rough decking, the lapel of his jacket pulled up over his face.

The descending whine of the turbine coincided with the appearance of a line of official vehicles that leveraged the darkness with a gyrating pulse of authority.

The far door of the helicopter slid open, forcing Jim to claw his way over the captain and Chief Williams. Agent Willard, visually agitated, frothed at the mouth, as he screamed an update into his satellite phone.

Jim reached Bill first, leaned in for a hug, and placed his mouth to his ear. "Trust me, don't say a *word*!" he urged, patting his partner on the back.

As the two parted, Willard, stepping between them, pointed to one of his nearby deputies and ordered, "Take this man into custody!"

Bill's immediate retort, aimed within an inch of Willard's glistening forehead, took himself and everyone else by surprise. Amid the swirl of debris and flashing lights, the detective's eyes remained calm, his outstretched hand steady as the falling rain.

The deputy took a step forward. As his gaze passed through the agent, Bill cocked the hammer, a move that summoned a dark vision of a young Victor Lawrence stalking his mother's car and firing a round into her unsuspecting head. The rich, the powerful and the criminally insane, always deferred their debts to humanity, seeking absolutions, first, in the bowels of wealth, ending in the hands of tolerant gods. But Bill had witnessed, first hand, the lengths the tiger would go to devour its young. Who, besides family, would miss an incompetent agent lost amid reports packed with deletions, omissions, and blackened paragraphs. It was easier to lift the rug or spin another lie.

The two seemed to have reached the same conclusion as Willard tactically rescinded his order. Head bowed, he ordered coolly, "Secure the scene."

The deputy, his youthful eyes full of anger, lowered his weapon and backed off slowly, offering those on the fringes a premature sigh of relief, unaware that Bill's weapon remained in place.

Catching the punitive stares of his superiors, Jim had seen enough. "C'mon Bill, don't waste the bullet. Imagine Afreet as your fuckin' roommate—for *life*!"

Seconds passed. Drawing a breath, Bill remembered the final words of the dying agent, lowered the weapon, and stepped back to collect himself.

Immediately, Master's colleagues moved to insulate him from further reprisal. Biding his time, Willard stared back, grinning with the patience of a vulture, as he ushered his team into the house.

"As you were, gentlemen!" barked the chief, his arms out like a traffic cop, as he stepped up to deflect the row of local officers intent on getting involved.

"Thanks, chief," Bill replied, relieved at their withdrawal.

"God damn you, Masters!" squawked his boss. "I should arrest you myself—pullin' a stunt like that! You might've cost yourself a job."

With respect and little contrition, Bill was firm with his superior. "*That* was no stunt, sir." He pointed towards Willard. "From what I've learned from that prick's dead partner, I'd say his interests are somewhat conflicted. Patterson had orchestrated this whole caper from the get go. He used his position as Willard's partner to manipulate Salaam and his pals, before he brutalized them and staged his own death." Anticipating the next question, Bill felt it prudent to leave the details of Willis's confession private.

"And this agenda?" asked the captain, tipping an eager ear.

Bill paused. "Forgive me, sir, but this goes much deeper than I'm willin' to say. It's for your own good. If what Patterson told me is true, I'm probably a dead man anyway." Bill paused and looked up out of the corner of his eye toward the chief. "Can I talk to Jim now?"

The chief rolled up his collar. "Get out of my sight!"

Looking over at Willard, who had moved to a nosey cadre of trench coats preparing to enter the garage, Jim shook his head. "Not here."

Taking a short walk into the woods, the two detectives found limited privacy under the scattered limbs of a stunted pine.

Jim didn't wait for an invitation. "I looked a bit deeper into Salaam's prison record, and was surprised to find that a <u>Mister</u> Groves visited him, ten times, for two hours a pop." He looked his partner in the eye. "Am I missing something?"

"Can you believe this shit?!" Bill lamented, seating his weary frame on a boulder under the tree.

He closed his eyes. "Looks like the professor flat out lied. Took the journal and played me for a fool."

Jim, closing the gap between them, fumbled with his tie. "There's more my friend."

Bill took solace in the emptiness of the night sky. He tried to take a deep breath but coughed instead. Containing himself, he lamented, "Of course there is."

"This *could* be an attempt to slow us down," conceded Jim with a shrug, "*but*, just as we were leaving, a package arrived, dropped off by—get this—a troop of Girl Scouts who were instructed by an old lady to give it only to *me*."

The consequences caused Jim to shutter like a wet dog as he found a seat next to his partner. Wary of those moving around them, he scooched-in closer, whispering, "The package contained a dossier on Groves. The cover had a gold seal with a two-sided head. Real official lookin'."

Without thinking, Bill cleared his throat and offered softly, "Janus."

" .... Yeah, Janus," Jim replied, impressed. "Rico said he'd heard the word before on a game-show. It's some sorta' Greek god with a two-sided head." He waited for an answer that never came. Jim evaluated the condition of his tired partner. "We can do this later."

Bill sighed. "I've waited long enough."

Jim pulled his lighter and a fresh Tiparillo from the pocket of his rain coat, took a few warm-up puffs, and began again. "Did you know the professor had a daughter?"

Masters was emphatic. "*No.*"

"According to the dossier, Groves had a daughter named Janice," Jim added, bracing himself. "It was corroborated by an attached copy of an *original* birth certificate."

Stung, Bill labored to his feet. Running his right hand through his hair, he began to pace. "This is so fucked! Groves is my mother's *father?*" He wanted to run.

"Keep it down," urged Jim, raising a gentle palm. He paused to look about. "Obviously, that was kept a secret for a reason. The dossier mentioned others who had changed their children's names. Close friends, associates, and those accused of being communists or spies."

Looking about, Jim noticed that Agent Willard was back on the front steps, preoccupied with an agitated Chief Williams, as their captain exchanged professional pleasantries with local law enforcement now assembling around the dead body in the drive.

"Hey, who owns that in the driveway?" Jim asked, taking notice..

Bill, feeling no remorse, offered nothing but an arched brow.

"Whew. . .when it rains it pours."

"Guy *shot* me, for Christ's sake," Bill protested, lifting his shirt.

"But forget about him! What do *we* know about Patterson?"

"Diaz called the marina where he *had* his boat docked. Guy on the phone described the Agent Orange as 'big and fast.' Said he was contracted two weeks ago to install extra fuel tanks and a state-of-the-art navigational system capable of shore-to-shore operations. Patterson paid him in cash."

"What does that mean?" Bill asked.

"No skipper needed."

"Great. Where'd he say the boat is now?"

"Left dry-dock, fully fueled, two days ago. No one's seen it since."

"Over forty-eight hours at sea and its registered captain's inside cluttering the rug." Bill paused and put out his hands. The rain had returned.

"With the present weather conditions, on auto-pilot, you figure, what, three, maybe, four hundred miles….tops? Lotta' wind out there."

"Blow you all the way to Africa," said Jim, recalling the words of Salaam's elderly neighbor.

"Not likely," Bill replied, convinced the wind's value came with altitude, not opposing current and wave.

Ending his conversation with Willard, Chief Williams turned and approached the two detectives with urgency. "There's been a bomb scare. Tomorrow's ceremonies at the U.N. have been officially canceled."

"U.N.?" asked Bill, unable to get a read on the chief's face.

"Negative. The threat was a warning to evacuate coordinates that cover ten-thousand square miles of the Atlantic."

"Coordinates?" interjected Jim, scratching the back of his neck. It didn't sound good.

"And, for the last eight hours or so," the chief added, "Coast Guard agencies, on either side of the Atlantic, have received numerous, unauthenticated, distress calls from both aircraft and maritime vessels just *outside* the location specified in the threat."

Pulling his coat tight around the collar, Bill tuned out the world as he sank into a relentless quagmire of racing thoughts and heavy emotion. He didn't believe the professor was a co-conspirator in this mess, but he was sure whoever was in charge needed a front man like Afreet, someone, willing to sever all ties to family—a motivated person of unyielding trust, who had access to money and military connections and knew how to navigate the political cesspools of the world. . . .

Paralyzed by the revelation, Bill grabbed blindly for Jim's arm as the warm taste of bloody vomit etched the back of his throat. "Holy shit, Jim! Patterson wasn't waiting for *someone*. It *is* over. They're gonna' run a *real*. . . ."

Among those present, there were no words to describe the flash and broad spectrum of light that corkscrewed across the heavens like wild fire, gripping the scene with the brilliance of a low-voltage dawn.

All electrical power on the ground failed, as the object's glowing core began to pulse unchecked--brighter then softer, brighter then softer—penetrating the clouds as its growing mass took the shape of a nautilus shell turning inward on itself, spitting and popping with continuous bursts of electrical flak.

Another second passed before the rain abruptly ceased, cuing the crickets and cicada into a forced silence as the once orbital motions of the trees and flora screeched to a sudden halt.

Attempting to shield themselves from the light, most men covered their eyes, as others, heads bowed, held their hands together in prayer.

The thought of summer fireworks danced in Bill's head as he braced for the finial bang, heeding the tiny voice that insisted on the need for immediate cover. "Hit the deck!" he screamed, grabbing Jim and the chief, pulling them to the ground.

The captain and those in the drive soon found themselves reeling as a warm pressurized wave of air engulfed them, knocking them to the ground, shadowed by a teeth-chattering super-sonic boom that cracked a score of windshields and turned the idling helicopter on its side.

With the smell of ozone heavy in the air and the taste of a nine-volt battery numbing their tongues, those who were able rose above the settling cloud of dust to behold the bright aurora that had morphed into an eerie array of sub-electrical dendrons that snapped and arced across the night sky with a rhythmic frenzy. The sight was beautiful as its warming rays left the crowd of men standing in awe, its fiery center sucking in the milky ether that separated our lives from the rest of the universe, its cloudy mass reduced to roiling balls of steam.

With the swiftness of a wave succumbing to its crest, the

phenomenon receded, fading to a mere twinkle, then vanished, plunging the faces of those on the scene into a strobe filled blankness.

Stunned by his epiphany, Bill stood and worked his jaw. Dusting himself off, he wondered how the years had treated his father, knowing firsthand he had aged a lifetime the day his mother was slain. Regardless, it was obvious his capacity to captivate a room had remained unswayed.

All stood and stared in silence. Some ran their hands around their persons to assure their mortality, as a warm rain recommenced and the animals of the night resumed their chorus, vying to be heard over every civil defense siren in the western hemisphere.

Willard was about to speak, when the sound of his satellite phone broke the silence. After a few bitter nods, he hung up and waved Bill and his colleagues towards the house.

"Chief Williams," he said firmly, "another directive's been given to seal this scene and order all those without proper clearances to be escorted back to the city for debriefing. Military and CIA personnel are only a few clicks out." He checked his watch.

With his arm jabbing toward the sky, the chief demanded, "What the hell was *that*?"

"What was *what*?" replied the agent coldly.

"A reckoning for *all* who have done us harm," Bill interjected. "The race is over, Willard," he added firmly, turning to address anyone willing to listen. "What you all just witnessed was developed by. . . ." He hesitated and cleared his throat. "By *private* initiatives, made up of ordinary people, not corporate arms of government, who're looking to preserve their freedoms at whatever the cost."

"Do *we* have it?" asked the captain, holding a bloody handkerchief to the swollen knot oozing on his forehead.

"The people have it," Bill replied.

"Enough Masters!" shouted Willard, "You sound like a fuckin' communist. That information is classified! National Security mandates require you to *cease* this conversation immediately!"

Bill collated the totality of the last forty-eight hours, needing a mere nanosecond to realize that his crime fighting days were behind him. The truth bared, he had no clue as to what type of pariah he would make.

Eyeing the disheveled agent with contempt, Masters wanted to leave the stark isolation of the federal arena with the warmth of at least one bridge blazing in his wake.

"My mother was murdered," he said, to all who would listen, "to prevent what you *all* just saw. But you already knew that, didn't you, Willard? At least that's what *your* partner told me before he died." Bill had caught the agent off guard. "Yeah, Willard, that's right." But he didn't stop there.

Bill could see the uneasiness settle in as Willard's eyes darted among the blank faces of those in his command, fishing for support that wasn't there.

Willard might have had fewer friends than a prison rat but his father had groomed him well. Head back, his gaze upon the night sky, he reached deep into his front pockets and paused. "....Then, I guess we shouldn't mention what *your* old man's been up to after all these years."

Bill felt the blow, but he parried with a strong silence.

"Yeah, take a breather wise-ass," Willard prodded, feeling confident enough to take some ground. "Your old man's public enemy number *one*, Masters! Has been for years. Washington can't wait to shack him up with your ol' pal Afreet. And oh, yeah, who's that other pesky little character who taught Salaam everything he knows?" He grabbed his chin in mock surprise. "Oh, that's right, as of yesterday, your professor friend, public enemy number two. And with you giving him Salaam's journal. Christ, you Masters make the Rosenbergs look like a clan of blue-blooded chauvinists."

Bill quickly moved his free arm to his ribs to stem the painful effects of an unexpected laugh. Willard flinched, producing many grins amongst his minions.

Masters took comfort in the fact that he was legally untouchable. His father, outside of a few nameless postcards, never *once* made physical contact or left any traceable ties between them. Outside of the initial investigation, Bill was hardly a regular at the professor's home. But he also knew the two had a plan. And if Bill was going to survive long enough for them to carry it out, he'd roll the dice and do what anyone with a brain does when the scales of justice begin to tip against them. He'd keep his mouth shut. Almost.

Willard wasn't through with his inquisition. "What was the purpose of giving Dr. Groves Salaam's journal?"

Before Bill had a chance to reply, Chief Willie Jones, dusting the knees of his pants, threw his hat in the ring, aping Willard's uncanny indifference with scathing aplomb. "What journal?" he asked, pointing listlessly toward the sky.

Jim, tired and wet, registered his allegiance by adding, "There is no journal, only notes forwarded in cooperation with your public enemy number two." As the men shared an insider's laugh, they gravitated towards Bill who had become noticeably shaken by their loyalty.

Bill's captain stepped up and put his arm around his favorite detective and looked Willard right in the eyes. "You starched collars'll never get it. When the chips are down, it's not what's right or wrong, it's the side you're on." He offered Bill a rare smile and an added squeeze, before he suggested, "We should get you to a hospital."

The thundering sound of additional helicopters startled a few who had yet to shake the stark reality of their earlier observances. Skimming the tree tops, two Apache gun-ships did a quick fly-by, trailed by three more in formation that descended from the sky, one landing in the drive, two others concealed beyond a bordering line of spruce.

Bill was pleasantly surprised to see Mayor Kravitz ducking under the blades, his remaining grays clinging desperately to his scalp like coral fending the tide. Walking sternly on the mayor's heels, Bill recognized, as did Willard, was an angered Director of the FBI.

As they entered the circle, Kravitz stood directly in front of Bill, who was sure he caught the wink, before His Honor ordered, "After you've seen a doctor, I want you and Tonto to go home and gets some sleep. Just keep your traps shut!" He turned for the director's blessing, which he received with a nod and added, "No radio, TV, no *Good Morning Today*. Silence is the order of the day." His roaming finger left no one out, as he tossed visual daggers at Agent Willard.

After a brief discussion with the mayor, the FBI director snapped his fingers summoning Willard to the house.

On cue, the copter pilot signaled the eager entourage it was time to go.

Before departure, the skinny navigator passed out headsets, informing his passengers of the need to climb to higher altitudes due to the lack of visuals, a result of what was initially reported as a tristate blackout.

Adjusting his flight-harness, Bill knew, after thirty years, *no one* had the juice to indict a family as powerful as the president's, or wealthy as the Willard's. Yet peering at the line of bumper-to-bumper traffic clogging the Turnpike to the horizon, they wouldn't need to. With Airmont's power grid totally off-line, the financial losses sustained would be devastating. Stock prices would tumble, consumer satisfaction would sink to new lows and any investor with a brain would retreat off their balance sheet with the speed of a French division. His father had bypassed the courts and hit 'em where it hurt.

Fatigued, his chest racked with spasms, Bill forced a smile and patted his partner's knee as he tilted his head back and closed his eyes, tuning into the whine of the turbine as the craft began its climb to altitude.

CHAPTER 33

Midnight was a distant memory when Bill arrived at his apartment during the biggest blackout in American history. It hadn't been the merchants on easy street who felt the wrath of the swarming crowds looking for appliance upgrades and other domestic luxuries not offered in the latest welfare package. They had been rescued by Western and Canadian power companies trampling each other to pick up the slack.

Amid the glow of emergency lights, half conscious, Bill checked his mail and walked carefully through the darkness, using the lobby wall as a guide.

Safely home, he routinely flicked the wall switch, dropped his belongings on the glass table, and took a seat on the couch. Bill rubbed his free hand over the bandage gripping his mid-section like a sausage casing. Unable to hear Kathy's tell-tale snore, he rose, headed down the hall, and ducked his head in the room. Her outstretched arm hung from the edge of the bed, her face was pressed into the pillow. She had slept through the whole thing.

Obeying the growl from his stomach, he moved through the apartment toward the kitchen. Without power, he settled for a few finger-scoops of peanut butter and chugged blindly from the milk container he had plucked from the darkness of the fridge.

Bill licked his fingers as he returned to the living room, retrieving matches from the end table, lighting the candles over the fireplace. Cupping the flame, he paced the floor lighting every candle he could find, supplying just enough light to keep him awake.

"Alone again," he mused, removing his shoes. His tired feet plopped upon the table; Bill emptied his pockets, flinching at the sound of the magnifying glass clanking off another bowl Kathy had left behind.

Sinking into the sofa, he wiggled his toes as the lids of his weary eyes bobbed in unison with the opaque flicker that danced before him. Sirens wailed in the distance as sleep summoned, defying closeted thoughts that yearned for a single shred of closure.

The return of power jarred Bill awake as the stereo pushed static and the answering machine played its message. Bill's eyes refocused on the candle that had leaked wax on the mail, most of it pooling on the picture of his latest postcard—a yellow ribbon wrapped around an oak tree.

Bill waited for the wax to cool before he peeled it off and rolled the card in his hands, inspecting it, like he always did, for something that might differentiate it from the last. The latest anomaly came in the form of writing found in the middle of the card that was entirely too small to read.

Fighting the pain of bending, Bill reached for the blue lens lying in the shadows of the cereal bowl. As the case opened, a sliver of glass joined the carpet, reminding him of what should have been. Placing the lens to his eye, he brought the card to his face.

Both the card and lens tumbled to the floor, as Bill inhaled to catch his breath. Frantic, he hustled to the fireplace, stumbling over everything in his path. He grabbed his cache of postcards and returned to the couch.

Shuffling through time, back to the beginning, he selected the first card and put the glass to his eye. In seconds, he tossed it down and grabbed the next one, then the next and the rest, each successive card producing a mixture of emotions that bounced from joy, to sorrow, to self-loathing.

From the first card, John Masters *had* told his story as it unfolded, written over the years in a solution visible only to the lens that had saved his son's life. He told of his plight for justice, starting with the murder of his wife and ending with the dramatics that had been played throughout the night sky.

Bill ran his hand through his hair. His mouth ran dry and his moistened forehead was warm as churned humus. He needed something to drink.

Passing the front hall, he sensed a presence that was confirmed by the shadow of feet moving at the base of his door. Bill pulled his gun, ready to rumble, when he was startled by an odd sound that had always fell short of a knock. As soothing as his mother's voice, the sound of a cane tapped the floor, erasing his fears, summoning the latent might of a childhood smile that pushed the heavy concerns of the world forever from his face. For Detective Bill Masters, yesterday was about to begin.